APPARENTLY, I'M TORTURE

APPARENTLY, WE'RE THE PROBLEM
BOOK TWO

DEMI BLAIZE

P.S. Want more laughs, love, and a little trouble?

Scan the QR code here to join my **Book Club**!

It's free, fun, and you'll get access to giveaways, behind-the-scenes extras, and new release alerts!

BOOZY BINGO

CROSS OUT WHEN	CROSS OUT WHEN	CROSS OUT WHEN
THE FIRST TIME '**POOR UNCAFFIENATED SOUL**' IS MENTIONED	THE MAIN CHARACTERS MAKE YOU WANT TO YELL AT THEM	THE MAIN CHARACTERS CALL WHAT HAPPENED '**A MISTAKE**'
MIA CALLS TREVOR '**TREVIBOY**'	LILLY SINGS HER COPING SONG	SHAWN CALLS LILLY '**MISS FARES**'
THINGS GET SPICY (KISSES, INTIMATE TOUCHES, ETC)	MIA CALLS SOMEONE A '**FIT ASSHOLE**'	THE FIRST TIME '**TORTURE**' IS MENTIONED

@demiblaizebooks

NOW

CHAPTER 1
LILLY
MONDAY AFTERNOON

South Bronx Classical
Bronx, NYC

I REALLY DIDN'T WANT to go in there.

Just the thought of being alone with Trevor–No. I couldn't let myself think about it. I had to focus on something else.

Anything else.

Okay, this wasn't working. Trevor was definitely in my head. But maybe saying it out loud would help me believe it?

"I'm not a bad teacher," I told myself. "I don't care what Trevor thinks. I'm *not*. I *know* I'm not."

This... wasn't working either.

So I squeezed my eyes shut and ran my favorite song through my head, mouthing the words. It helped me focus on my breathing. In and out, slowly, steadily, in and out, again and again.

It was the same song it always was, from the same movie I'd seen so many times.

After my mom died, it was all I had left of her. That song, and this school.

Just as I started to feel okay again, Mia popped her head out from behind the staffroom door. Her dark, straight hair swished around her shoulders, brown eyes widening just a teensy bit more when she caught me standing alone in the warm, empty hallway.

She said, "Hey," so gently that I almost couldn't hear the English accent in her voice. Easing out of the room, she closed the door behind her. "You okay, love?"

I forced a smile and nodded, but the look she gave me called me out on my bullshit.

Mia knew I wasn't okay. We'd been best friends since we'd met at our sorority years ago–I couldn't get anything past her.

She put her hands on my shoulders and squeezed. "It's just an update meeting. You'll be fine."

Just hearing the word 'meeting' made me feel nauseous.

"It's just... he makes me so–"

"I know," Mia said, cutting in gently. "But we're almost done with the school year. Get through this, and that's it. No more Trevor."

She let go of me, and I took another deep breath. She was right. I just had to get through it.

I stepped around Mia, opened the door, and walked into the staffroom.

Trevor wanted to speak to me, and whether I liked it or not, I had to show up.

CHAPTER 2
LILLY
MONDAY AFTERNOON

South Bronx Classical
Bronx, NYC

MAYBE IT WOULDN'T BE SO bad. Maybe it was all in my head.

Maybe Trevor would cut me some slack.

"Miss Fares. About time. You're *only* three minutes late," Trevor muttered as soon as I walked in.

Nope. No slack in sight.

I should've expected it. He *was* my ex-boyfriend. And my boss.

This meeting featured all my nightmares rolled into one gigantic ball of torment.

I forced my short legs into the small, boxy, air-conditioned room and plopped into the soft, mustard-colored chair across from him. Brushing my brown bangs out of my lashes, I pulled my shoulders back and flashed Trevor my perkiest smile.

"I read somewhere that people who are late all the time are actually good multitaskers," I told him. "Did you know–?"

"Lilly," he snapped. "Give me one more fun fact, and I'll give you sub duty."

I quickly shut my mouth. I had sub duty last week and wound up teaching ninth-grade math to kids who solved every equation before I could put pen to paper. They were so bored waiting for *me* to *catch up.*

Substituting for absent teachers was the worst. And math wasn't exactly my strongest subject.

But books? I could talk about books all day, every day.

I taught Literature at South Bronx Classical just like my mom did. Before her cancer set in.

Trevor cleared his throat. "Now that you're here, we can get started. It's our last week of the term. What have you got planned?"

It still felt weird to me that Trevor was asking questions like this. To me, he wasn't our Head Teacher. But it'd been a year since he was handed the role, so... maybe it was me? Maybe I was the problem?

Mia was doing okay with Trevor as our boss. But she wasn't the one who dated him in college.

And now he was giving me a blank, exasperated look. Probably because I was taking too long to answer.

"Let me guess," he muttered. "More of those pony movies?"

I could tell from the way he asked that he hated those movies. He hated them because I loved them.

"My students like them."

"The boys, too?" he drawled, irritating me, which actually worked in my favor. Being annoyed with him meant I wasn't anxious, and that was good because I really didn't want to let Trevor bring me down. Not with the school year so close to ending.

My students worked hard over the last few months, and they deserved a reward. Whether he liked it or not.

"They complain a bit, but once the film starts, they eat it up."

He leaned across the table, and I caught a hint of coffee on his breath. "But they don't have anything to do with the curriculum."

He wasn't wrong. The My Little Pony movies weren't part of our plan.

But that was the point.

They were an escape. They gave all of us a break. The students needed that at the end of the school term. And I needed it too.

The 'Cafeteria Song' from the original movie was the one I sang over and over. It was how I coped with my chronic anxiety.

No matter what I tried, I kept coming back to that song. Nothing else worked.

Maybe it was because watching those movies with my mom was the last time I felt happy before she died.

I had so much fun sitting with her on our two-person sofa, singing so loud that our neighbors could hear us. They ended up pounding on the walls, trying to get us to stop. I could still hear Mr Covoski yelling at us through the plaster.

I could still hear the sound of my mom's laugh as he pounded.

"Dissecting movies they enjoy helps them practice their critical skills," I reasoned. "You'll see it pay off in their exams."

He scoffed. "Isn't that what you said last time? A quarter of *your* freshmen are starting their sophomore year in the remedial class."

I shifted in my seat, trying to ignore the twinge in my chest.

"What other classes do you have?" he asked.

"Freshmen intermediate and sophomore advanced."

He looked from me to the door. "What do you think about giving sophomore advanced to Mia?"

Mia's voice floated into the room, the door shutting as she grumbled. I was instantly relieved that she was here.

"Treviboy, don't you even think about pushing her classes onto me."

I wished I could speak to Trevor the same way Mia did.

I knew she called him 'Treviboy' because it reminded him that we all graduated at the same time and had the same kind of experience. And I think he let her get away with it because so much of his disgust was pointed at me.

Even now, as he leaned back in his chair, I could see what he was trying to do, and it made my stomach churn.

I'm a good teacher. He can't take my classes from me.

"The semester's almost done," Mia said, and I pictured her standing behind me with her arms folded across her chest. "Changing things now will only confuse the students."

He met her gaze over my head as his lips thinned. Ugh. I couldn't believe I used to date him.

"All right, fine," he agreed, and just like that, my shoulders dropped. Maybe that was it. It was over, and I could get back to teaching.

But then he nodded at the door behind us and said, "I need a few minutes alone with Lilly."

Mia turned and left, and with every step she took, the more dread I felt.

Once we were alone, Trevor leaned back in his chair and ran his blue eyes over me like I was a piece of trash he was dying to throw out.

"I need to talk to you about The Educational Arts Fundraiser."

"Uh... oh, okay," I said, instantly confused. "It's six weeks away, isn't it?"

He nodded. "Yep. I need you to help them put the event together."

I frowned, trying to make sense of what he'd just said.

"But I can't–I mean, only the department heads run it, don't they? Isn't it... *your* job?"

I cringed at how I sounded and immediately wanted to apologize. I couldn't help it. When it came to Trevor, I was just trying to tread water at this point.

He tsked and rolled his eyes to the ceiling. I hated when he did that. It made me feel like a seventh grader in detention.

"We decided to pick teachers from our faculties this year, and out of all of us, you have the right kind of experience."

I tried to keep my voice even. "But I don't. Not... really."

He cocked his head at me, like every word that came out of my mouth was sheer stupidity. "Lilly, you sat on the Fundraising Board of Kappa Delta for five years in a row."

"But that was a long time ago. It's not like I can run an event like that now–I wouldn't know what to do."

It wasn't that I didn't want to do the work. It was what the work meant.

It meant spending six whole weeks with complete strangers, doing a job I hadn't done in years.

Just thinking about it put me in fight or flight mode. My shoulders were up by my ears, my nails were digging into my palms, and even my toes were braced, like I couldn't decide which one to go with: argue with Trevor on this, or run out of the room just to get away from him.

Trevor sighed and hung his head like a drooping balloon.

Oh, how I wished I could pop that balloon.

"Look, I didn't want to bring this up again, but this is getting serious. Parents are starting to complain."

That was all it took to shake me. Once the parents said something, that was it. Career over.

I forced myself to ask, "What... are they complaining about?"

He looked up and said, "What do you think they're complaining about? You know the principal and I aren't thrilled with the test scores coming out of your classes."

My stomach dropped.

I did know it. It was why I dreaded this meeting in the first place. I should've expected that at least one parent would've said something by now, but I'd hoped, since it was our last week, that Trevor would let it go.

I should've known better.

"But–"

"I can't fight her off forever. The principal needs results."

I could feel saliva building in my mouth, and I swallowed it down. I couldn't have an attack in front of him. I couldn't. I had to calm down.

"But I can't teach to the test," I told him. "You know that."

Trevor went on as if I didn't say anything.

"I talked it over with the principal, and I've set up a professional development module for you. If you're serious about your job–"

"I *am* serious–"

"Prove it. Complete the module, work the fundraiser, and you can stay."

"But–"

"And no more of those damn movies. They're a waste of time."

My eyes blurred, and I sat there in shock. If he noticed, he didn't care. All he did was raise a brow.

"Lilly, this is a warning. I don't care that your mom used to teach here. If your students fail the next round of exams–if this fundraiser doesn't work out–you lose your job. Do you understand?"

My fingers went numb; the back of my throat burned. But I managed to nod.

Trevor stood and left without another word, dismissing me. And everything he'd said hit me all at once.

Suddenly, there were tears stinging my eyes and my stomach was in knots.

I put my hand on my navel and dropped my head between my knees. But it didn't help. And how could it?

Trevor just told me he was about to take away everything I cared about.

I could lose my job.

I could lose my classroom.

My worn-in textbooks. My students. This was my mom's school. I was supposed to be here. I couldn't lose this.

If I did, I'd have nothing.

CHAPTER 3
LILLY
MONDAY NIGHT

Lilly's Apartment

"So, there's nothing I can do about it?" I muttered into my phone as I pulled a pair of lounge shorts out of my bedside drawer.

"Well, I read the contract you sent me, but it doesn't sound like workplace harassment or discrimination," Nikki said, her voice straining. She was probably picking up toys in her living room. Her two little girls played hard. "And Trevor can sign you up for professional development if he thinks you're not doing your job well."

"Really? So he's just allowed to send me to some fundraiser?"

"Sort of. You're supposed to work during school breaks, right?" she asked.

"Yes... on admin stuff."

"*And* career development?"

I wasn't sure I liked where she was going with this.

"Uh-huh... Like workshops."

"Like this fundraiser. Actually, I don't think this is the worst thing he could've done. He could've just fired you and dealt with the principal after."

Damn, Nikki had a point. She was so hard to argue with. Maybe that was why she made such a great lawyer.

"I know you have to give up half your summer break for this, but it could be a great opportunity," Nikki said, probably trying to help me find the silver lining.

Grunting, I trapped my phone between my ear and shoulder as my shorts made it up and over my ass. I'd gone straight home after the meeting and called Nikki to talk it over.

I thought maybe she'd help me come up with the kind of solution that would let me keep my job even if the fundraiser didn't work out. But this conversation wasn't turning out the way I'd hoped.

"But I don't want any new opportunities. I don't want to teach anywhere else. I love my students, and I love my classroom."

I dropped onto my couch and winced.

"What happened?" Nikki asked. "Are you okay?"

I must've made a noise. "Yeah, I'm fine. I just sat down."

"And that hurt?"

"My ass is eating my shorts," I explained. "I have a wedgie."

As Nikki laughed, I leaned to the side and tugged the hem, hoping to save the trapped fabric.

I was pear-shaped—slimmer on the top half, larger on the bottom—and no amount of exercise changed that genetic fact. But at least my ever-growing ass could be used to entertain Nikki.

As her laugh faded, she paused to say something to Tristan, her husband and one of my closest friends. When I heard her voice again, she wasn't Nikki-my-amused-friend. She was Nikki-the-no-bullshit-lawyer.

"Lilly, I know you love your job, and you think it isn't fair that Trevor is making you do this, but if you do this well, you can throw it in his face for the rest of the year."

"But what if I can't do it? Or... what if he makes me do it every year?"

I'd known Trevor long enough to know this was a lose-lose situation. I was doomed if I did well, doomed if I didn't.

"Well, next year you'll have leverage." She let out a breath and shifted her tone. Oh no. She was about to go next-level. I could feel it. "And you don't have a choice. Whether you like it or not, Trevor is your boss, and this is your job."

I groaned again. "*Niikkii.*"

"Sorry, but it's true. Just try and forget about

Trevor. Forget about the principal. Do your job and do it well. Prove them wrong."

I settled into my sofa and mumbled, "You're right."

And she was.

Trevor was trying to make me feel like a failure at the one thing I was good at. He was trying to force me out of my mom's school. If this was the only way I could stop him from doing both of those things, then I'd show up at that fundraiser with a smile on my face.

I could hear the satisfaction in Nikki's voice as she said, "I'm always right. So. When are you coming over again? The girls have been dying to see Aunty Lilly."

~

Tuesday Morning
South Bronx Classical
Lilly

"*He's on the Board?*"

I'd just come around to accepting the whole fundraiser thing when I was called into the staffroom. Trevor was there alone, hovering behind our round table with a bigger-than-usual smirk on his face.

I didn't trust that look—and for good reason.

He'd just told me who I'd be working with over summer break, and he knew I wouldn't be happy about it.

"He's not just on the Board; he's leading the event."

Trevor was firm, but I could just make out the hint of glee in his eyes. "Is that a problem, or can you be professional about this?"

Sometimes, it was easy to picture Trevor as the villain of my story. But then something like this would remind me that he didn't quite fit the role. He was a huge, irritating thorn in my side, sure, but he wasn't the villain.

That title belonged to Shawn Jackson.

I folded my arms. "I can be professional. He's the one who's been avoiding me for five years."

Trevor put down his coffee cup and smoothed a hand through what was left of his blonde hair. "I don't understand why that's an issue."

He wouldn't. Ignoring me for five years probably sounded like a great idea to Trevor.

I frowned. "I bet you gave me this fundraiser so you wouldn't have to talk to him."

He made a noise. "No, actually. If I knew he was going to run this thing, I would've signed up for it. But I already told the principal that you were going."

I made a face. "Wait, why?"

"Why did I tell the principal–"

"No, why would you want to see Shawn?"

He looked at me like I should've known the answer to that already. "Lilly, come on. How many years has it been since we graduated?"

I sighed. I knew what was coming.

"Five."

"And what've we done in those five years?"

"We've raised the minimum grade in language arts across all years–"

"Except your classes."

Fighting the urge to grind my teeth, I muttered, "Except for *my* classes. You and Mia have led professional development workshops–"

"And I've been promoted to head teacher."

I folded my arms and squeezed my eyes shut. "Yes, you've been promoted to head teacher."

"And what have you done?"

My eyes flew open and I glared at him. "Nothing, apparently."

I hated workshops. There was no way I could teach them.

Unlike with my adorable students, the thought of teaching people with more experience in literature than I had felt like this big, unreasonable thing that I just couldn't do.

I knew exactly what would happen if I tried. I would spend weeks before the event just overthinking and overthinking. I wouldn't sleep; I wouldn't eat. I'd probably puke at the sight of the agenda.

There were some parts of teaching I was always going to be comfortable with, like managing my own classroom and helping kids understand the magic of books.

But leading workshops? Nope.

He nodded, satisfied with my answer, and I shut down the urge to roll my eyes.

"And what's Shawn done?" he asked.

I thought I knew what he wanted to hear, so I started to recite the usual professional jargon: "Shawn Jackson is an educational leader in literature–" but Trevor cut me off.

"You know what he's done, Lilly. He's revolutionized our teaching standards, and now he's working on getting his Maslow initiative into every school in New York."

He paused, and I stood there, waiting for him to go on. Because there was more. There was always more.

"And that's on top of raising his school's test score average to an all-time high. His grades get better results than ours in literature every year. *Every* year. Without fail. No one else has that kind of track record."

And there it was. The end of Trevor's rant.

"Okay, okay. I get it." I waved my hands in the air. "Shawn's amazing."

The defeat in my voice seemed to have a calming effect on Trevor. He picked up his coffee cup and drifted to the door as he said, "He's a great teacher. He had the choice to work here, and that could've been huge for us. But because of you, he didn't. Instead, Mia and I got stuck with you, and all you do is teach students how to sing along to cartoon musicals."

I looked away, hoping Trevor couldn't see how hurt I was.

"I'm giving you a chance to fix things before you lose your job. Don't screw things up with Shawn a second time."

As Trevor walked out, Mia shot him a glare on her way in and gripped my arm.

"Don't let that asshole get you down," she told me. "I know what happened with Shawn, and so do you."

Mia must've heard what Trevor said, and maybe I should've been embarrassed by that. But honestly, I didn't care.

I was just glad to have her on my side.

Dressed in a button-down shirt tucked into a high-waisted skirt, Mia looked impressively put-together. Exactly like the kind of person parents wanted teaching their kids.

Not like me.

I was in a shapeless shift dress with a wool cardigan thrown over it. If our outfits reflected how well we did our jobs, then now more than ever, I deserved to feel like a failure.

Swallowing past the lump in my throat, I managed, "I just wish I knew why he hated me so much."

She frowned. "Lilly, he didn't hate you."

"Shawn said working with me was torture. And he must've meant it, because he still won't talk to me."

"Well, you have to spend the next six weeks together. Maybe he'll pull his head out of his ass long enough to apologize to you."

"Maybe." I pressed my palms to my eyelids and

tried to calm down. I still had three more classes to get through today. My students didn't deserve weepy-eyed, distracted Lilly. They deserved fun, on-the-ball Miss Fares.

But I couldn't deny that this whole thing was kind of crushing.

I'd dedicated five years of my life to this school, and I loved my job, but... was I really that bad at it?

Were my priorities all over the place? Was I just coddling my students?

Their test scores didn't lie.

Maybe I had it all wrong. Maybe I wasn't doing the right thing by them.

Whatever Shawn was doing was working. And whatever I was doing? It was about to get me fired.

Mia tsked, probably tired of watching my misery play out across my face. "Okay, you know what? This isn't working for me. You're not doing this alone. I'm going with you."

While still rubbing my eyes, I shook my head. "Mia, you don't have to give up your holiday time for me."

"Well, what else am I going to do anyway? Sit at home, alone, while my best friend is stuck in some dingy hall working with a man she hasn't gotten along with in half a decade?"

"You could bake cookies for your neighbor," I offered. "Maybe watch him tear up his floorboards?"

Mia sighed, her brown eyes wistful. "God, they don't make them like that anymore, do they? Those thick shoulders get me every bloody time." She straightened as the bell rang. "Come on. Let's get to class. We can talk about it on the way."

She offered me her elbow, and I wrapped my arm around it. "Mia, I can't drag you into this. They're not giving us overtime pay."

She yanked my arm and pulled me along. "Then consider it payback for all the times you've helped me put together a research paper or a whole unit. Trevor might not see all the work you put in, but I do."

A gaggle of freshmen zipped by, laughing and waving at us as they ran. But they didn't distract Mia. Her eyes snapped to mine as she told me, "You have to let someone help you for once."

"But what if I bring you down with me? What if it's a disaster?"

She waved a hand in the air. "Oh, don't be so dramatic. You've clearly been studying too much Shakespeare. Look, if that happens, then Treviboy better pull up his big-boy pants, because we're not leaving this place without a fight."

Well. Who was I to argue with the fiery Mia Walker?

It looked like we were taking on Shawn Jackson together.

CHAPTER 4
LILLY
FRIDAY MORNING

Last day of school
South Bronx Classical

RANDOM FUN FACT ABOUT ME: I loved fun facts.

As a kid, I used to write them down on small squares of cardboard until, eventually, I had a deck I could carry with me wherever I went.

It came in handy when I had to meet new people. Because my job sometimes meant I had to socialize. Which... I wasn't always comfortable doing.

Awkward silences were the worst. But that's where my deck of facts came in.

As soon as there was a lull in the conversation, I'd pull out a card from my collection. It kept the conversation going, and sometimes, it earned me a smile or two.

Being prepared helped me cope. It was something

my mom taught me. And when I started including them in my classes, the 'Fact Check' game was born.

"Okay, two points to anyone who can give me a new fact," I shouted.

Standing in front of my freshman intermediate class, I held a whiteboard marker to the firm, glossy wall.

"Your cat can be allergic to you," Michelle called out.

I pointed at her and said, "Someone check that for me, please. Blue team, true or false?"

Okay, I could admit it.

This silly end-of-semester game had nothing to do with literature, but it was great for warming up their working memory. It also gave them a taste of team-work, which, in my book, was never a bad thing.

From the blue team, Chris groaned. "Correct."

"That's two more points. Great job, Red."

Jessica and Michelle giggled behind their hands as Chris shot me a glare.

"Miss Fares, you're not supposed to take sides," he grumbled.

I held up my marker. "I'm not, I swear. But if you want to beat their four-point lead you've got to give me some facts, guys. Come on, what do you have for me?"

Lisa made an "ooo-ooo" noise before throwing her hand in the air.

"Lisa?"

"Oranges have the highest amount of vitamin C out of every fruit?"

Her hand slowly lowered as she spoke, and the way she ended her sentence told me there was a severe lack of confidence on her end.

I swung my marker toward Jessica's team. "Red, time to fact check."

Lauren gasped as Jessica's screen loaded. "Nope. Strawberries have more vitamin C. Ahaha, lose a point."

Lisa grumbled and ripped a paper from her notebook. As she wadded it up–no doubt to throw at Lauren's head–I threw my arms out.

"Okay, okay, I'm calling it. Red team wins today."

Some groans sounded from the blue team, but they were drowned out by the other team's cheers.

"Settle down, guys, settle down. Today's victory means Red chooses which movie we end our semester on. What's the verdict?"

Lauren, Jessica, and Michelle whispered excitedly as I shifted on my feet, staring down at my once-white tennis shoes.

I was probably going to need a new pair before I walked into the hall next week. Who knew what the situation might be like there. What I'd have to wear. Whether I was allowed to wear tennis shoes in the first place.

The head of our fundraiser moved quickly. Shawn already had his venue lined up–and I probably shouldn't have been surprised by that. This was an annual event, after all.

But it made me wonder what else he'd planned. And if he'd actually stick around to talk to me for the first time in years.

Without fail, no matter what the event was, he found a way to avoid me.

The first workshop he spoke at three years ago?

Once he was off the podium, he walked out as soon as he saw me coming.

Tristan's gallery showing last year?

He didn't show up. Instead, he made an excuse and treated Tristan to some private experience I was never invited to.

My own Uncle Henry's 70th birthday party?

He stayed for twenty minutes, *ignored me*, then left. I was too busy running the party to corner him.

Now he had no choice. He had to talk to me. My nerves pinged and rebounded at the thought.

"*Rainbow Rocks*," Jessica called out, snapping me out of it. "But can we watch it karaoke style?"

I turned back to the board, wiping their scores.

"Is there any other way to watch it? Blue team, are we happy with this choice?"

Chris shrugged. "We wanted that movie anyway."

I put a hand to my chest as I made my way to the desktop. "Aw, guys. I'm so touched. I really thought *Inside Out* was going to be the popular choice."

Projected against the whiteboard, the sound of the

movie filled my classroom, and my students fell into a hush.

We were at least a half hour in when Jessica's side-eye caught my attention.

I shot her a questioning glance, and she ducked her head, shimmied out of her seat, and crept toward me.

Leaning forward in my chair, I asked, "Everything okay?"

Jessica's bottom lip jutted out, and I could sense a soft whine coming my way. I looked at the rest of my class, but they were absorbed by the screen. I motioned for her to follow me outside.

In the hallway, she relaxed, her shoulders sagging in her pressed school uniform. "Miss Fares, my mom wanted me to…"

I scanned the empty hallway as she trailed off, mostly hoping Trevor wouldn't catch me alone with a student. A classroom management no-no these days.

"Is something wrong?"

"No… yes? It's about my book report. You gave me a B+, and my mom thinks I can do better."

"You *can* do better."

"I have to if I want to get into an Ivy League school," she muttered.

I shifted back, studying her. Jessica wasn't a bad student by any means. She was quiet in class, attentive, and always completed her work. She had dark brown eyes, jet-black hair, and a penchant for winged eyeliner.

She was a social butterfly and loved school. She thrived here.

But it wasn't a faculty secret that her mother wanted her to buckle down and raise her grades. I mean, I hadn't had the pleasure of a Mrs-Hernandez-parent-teacher-dressing-down, but it was clear from this conversation that my blissful ignorance was coming to an end.

"Is that what you want?" I asked. "You still have the rest of high school in front of you and Ivy League schools are a lot of work. The load is intense."

She lifted a shoulder, and that was my answer.

"Jessica, if you don't want to study at a school like that, you don't have to. Didn't you want to learn filmography?"

Again, another shrug.

"Is that still what you want?"

She nodded. Finally. A different nonverbal answer.

"Why don't you just tell your mom that?"

Jessica chewed the inside of her cheek for a moment, then said, "Mom says I should do my best just in case I change my mind. But I know what she's really thinking. If I bust my balls to get into an Ivy League school, then I'd be stupid to turn it down. I'd have to pick something worth studying at one of those places. Like law or medicine."

I frowned. "You could study film too, though."

She rolled her eyes. "No one goes to an Ivy League school to study movie-making, Miss Fares."

Ah, teenage sarcasm. I wouldn't miss this for ten weeks.

"Anyway, my mom wants to know if you'd tutor me. Like, over the summer break."

I shook my head. "Sorry, but I can't. Teachers aren't allowed to tutor their own students."

Her bottom lip trembled. "Please, Miss Fares? I need to get her off my back. She won't let me see my boyfriend until my grades get better."

I held in a groan. I knew what that kind of freedom meant to a teen.

"I could arrange for someone else to help," I offered, giving in. "Would that be okay?"

Her face pinched, but she nodded. "I think Mom might be all right with that."

"What about your other subjects?"

Ah, great–she was back to shrugging.

"I'm doing better in my other classes. I just can't wrap my head around literature. I thought I aced the last exam, but you know my results weren't great." With wide, horrified eyes, she whispered, "Mister Atkins called my mom and told her that I was almost dropped into the remedial class."

I remembered the results from that exam, and how disappointed my students were afterwards. Even now, I hated thinking about it. Maybe Trevor–known as Mister Atkins–was right.

Maybe my methods weren't working. If a student as

capable as Jessica wasn't getting it... what hope did the rest have?

"I'll find someone who can help, don't worry."

I wanted to pat her on the shoulder and tell her she was going to be fine, but instead, I nudged my chin toward the class and opened the door.

It looked like I had more work to do.

CHAPTER 5
LILLY
MONDAY MORNING

Verra Convention Center
Manhattan, NY

"Do you know a tutor who might be willing to work over the summer?" I asked Mia as we walked into the convention center.

The air conditioning was in full swing, and walking in here was like being thrown from an oven into a freezer.

"Oh, fuck me," Mia grumbled, hugging herself. "They couldn't turn down the fans, could they?"

Other than the air conditioner being aggressively good at its job, the center was nice. Cluttered, but nice.

The walls were industrial chic, painted with a thin layer of white that barely covered the red and brown brick beneath it. The flooring was a thick, grayish kind of wood. Stacks of chairs and folded tables lined the walls. They framed a boxed-in and curtained stage, and standing in front of that stage were about twenty teachers from other nearby schools.

My traitorous eyes were trying to pick out a six-foot-two, wide-shouldered, hard-chested, hazelnut-skinned man with great hair and an even better smile, when Mia let out a strangled noise and straightened her pint-sized legs.

"That bitch. I can't believe she's here."

That was when I found the pretty blonde with sharp, angled limbs and features. Stacey. Of course. Why wouldn't she be here?

"Looks like it's a reunion," I grumbled.

Without warning, Mia took off in her direction, and I swore under my breath before following her.

"Mia, wait. It's been so long, she's probably—"

"Well, well, well," Mia started, sounding like a cartoon villain as she stopped just behind Stacey. "Look who it is."

Stacey turned around, and her eyes went as wide as her smile. "Mia? Mia Walker? No way." Her excited squeal was very familiar, very loud, and I almost covered my ears at the sound of it.

Stacey gathered Mia up in a hug, and Mia fought her off with more force than I would've expected. "Don't you try to hug me. Not after what you did to Lilly."

Confusion crossed her face as Mia pulled herself free.

"What? You mean Trevor?" she asked.

"Obviously."

Stacey rolled her eyes. "Who cares about my cousin?"

"I care." Mia slapped her chest for emphasis. "We have to work with him, and Treviboy is awful."

"Is he?" She laughed it off as her gaze landed on me. "Lilly Fares? Oh my god. It's been years."

She pulled me into a hug and, unlike Mia, I didn't fight it. What was the point? But as I stiffened in her arms, Mia latched onto Stacey's shoulders and yanked her away.

"You don't get to hug her until you apologize–"

On instinct, Stacey struggled against Mia. Their feet tangled, and they lurched sideways. Into me.

I stumbled, grunting, taking them down with me. The three of us hit the stack of chairs by the wall with our full weight, which then knocked into another stack, sending chairs crashing to the ground, clattering around us. One swiped Stacey on the shoulder, another caught Mia on the leg, and I was on the ground with a pile across my lap, my view of the center now filled with dark green plastic.

Pain shot through my head, down my back, and rang through my right knee.

All I could hear then were Mia's and Stacey's groans, my own whimpers, and the noises our colleagues made as they started digging at the heap of chairs.

"I can't leave the room for five minutes without something like this happening?"

A dark, deep, velvety voice.

I knew that voice.

Instantly, my nerves lit up and scattered, just like that.

It was him. He was here.

And he was about to see me like this.

One of the other teachers said, "Sorry, sir. We had no idea–"

"Just get down here and pick up a chair," he interrupted, and his voice sent me back to a place filled with pastries, coffee beans, and paintings.

A place and a time when he didn't hate me.

I braced myself, ignoring the pain as I fiddled with my freshly trimmed, washed, and styled hair before wincing down at my bare knee. My sundress wasn't going to be long enough to cover the bruises I'd have after this.

I probably looked terrible–disheveled and hunched after my battle with these chairs. And did I have a bump on my head?

As the last chair lifted away from me, I touched my sore scalp. It felt more... indented than anything else?

God that was weird. But maybe I'd always had a misshapen skull?

That made sense. What about me wasn't defective at this point?

I wanted to groan, shut my eyes, and lean against

the brick wall, but fought the urge. It shouldn't have mattered that this was the version of me he'd see after all these years, but it did.

Mia and Stacey stood to the side, holding their arms and checking their knees.

And in front of me, leaning down in a pair of black trousers, a matching blazer, and a white button-down, was Shawn Jackson.

Dark-eyed, ticked-off, Shawn Jackson.

Even while angry, he was just as perfect to look at as ever, and I was irrationally annoyed at him for that. It just didn't seem fair.

And it was even less fair that my lungs had seized up, tightening as I recognized the way he smelled. A fusion of caffeine, wood and musk hit me, so familiar and heady, that before I knew it, his hand had wrapped around mine.

FIVE YEARS AGO

CHAPTER 6
SHAWN
MONDAY AFTERNOON

Tristy's Coffee Shop
Downtown Manhattan, NYC

TRISTY'S WOODEN walls were laced with artwork, lined with the faces of people I counted as family. Ancient Greek replica earthenware and Lebanese tapestries filled every available surface, and the yellow overhead lighting bathed it all in a warm glow.

When the coffee shop reached this hour in the afternoon, it felt like being wrapped in a blanket on a rainy day.

The pat, pat, pat on the windows combined with prickled skin, shivers tracing your spine as warmth draped over you—that's what *Tristy's* felt like.

The smell of roasted coffee and freshly baked pastries hung in the air; a permanent cozy fixture. This place, and the people here, were home.

But it didn't exactly feel like home right now.

I stood over Lilly, my jaw locked tight as I stared at the ground.

We were hidden from customer view in the small inventory room just behind the counter–the back room–surrounded by shelves of coffee beans and cleaning supplies.

The back room didn't have the same warmth to it that the shop itself did, but that didn't make it any less comfortable. Usually.

Today was an exception.

My muscles tensed as Lilly sat on the sofa in front of me and ripped a croissant to shreds on her plate.

"You dumped Stacey over a text message, Shawn," she complained. "You have to know that's not okay."

I ran a hand over my face and looked up at the ceiling. "How could I have dumped her if we never went out?"

"You could've at least called her."

"Lilly, I don't know the girl. Why would I call her?"

She shifted on the cushions and glared at me, balancing the plate on her lap. "It's basic courtesy. It's the least you could do."

"No. The least I could do is send a text–which I did. Now the least you can do is stay out of my business."

She yelled, "You *are* my business, you big doof!" at my back as I left.

I'd heard her say that too many times. She meant it

to show that she cared. That I mattered to her. But it never meant what I wanted it to mean.

I walked to the shopfront, stopping when I reached the counter. Pressing my palms flat to the surface, I let the wood take my weight as my boss, Tristan, turned and clapped a hand on my shoulder.

"You okay?"

"Yeah... just Lilly being Lilly."

I was wound too tight. I rolled my shoulders, trying to loosen up, but Tristan could tell I was agitated. He gave me a quirk of his lips but didn't say anything.

Knowing he'd get it, I waved a hand at the room Lilly still sat in, and told him, "Graduation's coming, and she won't..."

"Relax?" Tristan finished, his smile spreading to a full grin.

"Yeah."

He tilted his chin, and I felt his dark eyes on me. He was looking for more, probably trying to figure out why my argument with Lilly bothered me so much.

"Are you sure that's what you're upset about?"

I crossed my arms over my chest, admitting, "I don't know anymore. All I know is I can't keep doing this."

Lilly's voice quietly trembled as it drifted through the open doorway, and Tristan's attention snapped toward the back room.

"Jump up, make a sound, hey, stomp your boots, turn around..."

I ran a hand along my shorn, stubbled black hair and took a step closer, trying to see in. "Is she...?"

If Lilly was singing, it meant she was trying to calm down. Was she that upset?

Tristan shook his head, his hand still on me, keeping me in place. "She's fine."

A grumbly, "I'll go," rolled out from behind me, and a short, stout, balding man with gray hair and bushy brows waddled by us.

Lilly's uncle, Henry, rounded the counter in a brown cardigan and black apron, shuffling into the back room to get to his niece.

Tristan let out a breath. "Two more months and you're both leaving. Think you can hold out 'til then?"

Could I?

Staying here meant two more months of feeling like this. It meant pretending that being this close to her wasn't killing me.

But Tristan needed me to stay, so... it wasn't even a question.

"For you? I'll try."

His grip on my shoulder tightened, and I gave him a smile I didn't feel.

Tristan was my boss and closest friend. No matter what I did, he was there.

He meant a lot to me. The last thing I was going to do was let him down.

I'd keep working here at *Tristy's* with Lilly until our time was up.

Once we left, we'd take on careers as teachers, and everything would change.

I could keep it together until then.

What other choice did I have?

NOW

CHAPTER 7
LILLY
MONDAY MORNING

Verra Convention Center
Manhattan, NY

Shawn's expression was blank as he lifted me to my feet, but it didn't stop my stomach from flipping.

This was the first time Shawn had looked at me, let alone touched me, in years. Goosebumps raced along my skin as his thumb slid over my knuckles. Then he dropped my hand, and I felt his eyes on me as I straightened my dress.

Heat spread from my toes to my cheeks as I mumbled, "Sorry... I'll fix the chairs. If you want me to, I mean."

His frown deepened. "Are you hurt, Miss Fares?"

His tone caught me by surprise. It was cold and firm. After the way he'd held my hand, I thought maybe—but who was I kidding?

Five years without a word, and now he called me by my teacher name. That was probably how he wanted it. Distant and professional.

My embarrassment whittled down to frustration.

"No. I'm fine... *Mister Jackson*."

His dark eyes glinted. Did he think this was funny?

Ugh. I hated this. My emotions were on a rampage, and I still didn't know how to feel.

Shawn was... here. Tall, broad-shouldered, chiseled Shawn.

He had the kind of shoulders my teeth could sink into, the kind of hands that could dwarf my waist. There wasn't any point in denying he was as devastating as ever, but how could I care about that when the first thing he'd said to me in years was so stiff and formal?

Then, as if on cue, he turned from me to Mia, and I flushed from head to toe. Did he just snub me?

"Miss Walker, this is a work event. You will treat it as one. And you, Miss Atkins. This is not a sorority reunion."

I watched them as a warm prickle crept along my arms. Other teachers drew closer as he spoke, their faces blank, like they weren't even aware of it. I couldn't blame them. Shawn was magnetic.

He was calm and focused as he spoke. He didn't yell, and he didn't need to. His tall, broad frame took up space, sure, but it was his confidence that kept their attention.

When we were younger, working together at *Tristy's Coffee Shop*, it was pretty much the same. But instead of leading rooms full of teachers, he was roping in phone numbers. He was the hottest guy at Pace University.

And me? I was... just there, I guess. Trying to get to graduation.

"This fundraiser isn't an excuse to act like–" He cut himself off and gestured at Mia and Stacey.

Mia rolled her eyes. "Oh, relax, Shawn. Don't get your panties in a–"

"What is it that you don't understand, Miss Walker? We need this to go well. I won't tolerate anyone who isn't here to take this seriously. Do you understand that?"

I drifted closer, finding myself shoulder to shoulder with everyone else. Mia's glance ping-ponged around, finally settling on me as a bright pink flush spread across her cheeks.

Was Mia actually embarrassed? She was never embarrassed.

"Of course I do," she snapped. "You're not the only one who cares, you know."

He turned away from her, taking in the small crowd. "We all know what this fundraiser is about, don't we? We're here to make this the best Educational Arts Fundraiser New York has ever seen, aren't we?"

There were nods all around. I tried to meet Mia's eye, but she was too busy glaring at Shawn. Not that he noticed. He went on as if she weren't there.

"Over the next six weeks, it'll be our responsibility to make sure this fundraiser is a success. Our goal is ambitious, but I'm confident we'll get there."

As his deep, smooth voice rumbled through the hall, the teachers around me fell into a hush.

"So. We all know why we're here. But you don't know what you're going to do. Miss Atkins, could you please hand out their information sheets?"

Stacey straightened with a jolt and quickly went to a nearby table, returning with an armful of papers. Threading through the crowd, her footsteps were soft as she handed out sheet after sheet.

Mia found her way next to me, her shoulder bumping into mine. "That asshole," she whispered. "I've never been so embarrassed."

I grimaced. "I'm sorry."

"It's not your fault, Lilly," she spat. "It's his."

She looked over her instruction sheet. Our names were written on the top margin, and Mia's instructions were different from mine. Shawn modified his plan to suit each of us. I almost wanted to roll my eyes because *of course* he did.

It looked like I was in charge of merchandising for the event, which was better than doing something I'd never done before.

It used to be my specialty, back when I was a young and eager Kappa Delta. Maybe stepping into these duties would be like riding a bike. Maybe I just needed to—

Mia grumbled under her breath. "He's got me looking after the entertainment. Looks like I'll be spending the next six weeks getting coffee for a group of men with a celebrity complex."

Shawn spoke with such authority that it snapped our focus back to him.

"You'll have separate duties ranging from catering, invitations, marketing, entertainment, and merchandising, and each task is important. Your individual skills are what will make the difference between getting the job done and getting it done well."

He gave the crowd a small smile, and my heart shuffled as I caught sight of a dimple.

"Thank you all for volunteering your summer break like this. Your time is valuable, and you could've spent it doing anything else, but you're here. It won't go unnoticed."

A small applause rippled through the gathered teachers, with Stacey clapping loudest of all. I cocked my head at her. Was she... working with him? Assisting him? Or was it more than that?

I hugged my paper to my chest as Shawn said, "If you'll follow me, our office is on the upper floor."

With that, Shawn turned and walked toward an inconspicuous elevator, half-hidden behind another stack of chairs. He didn't look over his shoulder to make sure we were coming. He knew we'd follow.

What I would've given to have that kind of confi-

dence. Maybe I would've done more with my career if—
come on, Lilly.

I wasn't here for a pity party. I was here to prove I could be the teacher my students deserved.

A group of us crammed into the elevator, leaving the other half to wait until it came back. Even with all of us split like this, there wasn't a lot of breathing room. But, somehow, we managed to give Shawn a bit of distance. It wasn't until the carriage jostled that someone burst his personal space bubble.

Guess who that person was?

Little old me.

"Uh, sorry."

Geez. Bumping into Shawn was like face-planting into a brick wall. Or an electric fence. Sparks skittered across my skin as I steadied myself.

It wasn't until I looked up at him that I realized I still had my hand on his chest, and I jerked back like I'd touched a hot plate.

Every bit of me was covered in sweat; I could feel it weighing down my bangs, sliding down my spine, settling in my armpits.

I muttered my apologies again, and he softened as he looked down at me.

A strange development. His slight smile was stranger still.

My lower belly fizzed, like hundreds of tiny bubbles decided to pop all at once.

"It's fine, Miss Fares."

But then he had to use my damn teacher name again.

"Are you... still mad at me?" I asked, almost whispering.

His brows shot up. "We're here for work, Miss Fares."

"But I just want to know–"

I cut myself off as I noticed that we'd caught the attention of a few teachers. Their squints moved from me to Shawn as the elevator doors opened. And they didn't stop until he gestured for them to step out.

We shuffled into a room filled with soft beige carpet, large windows, and wooden cubicles lined with desks, chairs, and computers.

It was freezing in here. I hugged myself as I followed Shawn inside.

The elevator disappeared and reappeared, bringing more teachers in.

"There's a workstation for each of you, and to avoid confusion, your desks have been labeled. For now, I want you to find your place, boot up your computer, and get comfortable. If there are any technical issues, I'm your point of contact."

He sounded so robotic.

Where was the fun, carefree, goofy Shawn I knew and loved?

The professional tone made sense when he was up on a podium, delivering a well-rehearsed speech to hundreds of teachers, but we had to work together for the next six weeks.

He could ease up a little, couldn't he?

If Mia and I couldn't–

Mia.

I looked around the small crowd and found her grumbling under her breath, shooting Shawn daggers.

I took her by the elbow as everyone scattered, searching for their desks. "Come on, let's find ours."

"I bet that bastard sat us as far away from each other as possible," she muttered.

"Why would he do that?" We weren't naughty kids who needed to be separated.

I found my desk, which was sandwiched between a teacher from an art school, and another from a tech school.

Mia kept walking, and when she stopped at a desk that was on the other end of the room, she stared pointedly at me from across it.

"Well... maybe we are the naughty kids," I mumbled.

Behind me, a deep rumble caught my attention. I turned, flushing as Shawn raised a brow at me.

I tried not to stare. At his sharp jawline, defined cheekbones, and full lips.

It really wasn't fair that he still looked like this.

It was so intimidating. *He* was intimidating.

It was harder than ever to believe we were once friends.

My lower belly fluttered, and as he watched, I backed up against my desk.

He cleared his throat. I licked my bottom lip. His gaze dropped to my mouth. That tiny shift in focus jolted me, and just like that, I wanted him closer. And that was just... so irritating.

What was wrong with me?

I didn't like Shawn anymore. He called me torture, ended our friendship, and avoided me for years.

All I wanted was to know why.

Why was he treating me like this?

But I'd gotten nothing that came close to an answer from him so far. So why couldn't my body let go of this frustrating pull toward him?

"There's just one last thing, Miss Fares."

"Oh?" I breathed out.

"There's a break room down the hallway. Please use it if you need to."

Confused, I glanced around the room, until I noticed a quiet space peeking out from behind the corner. Did he think I needed it–

"Because of my anxiety?" I asked, finishing my thought out loud.

His lips fell into a flat line, like this was the last thing he wanted to talk about. "I'm giving you space." His voice dropped lower, making me lean closer. "If you need it, I want you to use it. Okay?"

I swallowed and nodded. "Yes, Shaw–"

"It's Mister Jackson."

Heat spread, pulsing in my lower belly. I was instantly flustered.

"You can't keep pretending we don't know each other, *Shawn*. You have to talk to me at some point."

He was infuriatingly professional as he said, "Have a good afternoon, Miss Fares. I look forward to seeing you tomorrow."

Then he turned and walked away, and there it was. That feeling again.

Disappointment.

But that was fine.

I wasn't here for him. I was here for me.

And for the next six weeks, whether he liked it or not, Shawn would just have to deal with that.

CHAPTER 8
LILLY
FRIDAY NIGHT

Lilly's Apartment

FUMBLING WITH MY KEYS, I opened the door to my tiny apartment and stepped inside, mumbling, "Home sweet home," to myself.

Scorched candle wicks and cinnamon wafted toward me, and my nerves instantly settled. It was a relief to be alone like this. With no people, no expectations, and no surprises. I ran my hand through my bangs and sat on my soft, worn-in, two-person sofa.

My first week working this fundraiser hadn't exactly been stress-free.

On Monday, Shawn made it clear we were there to work. I tried to talk to him, but he wasn't interested.

Day two, I wobbled into the center wearing a white button-down tucked into a waist-hugging black pencil skirt. The heels I tottered in were a new buy, one I instantly regretted as I tripped across the subway plat-form earlier that morning.

I remembered walking in just in time to watch Mia's mouth drop open.

"You look amazing."

I studied the cute beige dress that hung from her shoulders. "Uh, thanks but... weren't we all supposed to dress professionally, Mia?"

Her face pinched. "I don't know. Were we?"

I looked around the center, taking in the varied display of jeans, tank tops, sneakers, and summer dresses.

"It was in the information packet he gave us. Wasn't it?"

Mia pursed her lips as I spotted Shawn–sorry, Mister Jackson–speaking with a casually dressed Stacey.

He was actually smiling at her. But he couldn't have a simple conversation with me?

I was getting tired of this.

I made it to his elbow and cleared my throat. "Excuse me, Mister Jackson?"

He and Stacey shared a glance before she hurried over to another group of teachers.

He put his hands in his pockets and said, "Yes, Miss Fares?"

"Are we supposed to dress like this?"

His gaze dropped, taking in my heels, pencil skirt, and blouse. I looked like I'd robbed Mia's on-duty wardrobe.

"Yes."

"But I'm the only one."

He frowned. "You're not the only one."

"Okay fine. You and me, then," I said while rolling my eyes. "But if it's okay, I'd like to wear *my* clothes."

His lips parted, and a small, breathless laugh escaped. I crossed my arms, hating the way the sound slid through me.

"These aren't your clothes?"

I opened my mouth to answer, but he turned his shoulder until I was blocked from view.

I flushed instantly. What made him think it was okay to treat me like this?

"Everyone, could I have your attention, please? For the next six weeks, it's business as usual. That means I expect you all to dress like it's just another day in the classroom."

The teachers around us grumbled, and Shawn raised his hands.

"I know, I know. It's summer break. But this is a work event. Let's treat it like that from tomorrow onwards, all right?"

As he turned to me and raised a brow, some of the other teachers gave me a few mean stares of their own. Oh, good. They probably thought I'd complained about what they were wearing. My shoulders slumped. I wasn't off to a great start here.

"Happy, Miss Fares?"

"No, I'm not." I really would've preferred to wear my shifts and sneakers. "Can't we just talk?"

Stacey reappeared next to him, snagging his attention. "Shawn, the clean-up crew is here."

Pouring through the doors were men of varied sizes in overalls, and Shawn gave me a brief look before walking away. I twisted my lips and glared after him.

Stacey called him by his first name, and he didn't correct her. Why did that bother me so much?

Ugh, between the stomach flutters and all this dodging, he was driving me crazy. I hated not knowing how to feel about this.

I wound up spending the rest of the afternoon tied to my desk, trying to figure out how to get my email to work on my damn computer.

My third day wasn't much better. I couldn't access the server, and I needed to see the project plan so I could track my tasks.

Mashing my hands against the keyboard, I stood and stomped my sore, heeled feet into the meeting room. Shawn was in there, busy giving a teacher advice on how to handle a class full of rowdy ninth graders, so I stood in the doorway, shifting from foot to foot as I waited.

My hands found their way to the seam of my skirt, and I flinched at the way the stitches stretched around my ass. Fitting in this was a feat all its own, and I'd probably have to size up soon. Especially if I kept eating the pastry-filled care packages Tristan sent over.

My feet were burning. And they were still talking.

But maybe they didn't know I was there.

Neither of the men looked my way. At all.

Well, since they weren't looking... I toed off my shoes and let my bare feet thread through the carpet. I almost groaned, it felt so good.

But as if they could smell my sweaty toes, the two men turned to face me, and I bit my lip.

Now they looked at me?

Shawn's eyes walked the length of me before settling on my feet, and, of course, heat burst under my skin.

"Could you give us a second, Jack?"

'Jack' nodded and walked by me with a smile on his face. So, it wasn't just Stacey he was on a first-name basis with.

I crossed my arms over my chest and scowled at Shawn, but he didn't seem bothered by it.

He thrust his hands in his pockets and asked, "Yes, Miss Fares?"

"I can't access the server," I snapped. "Or set up my email."

"Okay. I'll get someone to help–"

"I need it fixed today." At his slightly incredulous stare, I added, "Please."

"I'll take a look at it," he answered, but didn't move from where he stood.

I hiked a thumb over my shoulder. "I'm sitting over there."

He smirked. "I'm aware of where your desk is, Miss Fares. I don't need you to point it out for me."

He came closer, and my stomach swooped.

"But in future, if you could keep your shoes on, I think our noses would appreciate it."

My mouth dropped as a hint of his familiar teasing smile appeared, but then he was out the door before I could think of a single thing to say.

By the fifth day, my email was working and I finally had access to the server, but my computer started rebooting every half hour. As my head thudded against the keyboard, I decided I needed another coffee.

Picking up my mug, I slowly made my way down the hall. As painful as these heels were, I thought I was finally starting to get used to them.

"Can't you cut her some slack?" Mia's voice floated out of the kitchen. I paused by the doorframe.

"I can't just forget what happened." Shawn's voice. And it was warm. Kind, even. I took a breath and held it.

"I'm not asking you to. Look, Treviboy—"

"You mean Trevor?"

"Yes. Him. He's been a nightmare since the two of them broke up, but after he got his promotion, he's been worse. The asshole doesn't let her get away with anything."

"Like what?"

"Like her test scores. He set her up with a module to study, and it's based on teaching to the test, which we both know is complete horseshit."

"Well... yeah. That goes against everything I'm trying to do."

"Exactly. And it's gotten so bad that he's even tried banning her from watching movies with her students."

A short burst of deep, gravelly laughter. Shawn was laughing. With *Mia*. Which made no sense. They couldn't stand each other.

"You mean My Little Pony? She still watches those movies?"

I could hear the smile in Mia's voice as she said, "Are you kidding? Thanks to her, I know every word of *Camp Everfree* and it isn't even my favorite one."

Another laugh. "Which is your favorite?"

"*Forgotten Friendship*, of course."

A bit of the old Shawn—the person I knew and missed—came through in his voice just then.

"I don't think anything will ever beat the original movie. That 'Cafeteria Song' lives rent-free in my head. Do you remember how many times she sang that?"

I squeezed my mug handle. Maybe... maybe he didn't hate me like I thought he did. Maybe I was wrong.

"She still does. Mostly when Trevor's around. That's what I'm saying here. I need you to stop making things so difficult for her."

"I'm not."

"Then how do you explain all the computer problems?"

"You think I'd do something to stop her from doing her job?"

"Oh, for Cripe's sake, Shawn, you haven't exactly given her a warm welcome the past few days."

She let out a breath, and I could picture her hands on her hips as she spoke.

"You're *Shawn Jackson*. If this fundraiser goes up in smoke, your career could swallow the bump without a problem. But Lilly's? We both know South Bronx is everything to her, and Treviboy wouldn't let her get away with it if she failed here."

A teacher walked by me, eyeing me strangely as he stepped into the kitchen.

"You've got an audience," he mumbled, and I stepped out from behind the doorframe, shame rippling through me until I thought steam was going to shoot from my ears.

Shawn and Mia stared at me until I felt obligated to say, "Sorry... I wasn't eavesdropping... I think? I just wanted coffee."

Oh, wouldn't the ground just open up and swallow me whole, please? Please, beige carpet, please?

They swapped glances and Mia was the first to slide by, shooting me a meaningful squint on her way past. Shawn was slower, choosing to study the table before eventually closing the distance between us.

"Miss Fares," he greeted while giving me a surprising smile.

He looked like he wanted to say something else, but

then changed his mind, walking out without another word.

I couldn't find a minute to corner him or Mia for the rest of the day. When we were finally funneling out through the front doors, I looked up to find him watching me. But as soon as my eyes met his, he looked away and stepped outside. I was about to call out to him when my phone rang.

"Mrs Hernandez," I answered. "How are you? How's Jessica?"

The busy street was full of cars honking in the summer heat. I covered my ear so I could hear the distaste in her voice.

"The tutor you sent isn't going to work out, Miss Fares. You sent a man to my house."

"O-Oh. Well, uh, I'm sorry... about that? I didn't think that would be an issue–"

"You didn't think sending a man to tutor my daughter would be an issue?"

"No, I didn't. What's the problem, exactly?"

Mrs Hernandez heaved a sigh so frustrated, I almost stopped in my tracks on the busy sidewalk, the urge to apologize right on the tip of my tongue.

"I saw the way she looked at him, and now I can't leave them alone."

I was confused, but the urge to apologize won out. "I'm so sorry, Mrs Hernandez. What can I do to fix this?"

She was quick to answer. "You can find me another

tutor. A female this time. And for god's sake, get me someone who knows what they're doing."

I swallowed and nodded, picking up the pace and ending our call.

Now that I was back home in my apartment, I took stock of what the weekend held in store for me:

1. I needed to find a new female adult literature tutor for Jessica to satisfy Mrs Hernandez.

2. On Monday, I needed to start contacting suppliers for the fundraiser.

3. Tonight, I needed to finish the seventh lecture on teaching-to-the-test to meet Trevor's timeline (He was *actually* tracking me. Like I couldn't be trusted to finish the damn lessons on my own).

Task list done, I let out a breath and stretched my feet across the sofa.

Did Shawn hate me?

On one hand, we had years of friendship behind us. We used to work side by side, getting in each other's way, poking and tickling. Laughing, too. My Jim Carey impression once made coffee shoot out of his nose.

He knew me. He knew my faults, my flaws, my weaknesses, and back then, I didn't think he judged me for them. Other than Mia and our little coffee shop family, he was the only person who knew about my mom and my anxiety.

It was clear from his conversation with Mia that he hadn't forgotten any of it.

So why was he still acting like this?

Yes, five years ago, right before graduation, we had a... disagreement. But I didn't think he'd meant it. I didn't think he'd cut me out of his life.

A year after graduating, when I saw him at our first workshop, I thought we were finally going to get over this. But that didn't happen.

He treated me like I was the last person he wanted to see. So, what else could that mean? Other than the obvious?

But he didn't sound like he hated me when he spoke to Mia.

Although, it did seem like she was pinning my tech issues on him.

But... Shawn wouldn't make my job difficult on purpose, would he? He couldn't be that desperate to get rid of me.

I snorted. Maybe he was. Maybe working with me really was torture. Maybe he'd let the merchandising part of the fundraiser slip just so he could find an excuse to push me out of his orbit again.

My anxiety hummed, beating at a steady rhythm.

I wasn't going to solve this tonight. The only thing I could do was finish Trevor's lecture.

I pulled my laptop toward me and settled deeper into the cushions.

FIVE YEARS AGO

CHAPTER 9
SHAWN
THURSDAY AFTERNOON

Two Months Until Graduation
Tristy's Coffee Shop

LATELY, I couldn't look at Lilly without staring at her. Without picturing what she'd look like naked underneath me.

I couldn't hear her husky voice without imagining her moaning into my shoulder, biting into it.

And I couldn't be near her without wanting to know what her waist felt like in my hands.

Which was a problem. A pretty big fucking problem. For me, at least.

But I didn't always see her this way.

Lilly and I spent years studying and working side by side, and neither of us had ever made a move. The urge just wasn't there.

I didn't know why—Maybe because I was a nineteen-year-old idiot when we met, and my head was wedged too far up my ass to notice how stunning she was at the time.

She kept her long brown hair tied in a lopsided ponytail or bun, with bangs that brushed the tips of her soft cheeks. She had two crooked bottom teeth that only showed when she was really smiling, and wide green eyes framed with thick lashes. With those bold, full brows and freckles, she was beautiful in a quiet, understated way.

I didn't see it, though. Not at first, and not for years.

But when that changed—and it sure as fuck did—all it took was a single afternoon.

We were in the back room one Tuesday last August, and she'd just finished mopping while I packed away the rest of the food.

Lilly was teasing me about this customer I'd been eyeing, and I couldn't resist teasing her back.

"You've never thought a customer was hot? I bet you've got a thing for one of them. What about James? The tall, hairy guy who orders a mocha every morning?"

She hung up her apron and laughed. "Shawn, come on."

"Maybe it's Extra-Foam-Guy? Does the extra foam do it for you, Lil? Do you want to feel those foamy bits all over you?"

I tickled her ribs, and she grabbed my wrists,

laughing and tripping backward, dragging me with her until we both fell on the sofa.

I kept tickling, trying not to make it weird, but she was on my lap somehow, wriggling while she laughed, and–

It was like opening my eyes for the first time.

I noticed the way her breath rose and fell, her breasts shifting under her shirt. I noticed the way her body curved over the cushions. I noticed how cute her nose was beneath all those freckles, and how perfect her lips were when she smiled.

Fuck... I *noticed*.

I wanted to run my hands over her soft skin, watch that smile fade as she bit her lip, arched for me, and silently begged for more, her breath sharp on my jaw as I dragged her closer.

But Lilly was taken.

She was dating some guy named Trevor, and... no matter how badly I wanted it, nothing could happen between us.

So I jumped off that sofa and let her thud to the ground.

She groaned, rubbed her ass, and said, "Damn it, Shawn," while I tried to think of the eighty-year-old woman with the hairy chin who kept asking to feel my biceps.

Now, months later, here we were, and I still had to talk myself down when she smiled at me.

If she smiled at me.

After our argument about Stacey, I was starting to think I'd never get a smile from her again.

The hiss of the coffee machine snapped me back to the shop. Tristan yanked his hand back. Too late.

I sucked a breath between my teeth and winced at his shiny new burn. "That'll need some ice. It looks bad."

It was proof of how little the poor guy had been sleeping. I couldn't remember the last time he'd burned himself.

Uncle Henry let out a snort and shoved his scarred fingers in my face. His Greek accent curled thickly in my ear. "Is nothing, see? Is part of job."

Tristan shrugged, pulling his hand away. "Yeah. It's nothing."

I shook my head and went to the back room. "Nikki wouldn't want you working through pain like that."

Uncle Henry's laugh pelted my back as Tristan called out, "Shawn, it's fine." But I brought the first aid kit back to the counter anyway and held out my hand.

He was fighting a grin. I could see it under all that carefully structured stubble he wore. But he put his hand in mine and let me treat his burn.

Lilly's uncle silently went to work behind the coffee machine, shooting me some amused side-eye while working faster than any of us ever could.

Just then, Lilly burst through the door, which startled the customers sitting in their cozy booths. She mumbled, "Sorry, sorry," to them as she hurried to join us behind the counter.

Nerves exploded in my stomach at the sight of her, and I barely held back a laugh when she winced at Tristan.

"Took you long enough," I teased.

She shot me a glare as she threw her jacket up on a nearby hook.

"Sorry, I was busy helping Mia with–" She shook her head, cutting herself off. "What did I miss?"

Uncle Henry kept working the machine as I muttered, "Tristan burned himself." She whirled to him. "Are you okay?"

"I'm fine," he said. "But Karim left early, so we're short. Can you and Shawn handle front for a bit?"

She nodded as Uncle Henry stepped back from the machine. Both the older man and Tristan shuffled to the back room, grumbling as they went.

Before our first customer reached the counter, I asked over my shoulder, "Done being mad at me yet?"

She moved to my side. "I never said I was mad. I'm just frustrated. I don't get why one date with Stacey was such a big deal."

I clenched my jaw so tight, I could feel my teeth grind. This again.

"Lilly, I'd do anything for you, you know that. But I'm not interested. She'll get over it."

By the time the customers reached us, I was behind the machine and Lilly was taking orders, passing me receipts between handing pastries over the glass divider.

"I can't believe you're not interested. She's your type."

I held in a laugh.

Stacey wasn't my type. No other woman was.

Lilly was the only one I wanted.

Even now, the closer she got, the more my muscles tensed. I wasn't used to wanting something this badly, and it was unbearable.

Every day, Lilly worked next to me, her body inches from mine. She was right there, *right there;* something I could see, smell, hear.

And I couldn't touch her. I couldn't taste her. I couldn't have her.

It was killing me.

"No," I muttered. "She isn't."

"Really?" She let out a short huff as she pulled a warm muffin from the microwave. "I don't believe it."

After bagging and handing over the baked good, she folded her arms and stared at me. I could feel her gaze on the side of my face, like she was poking me with it.

"What?"

"What kind of girl *is* your type, then?" she asked with a playful smile.

I tried to play her question off with a shrug.

"I'm too busy focusing on graduating to have a 'type'. Maybe you should focus on that too."

She surprised me then. She stopped, groaned, and

dropped her arms, letting them dangle by her sides. It was sudden enough that I shot her a look.

"What? What did I say?"

"Nothing," she said, her voice a little too high. "It's just... I haven't started studying yet."

Right. For her exam.

Lilly had one final exam, and she'd already failed it once before. If she didn't pass this time, there was a very real possibility she might not make it to graduation.

"Why not?" I asked.

As she shook her head, her face paled. Her hands wandered to her stomach; her shoulders tensed. Those weren't good signs. She was panicked, and I bet I knew why.

"I just have so much to do, and I haven't–"

Her voice cut off as I brushed her bangs from her lashes, instantly regretting it. Her cheek was so soft, it only made me want to touch her again.

A pretty dusting of pink spread beneath her freckles, but then she pushed my hand away as I said, "You've been helping everyone else with their work instead of worrying about yours."

It was the same problem she'd had since we met. She gave too much of herself to everyone around her.

"I *am* worried about my work, but I just need to help them with theirs too."

Obviously, I didn't agree.

Lilly, Mia, and their friends belonged to Kappa

Delta. The sorority had strict rules on what grade average they expected from their members, which was fine. But it wasn't Lilly's problem. She shouldn't have had to do the extra work to lift everyone else's grades along with her own.

It was burning her out. And with her exam only weeks away, she couldn't afford to let that happen.

"They should do it themselves," I grumbled. "And I bet they would if they knew how tired you were."

Uncle Henry leaned on the doorframe and muttered, "Never tell a lady she tired. I thought you good with women?"

Somewhat surprised, I laughed while Lilly rolled her eyes.

Her usually playful voice was coated with frustration. "I can't disappoint them. I'll be fine."

I knew she'd say that.

Lilly would rather run herself into the ground before she let anyone down. It was one of the things I loved about her—that she cared so much about other people.

But I didn't love it when it went too far. When she took on more than she could handle, and helping others meant hurting herself.

"I can handle it. Really." She put a hand to her stomach and breathed. "I just have to pass an exam a month before graduation. I can do it," she mumbled.

And she could.

She could do anything if she just stopped trying to make everyone else happy and looked after herself first.

But would she?

This was the part where I'd usually offer to help her study. The words were right there, on the tip of my tongue. But I couldn't make myself say them.

Lilly was with someone else, and being alone with her in a tiny, cramped study room, knowing I couldn't touch her... yeah, that would be torture.

I wouldn't be able to sit there and pretend I didn't want her, and right now, pretending was the only thing keeping me sane.

I had to let her figure this one out on her own. But standing here, knowing I couldn't help her, annoyed the shit out of me.

Because if she failed this exam again, that was it. No second chances, no diploma. Just more disappointment that she didn't deserve.

CHAPTER 10
SHAWN
FRIDAY MORNING

Tristy's coffee shop

THE RICH CHOCOLATE-BROWN cushioning on our chairs and booths was still immaculate after the last renovation Tristan managed a few years back.

I liked the way the surfaces reflected, slick and smooth, without a scratch in sight. There was something soothing about cleaning this place.

Except when Lilly was stacking cups and plates on a tray alongside me.

She'd been vibrating all morning, like she was about to burst. I loved seeing her like this. Her mood was infectious.

Even now, she lowered her voice and inched closer, like she wanted to tell me a secret. It was fucking adorable.

But then she asked, "Did you get a letter too?" and my chest sank.

I stared at the rag in my hands and kept cleaning.

"You mean the letter from South Bronx?"

From the corner of my eye, I saw her nod. "Yep, that one." Excitement crept into her voice. "Mia got one too. Can you believe it?" She squealed. "All of us teaching at my mom's school?"

I walked back to the counter and she followed. As I emptied the cups from Lilly's tray, I said, "Yeah. What're the odds we'd get picked to teach at the same place?"

In the same faculty.

I'd see her every day if I took that job, and I had to admit, the thought of that was pretty tempting. Even if taking the chance to be near her meant... more of this.

But the offer from South Bronx wasn't the only one I had. Brooklyn wanted me too. And the opportunities they'd laid out for me in that letter were hard to ignore.

"You're accepting, right?" she asked, and from the corner of my eye, I could see she had her hands on her hips.

I took a chance and looked up at her, instantly wishing I hadn't. She was so happy about getting this placement at her mom's school that she was glowing. That letter probably made her forget about the test she still had to pass.

But fuck. She really was beautiful. How did I manage to go so long without seeing it?

My head really was wedged up my ass.

"I'll think about it," I told her, and that was definitely not what she wanted to hear.

She rolled her eyes and put her hand on my arm. The warmth of her touch was so shocking, I had to fight the urge to pull away.

"I can't wait to teach there." She squealed again.

And now I had more urges to fight. This was getting ridiculous.

Her smile was so gorgeous that it was making me hard. At work.

Fuck me. What was I supposed to do with this in the middle of the day?

I'd never been so relieved to wear a black apron in my life. It was the only thing that hid what she did to me.

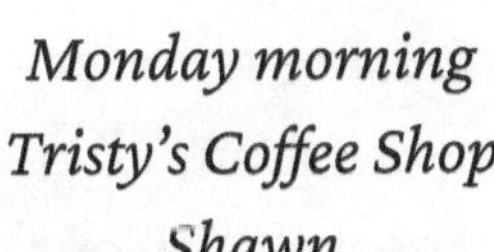

Monday morning
Tristy's Coffee Shop
Shawn

THE WEEKEND SPED by in a blur, and I was back at Tristan's coffee shop with my black apron tied at my waist, checking for Lilly every time there was movement outside our glass-paned wall.

I had to make a decision.

I reread both offers from Brooklyn and South, and if I based my choice on opportunity alone, Brooklyn was the better option.

They lined up workshops, mentorships, consistent classroom timetables, and a flexible substitution system that meant I could do something to help kids outside of the classroom, too.

But South had Lilly.

South Bronx was important to her. When she was a kid, her dad ran out on her and her mom, leaving them for a second family he'd hidden in Greece. I didn't know her then, but I heard Lilly didn't take the abandonment well. Tristan told me about her anxiety and how her mother helped her find ways to cope.

I heard that her mother, Harriet, was the entire inspiration behind Lilly's decision to teach. She was also the reason Lilly loved those cartoon pony movies so much.

I had an embarrassing amount of knowledge about My Little Pony. After we spent all those hours watching them together on the sofa in our back room, it was impossible not to memorize every detail of those movies. And I would've watched them for a thousand more hours if it made her happy.

I knew all the words to the song she loved most. I knew that when she sang it, it helped her get a handle on her anxiety. It was one of the techniques her mom taught her.

But, eventually, Lilly's mom died of cancer, and Uncle Henry stepped up, taking in his niece. He supported her in every way he could. So when Lilly told him she wanted to teach at South Bronx just like her mom did, he put her through all the right programs to give her that chance.

I knew what being there meant to her. And I wanted to do it with her.

But an opportunity like this might never come around again. Brooklyn Classical was offering me the career of my dreams, right there on a silver platter.

Now, it was Monday morning, and I didn't have much time left. Both schools were waiting for an answer.

Just then, Lilly burst into the shop, and I looked up. She made it to the counter, rubbing the sleep from her eyes and ruffling her bangs.

Without saying anything, she took off her jacket, threw it over the display case, and... moved so fast that, suddenly, she was just... *close*. Her face was inches from mine, her eyes pinned on me, like she could stumble into me any second. I had to curl my hands into fists to stop myself from touching her.

"What... are you doing?" I asked, trying to sound put off.

"We need to talk about this, Shawn. What're you going to do?" she asked, staring me down.

"What are you talking about?"

She leaned closer, if that was even fucking possible, and I had to hold my breath.

I didn't want to take in her toasted cinnamon scent. I didn't want to fight staring at her lips. I didn't want to struggle to keep my hands to myself.

This was exactly why Brooklyn should have been an easy yes for me.

"I'm talking about South Bronx. I've accepted, and so has Mia. But you–" she poked my chest "–might lose your spot to Trevor if you don't hurry up."

I was completely thrown. "Trevor's going to work there?"

Trevor was Stacey's cousin and Lilly's boyfriend. He was an okay guy, a decent teacher. I had nothing against him, aside from the fact that he was smart enough to ask Lilly out before I could.

"He will if you don't."

From the corner of my eye, I caught Tristan walking in, holding our two bowls of oatmeal.

Lilly wasn't fazed by our sudden lack of privacy. She kept her stare on me as she said, "And I want *you* there."

Having Lilly this close made it hard to breathe. It felt like air was being squeezed from my lungs, and I couldn't think straight. I was starting to sweat, annoyed with the fact that my body refused to calm the fuck down around her.

"You'd both better eat before the morning rush starts," Tristan said, handing each of us our meals.

Saved by the boss. I took my bowl and backed away

from her, thanking Tristan for more than just the food as Lilly mumbled under her breath behind me.

I want you *there.*

I knew what that meant. This was big for us.

We were about to change jobs, where we lived, our priorities. Everything.

On top of all that, Lilly was trying to wrap her head around working in the same faculty her mom once worked in.

I knew that if she could prevent one thing from changing, if she could keep working with me, she believed maybe she could cope with the rest of it.

And I wanted to be there for her. But, maybe I wasn't the one she needed.

NOW

CHAPTER 11
LILLY
MONDAY MORNING

Verra Convention Center

WITH MY PHONE strapped to my ear, I sped to my desk.

9:05am.

I wasn't late. Not really. Was I?

Crap, what if I was? What if Shawn called me into his office like I was a tardy truant? What if he yelled at me in front of the other teachers?

Arrrghh. This was what being a student felt like. It had been years since I felt like this.

I angled my butt into my seat, and it groaned, offended, like it was begging me to lose the five pounds that'd gone straight to my ass last summer.

Sorry, pal. Not today.

"Did you make it?" Nikki asked, still on the line.

"Yeah... hang on a sec. I can't breathe in this skirt." I

held the phone away as I sucked in a lungful of air and adjusted the waistband of my outfit.

"Didn't buy that new one, did you?" she drawled, on the verge of laughing.

"No," I answered, trying to sound annoyed instead of panicked. "I spent the weekend looking for an adult, female tutor who specializes in literature instead. Want to guess how many of them are in Manhattan right now, itching for the chance to teach a high school student over summer break?"

"Fourteen?" Nikki teased.

"Zero. I have zero people lined up for this. And Mrs Hernandez won't raise the rate from twenty dollars an hour. So, you know, as enticing as the job sounds, I can't really blame anyone for rejecting it."

Nikki made a noise of agreement as I booted up my computer.

"It's my fault for not setting boundaries with the parents. I offered Mrs Hernandez my number. My *number*. I mean, I can't blame anyone but myself."

"You're not wrong about that." Strike one for No-Bullshit-Nikki. "And Mia doesn't have anyone she can recommend?"

"She sent me the first tutor. And you know that didn't go over well."

Nikki hesitated, then asked, "What about Shawn?"

Acid crawled up my throat.

"I'm not asking him for help, Nikki. It's bad enough

that I've been nagging him about my computer since last week."

I clicked on my email and the server files.

Bong, bong. *You do not have permission to access this file.*

A scream of frustration died in my throat.

"What is it?" Nikki asked.

"Error messages," I groaned. "I thought this was fixed. I can't get anything done if my computer doesn't work."

"Is there anyone else who can help you?"

"No. Only Shawn."

Nikki playfully purred, "Well, you better go and say good morning then."

I groaned again and face-palmed. "He still hates me, Nikki."

"He never hated you. He just couldn't handle working with you." Her tone sounded so reasonable I wanted to laugh.

"And that doesn't sound like hate to you?" I sighed. "I've got to handle this."

"Give Shawn a kiss for me," Nikki crooned.

I scoffed and hung up. The last thing Shawn Jackson wanted from me was a kiss.

I stood and looked around the office, finding bowed backs and poorly-postured teachers tapping away at their keyboards. Across the room, Mia picked up a tiny bottle and waved it around.

I was too frazzled to laugh.

"Mia, what are you doing?" I whispered, eyeing the small bottle of whiskey. "If Shawn sees you with that, he's going to freak."

She laughed and showed me a paper with printed boxes. "But if I don't have my drinky-drinks, how am I supposed to play boozy bingo?"

At the look on my face, Mia rolled her eyes and said, "Don't worry, I'm not actually going to drink here. I'm saving them for later. It doesn't hurt to be prepared, you know."

I leaned on her desk and studied the paper. "Cross out every time Shawn says: 'Miss Fares'. *Mia.*"

She shrugged. "The man is nothing if not predictable."

I looked around the office, but he wasn't anywhere in sight. "Have you seen him come in?"

"Nope, not yet. Why?" she asked. "What's the plan? What do you need?"

I gave Mia a small curve of my lip, but I was too tense to make it look genuine. I gave up and went with the truth. "My computer isn't working again, and I'm so behind. If I don't get this fixed, I can't get my work done."

Mia's gaze went straight to my hand as I pressed it against my stomach. She stood from her chair and squeezed my arm. "Hey, it's all right. We'll figure this out. I'll print a copy of the project plan so you can get started."

I shook my head. "I need access to the department

email addresses, and I don't have that either." Acid swirled, burning my chest. "I could take the subway back to South Bronx. My email should be working there."

Mia frowned. "You shouldn't have to go all the way there just to use it. What about your phone?"

I opened the email app and showed it to her. I couldn't get it to load. My password wasn't working and I had no idea why.

Her frown deepened. "What's going on with you? You're like the Bermuda Triangle of technology."

I groaned and rubbed my eye with the heel of my palm. "I know. And Shawn isn't even here yet. I was worried about being late for nothing. I can't do anything until this is fixed."

"Okay, we can figure this out. Shawn isn't here, but his right-hand man is."

"Who's the right-hand man?"

"Stacey." Mia spat her name like it was a sour gummy worm. The one candy she couldn't stomach. "Who else?"

Leaning closer, I asked, "Do you know what's going on with them?"

She looked over my shoulder. "No idea. She might just be working the fundraiser with him, but we know they teach at Brooklyn together too."

"Ugh." My stomach swirled. "I have to sit down."

Mia gave me her chair, and I sank into it. I was

grateful that she was here, but it was hard not to focus on everything that was going wrong.

"What am I going to do? I need to get the merchandising organized in the next five weeks, Mrs Hernandez is hounding me for a tutor, and this module Trevor's got me studying is going in one ear and out the other."

"You're not absorbing anything?" she asked, her hand on my shoulder.

"No. The lessons are based on total crap. I can't believe I'm so bad at teaching that–"

"Lilly Fares, you are *not* a bad teacher," Mia interrupted, her voice firm. "I never want to hear you say that again. Your kids love you."

I started mumbling lyrics as Mia grumbled under her breath. I was too frustrated, tired, and anxious to argue with her. I just wanted things to start working so I could do my job.

I needed this to work.

If it didn't, if I lost my job, I'd lose everything.

My students, my classroom, the last reminder I had of my mom. I'd eventually lose my apartment unless I found another position fast.

But what school would hire a teacher who was fired for being bad at her job?

My chest squeezed. Feeling every bit of air that moved through my throat, I struggled to sing under my breath.

Both Mia's hands were on my upper arms now,

squeezing, and I shut my eyes, focusing on it. Her voice joined mine and we sang together.

"Jump up, make a sound, hey, stomp your boots, turn around. Start now, make a change, gonna make that sound—"

"Uh. Is everything... okay here?"

My eyes blinked open to find Stacey staring down at us. She looked confused and uncomfortable.

"Everything is just great," Mia drawled, folding her arms. "Except Lilly's computer isn't working again. Where's Shawn?"

Stacey hugged her notebook to her chest. "He's meeting with the Education Board. They're working out how much money to put into his new initiative."

She softened as she spoke, her shoulders relaxing, curving into her book as if it could hug her back. "But maybe I can take a look?"

I wasn't in a position to turn down help, so I nodded and followed her back to my desk, giving Mia a look over my shoulder. But she was staring at her tiny bottle of whiskey and bingo card, disappointed.

I almost laughed. Poor thwarted Mia. Did she really want to play that badly? I almost wished Shawn would show up just so she could cross off a few boxes.

"So, how are you going with your tasks?" Stacey asked as I sat at my desk and logged in. "We're on a strict timeline."

"I know," I sighed, trying not to take my frustration out on her. It wasn't Stacey's fault that I was in this mess. At least, not directly. "I haven't started. By the time things were working last week, I had to leave."

"So, you haven't done... anything?" she asked, with obvious judgment. "That's not like you. You used to be so on top of things."

My eyes snapped up, straight to her face.

I knew what she meant. She meant that I used to be on top of things back when we were students in the same sorority. But that was five years ago, and I was definitely *not* on top of anything back then.

"Because I had to be. I had to stay on top of my work and everyone else's, because you said you'd kick me out of the sorority if I wasn't."

Stacey's brow arched. "It was your job, and it was good for you."

My grip tightened around the desk. "No, it wasn't. I was struggling."

"Oh please, you wanted to help."

"Not like that, Stacey. I told you I needed time to study, remember? And you said I had to figure it out."

"And you did, didn't you?"

"Yes, but–"

I cut myself off as she rolled her eyes and said, "Lilly, come on. It's not like I forced you into anything."

I blinked at her, surprised. That was exactly what she did. And not just with the sorority.

"Stacey, you know I never would've dated Trevor if you didn't set us up. And now he's my boss."

She put her hand to her chest. "I set you up on one date. Everything that happened after that was on you."

My mouth opened, but I didn't know what to say.

Was I in the wrong here?

Were Mia and I living in some alternate reality where Shawn and I were never friends, and Stacey never forced me into doing all that work?

She paused, thinking, then shook her head. "Let's refocus here. You're not connecting to our files?"

Stiffly, I dropped my shoulders a notch and nodded. "Or my email."

She bent over me, and I caught a whiff of the sweet perfume she wore. I bet it was the same one she practically bathed in five years ago. Bubble-gum sweet, just like she pretended to be.

"I don't think I can fix this. We should wait for Shawn."

"When will he be back?"

She shrugged. "I'm not sure. It's an important meeting. Can you do anything else while you wait?"

As I shook my head, hot tears pricked my eyes. My phone buzzed, and Stacey took it as her cue to leave.

The name on the screen flashed, and I dreaded answering it, but I didn't have a choice.

"Hi, Trevor."

"I'm calling for an update." He was straight to the point, as always. "How's the fundraiser?"

I blinked, trying not to cry. "Okay so far. I guess."

"You guess? Or you know?"

What could I say here?

If I told him the truth, he'd hold it over my head. If I lied, he'd find out eventually.

"Your silence isn't exactly comforting. So things aren't going well?"

I sniffed. My throat closed in on itself, and I wasn't sure I could say anything even if I wanted to.

"I'm going to take that as a yes," he sighed, and I pictured him swiveling in his desk chair. "Lilly, I'm going to tell you this one last time. If you screw up this fundraiser, you can forget about coming back to South Bronx after summer break. Do you understand?"

"Yes," I breathed.

"Good. The next time I call you, I want to hear that you're nailing this. Got it?"

"Yes," I repeated.

He hung up without another word, and I dropped my head into my hands.

CHAPTER 12
LILLY
MONDAY AFTERNOON

Verra Convention Center

I BOUGHT the biggest slice of pizza I could find. One bite in, and I was already moaning. So damn good, and exactly what I needed.

My phone was on silent, strapped to my armband, playing my playlist. Between the saucy carbs and the music blasting through my brain, I finally felt like a normal, solid person again.

Another day wasted. But I wasn't going to give up.

Shawn had to come back sometime, and when he did, I'd ask him to fix my tech issues. Then I'd crush my to-do list, even if it meant ordering dinner straight to the office.

I'd sleep there if I had to. I wasn't going to let Trevor beat me.

Maybe he was the villain in my story after all.

Maybe he and Shawn were in cahoots to ruin my life. Maybe I had two bad guys to deal with instead of one.

It was times like this that I wished I had some kind of fairy godmother looking out for me. I'd look up at the sky and mutter, "Please, just tell me what to do?" And the answer would come to me, like magic.

But for now, the only thing coming to me was heat-stroke. I wiped the sweat from my forehead and walked back to the center, grateful for the blast of cold air, then shivering because of it.

Making my way past the maze of cubicles, the first thing I noticed was the quiet. I looked around but couldn't see anyone. Keyboards and desktops were abandoned under the fluorescent lighting.

Where was everybody?

I walked down the short hallway toward the meeting room, and before I could look through the frosted glass, the door swung open and sound burst free. Teachers were laughing and chatting, excited and motivated, while I stood there in total confusion as they squeezed by.

Mia detached herself from the group and waved her bingo card at me. "There you are. Check this out. I'm going to drink until I can't feel my toes."

The boxes she'd crossed off had things like, 'Drink every time Shawn gives a speech' and 'Drink when Shawn says *appropriate*'. I would've laughed if I wasn't so stunned.

I pointed to the room she just came out of. "What was that about?"

"Oh, nothing too crazy. Just a progress meeting. He set these up so we'd have a chance to go over our tasks." Mia crossed her arms. "I have to admit, the fit asshole has a knack for leadership." She cocked her head at me. "I sent you a text about it. Where were you?"

Unease unraveled in the pit of my stomach. "I didn't get a meeting invite, and my phone was on silent. I didn't see your messages."

Mia must've sensed something in my tone. She gripped my wrist and gave it a slight shake. "He's here, and I've told him about your dickwad computer. Get in there and sort this out with him."

I nodded, taking a steadying breath. This was what I'd psyched myself up to do. I was going to handle this. I *had* to handle this.

Mia gave me a final squeeze and left. Around the corner, I could hear teachers sliding into their desks, loading their computers, chatting, and laughing. They were making happy, productive, efficient sounds. The kind of sounds people made when they were content with being led by the great Shawn Jackson.

Maybe that was why the sudden whine coming from the meeting room snagged my attention like nails on a chalkboard.

"She blamed me for what happened with Trevor." That was definitely Stacey. And she was definitely talking about me.

"She was probably just upset." Shawn sounded as calm as he usually did.

"Upset or not, it was unprofessional."

"Unprofessional?"

"Yes. And I've been trying, you know I have. I've been trying since they got here. But between Mia pushing me into that stack of chairs, and her–"

I pictured Shawn's hands on Stacey's shoulders as she stuttered. He was patient but firm as he said, "I get it, but I can't kick them out of here. Mia's doing her job well, and–"

"Lilly isn't."

"Well..."

"She didn't even show up for our meeting."

"How about you get a coffee?" he deflected. "I'll talk to her while you're out."

Their footsteps were muffled by the carpet, but I could still make them out. They were leaving the meeting room.

I was standing in the hallway, just out of view, but as soon as they saw me, it'd be obvious that I'd heard every word they'd said. My accidental eavesdropping was turning into a bad habit; one I didn't want to get caught doing.

So what else could I do but try to escape before they noticed me?

I turned and made it about seven steps before Stacey started drawling at my back.

"Well, at least you won't have to look too hard to find her."

Bracing myself, I turned and lifted my hand in an awkward wave. "Hi."

Stacey passed by me with a pinched face. Behind her, Shawn stood, tall and intimidating, hands in his pockets as he watched me. My skin felt hot, like it was turning the brightest shade of pink just from having his eyes on me.

He stepped closer, and my breath caught in my throat as he gestured toward the now-empty room.

I wasn't sure I wanted to go in there.

Because based on what I'd just heard, it sounded like I was in trouble, and this felt a lot like being called into the principal's office.

The sexy principal's office? What did sexy principals even do? Give spankings? Was Shawn going to put me over his knee and spank me? Oh no, that was *not* an okay thought to have. What was wrong with me?

He held the door for me as I walked in, then shut it behind us, and I could swear that the hairs on my arms stood on end.

I had no idea what to expect, but being alone with him like this couldn't be a good thing.

"You weren't at our meeting today."

Sweat beaded under my bangs as I admitted, "I didn't get the invitation."

He cocked his head, still studying me. "Mia texted you."

"I know, but I didn't get her message."

"Because?" he asked, drawing out the word.

"Because I *didn't*, okay?"

Hot embarrassment flared, and I just couldn't look him in the eye anymore. Putting my hands on my hips, I turned away and started to pace nervously on the carpet. The lack of sound almost made me miss the soothing clack, clack, clack of my heels.

"My computer still isn't working, and I don't want to keep nagging you, Shawn, but–"

"Mister Jackson."

I stopped and stared at him. "Are you kidding?"

"No. I'd prefer it if you called me–"

"I don't care what you prefer," I yelled, all control gone.

Everything was crashing down around me, and all he cared about was what name I called him?

"My computer isn't working, and I can't do my job, and your assistant is telling you to fire me, and Trevor is threatening to take my job away, and Mrs Hernandez won't stop calling me–"

I burst. I physically *burst*.

"And on top of all that, you're acting like a huge dick, Mister Jackson. You're treating me like you don't know me. Like we never..." I trailed off, watching Shawn's face shift from concern to frustration as I palmed my stomach and curled over.

Acid scraped my ribs, eating into the pizza I'd enjoyed only minutes ago. I tried to steady my breathing, but was jolted out of it when Shawn turned and left the room.

He. Left. The. Room.

I slapped both hands to my mouth and screamed into my palms, letting my voice scorch my throat.

I HATE him.

I hate him, I hate him, I hate him.

My phone vibrated against my hip, but I couldn't answer it. I really couldn't. Tears pushed against my eyes, hot and urgent, and I brushed them away, trying to keep them back. It wasn't until Shawn reappeared with a bucket and a look of pure horror on his face that an actual sob slipped from me, and I sank to the ground.

He grunted, and the next thing I heard was the door slamming. A small thud hit the carpet, then his hands were on me, lifting me. His fingers squeezed my waist as he sat me on the table, and all I could do was blink as he cupped my face.

His thumb grazed my wet cheek as he whispered, "Lilly, don't cry. Please."

When I opened my eyes, his blurry face was tight with misery.

His touch was a drug. My skin thrummed under his fingertips, and it was surprising. All of this was. After days–years–of him ignoring me, here he was, comforting me.

I didn't know how to feel about it.

But I did manage to shake myself free of him, sniff, and rub my face.

"Sorry." My laugh was brittle. "Stacey's right. I'm not really acting like a professional, am I?"

Looking away, he said, "I brought you a bucket. In case you needed it," then stepped back and put his hands in his pockets.

I looked over his shoulder at the silver metal cylinder on the ground and said, "Oh."

Because what else could I really say here?

He remembered how bad my anxiety could get. He knew it could make me sick, and he brought me a bucket. He was trying to help. And there I was, screaming into my hands, bursting into tears over how much I'd hated him.

The tips of my ears burned beneath my hair. This was not my proudest moment.

"And I checked your computer earlier this morning. I don't know how it happened, but you've been locked out of our servers again." He looked at me like I was a puzzle. "I'll fix it, and then we'll sit together until you've caught up."

I shook my head. "You don't have to sit with me. I can do my job as long as everything is working."

"I know you can. But if you need anything, I could... help."

He drifted toward the door, like he couldn't wait to get away from me. Like he couldn't believe he'd just brought me a bucket and held my face in his hands, and was mad at himself for it.

"I'll be at your desk, but I should be done in twenty minutes."

Two tears slid free, and I caught them before they could drip down my chin. "Thanks. And, um, I'm sorry about–" I waved my hand in front of my face and sniffed, "–this. I can be better than this."

He frowned, then left the room for a second time.

I let out a deep, shaky breath and let my fingers trace my waist, cheeks, and chin. The same places Shawn smoothed, touched, squeezed.

He looked so sad. And he called me Lilly. I had to hope that meant something. That maybe he was finally done with treating me like he didn't know me.

In any case, I felt better after my emotional outburst. Less heavy.

Until my phone vibrated.

I pulled it out and stared at the screen. Mrs Hernandez. Again. Could I handle this conversation? After sending her to voicemail eight times this week, I guess I had to.

Bracing myself, I answered.

"Hi, Mrs Hernandez. I'm sorry I haven't been–"

"Finally. Why weren't you answering your phone?"

Resentment dripped from her. I was pretty sure this woman hated having to rely on me as much as I hated having to deal with her.

"I've been busy working on a fundraiser over the

holidays, but I've been looking for the right tutor for Jessica."

"Have you found anyone yet? A woman who knows what she's talking about, remember?"

"I remember, Mrs Hernandez. But no, I haven't found a tutor who matches your requests yet."

A deep sigh blew through the speaker, and I pictured Jessica's mother pinching the bridge of her nose. "Miss Fares, my daughter didn't do well in her last exam. She needs to raise her grade."

"Well, actually, she's only–"

"And if you were doing your job properly in the first place, she'd know more about Shakespeare and less about ponies with powers."

She sounded just hostile enough to make me clamp my mouth shut.

"If you don't find a tutor I approve of by the end of this week, I'll be making a formal complaint."

The end of *this* week?

There were only three days left. Three days to find a tutor. That was impossible.

My heart started up again. I could feel it pounding. I was genuinely afraid, because there was no way I could meet her deadline. But I gave her the only answer I could.

"I understand. I'll do my best."

"You'd better," she said, hanging up.

I sat and stared at the phone in my hand. The blank

black screen reflected back a tear-stained, red-eyed woman.

Was that who I was now? I looked pathetic.

Why was I even doing this?

Why was I putting up with being treated like this by Mrs Hernandez, by Trevor, by Shawn, by Stacey?

Maybe I should just quit. Maybe they were right, and I was never meant to teach at South Bronx.

If my mom were here, if she could see me like this, what would she say?

I almost laughed, because I already knew.

I could see her lying there now, in her hospital bed, so exhausted from her radiation treatment that she couldn't even cry about the pain anymore.

She would hold my hand, and it'd feel cold and stiff. Shaky enough in mine that I'd loosen my grip, careful not to hurt her. She seemed so fragile, and she was.

But that didn't stop her from telling me, "Those kids need me. And I'm stuck here. Who's going to help them now?"

"I will," I told her. "So you don't have to worry about them, okay? Okay, Mom?"

She was always worried about her students.

Always.

When I was growing up, it was all we'd ever talk about.

James, who surprised her with his grade on a book report. Wesley, who cried when he was told he'd be moving from a standard class to an intermediate.

Veronica, who needed someone to remind her to eat lunch because she spent every spare moment reading.

She was my mom, but she took care of them too. And she made me want to do the same. The kids were what mattered. They were why I did what I did.

I had to forget about Mrs Hernandez–Jessica was the one who needed me.

A dull thud vibrated against the glass wall, and Stacey's bright blonde head appeared, snapping me out of my thoughts. "Oh, you're still in here. Your computer's been fixed, so, you know. Time to get back to work."

She left as quickly as she came, barely sparing a glance for the emotional shitshow in front of her.

I pocketed my phone, smoothed a hand down my bangs, and stood. If it took sitting at my desk for the rest of the night, I'd find a way to get the work done.

FIVE YEARS AGO

CHAPTER 13
SHAWN
FRIDAY EVENING

Tristy's Coffee Shop

I WAS SO FUCKING FRUSTRATED, and I couldn't shut it off.

I'd been on my feet all day, serving customers, cleaning, training, restocking.

It was a good day. Busy. Distracting. But it wasn't enough. Everything I did felt pointless.

Because the entire day went by without her.

And I still hadn't called South Bronx.

I decided to take the job with Brooklyn–it was the best choice for my career.

But I couldn't do it yet.

Not until I knew for sure that Lilly would be okay on her own.

Tristan and his wife, Nikki, left the shop early. Nikki waddled in, her pregnancy slowing her usually quick pace, and they left for a gallery show featuring Tristan's latest piece. He said he'd stop painting until the burn on his hand healed, but I didn't think anything could've kept him from it. He was a man possessed–*obsessed*. I knew what that felt like now. I just never thought I'd feel this way over Lilly.

Uncle Henry was gone too, trusting me to close the shop without him. I was expecting a quiet night, so when the door chimed, my head snapped up in surprise.

"See? It isn't closed yet."

"Oh good, are there any of those crullers left? I love a good cruller."

The two girls were dressed in costume, but I'd know their voices anywhere. Lilly and Mia.

"What're you guys–"

I was cut off by their screams. Then they clutched their chests and laughed.

"You scared us, you fit asshole," Mia cried. Her Sussex-style English accent was strong, even when she swore. "What're you doing behind there?"

Lilly giggled, and I took the chance to let myself stare at her.

She was wearing a white tee with a cloud and a rainbow lightning bolt plastered to her chest. It was tucked into a short black skirt with pink and white stripes stitched on either side. The outfit was skin-tight, clinging to every curve.

Her skin was painted blue, her face outlined with makeup that framed her green eyes and plush lips.

Despite the rainbow wig on her head, she was the sexiest blue woman I'd ever seen.

"Nikki and Tristan are at a gallery show, and I'm about to close. Why are you guys here?" I couldn't stop myself from smiling as I added, "Dressed like that?"

Mia adjusted her long red wig. "We're here because this one—" she pointed at Lilly "—ate the last Pop-Tart, and I'm starved. I can't survive a party without something in my stomach."

Lilly smothered a yawn. "And I really need a coffee. I'm running on empty."

I folded my arms and sighed. The shop was supposed to be locked tight by now. But what else could I do? I wasn't going to let them starve.

I flicked on the coffee machine, and the noise it made clashed with the whooping the two girls did in front of the counter. As I picked up the tray of leftovers and started unwrapping it, a prickle of awareness told me Mia was staring at me.

"Aren't we lucky, Lilly?" she teased. "The famous Shawn Jackson is making us coffee. The same man who knocked our Stacey back."

As uncomfortable as Mia was making me, I didn't want to squash their pastries, so I set the tray down and flexed my fingers.

"You get fitter and fitter every time I see you, Shawn."

"Thanks," I grumbled, still tense.

"I'm looking forward to seeing more of you at South Bronx. Work should be fun."

I looked at Lilly, desperate to talk about anything else. "What're you supposed to be, anyway?"

She let out a playful scoff and looked down at herself. "Isn't it obvious?"

It was.

I couldn't know Lilly Fares without knowing every one of her childhood obsessions. But I couldn't help it. I was aching to tease her.

"You're Smurfette on a rave night?"

This time her scoff was real. "I'm Rainbow Dash. And Mia's Ariel."

I bit back a smile. "I knew who Mia was—she's wearing fins. But I had no idea who you were supposed to be. Is that a rainbow coming out of your ass?"

"Oh, Shawn." Lilly leaned over the counter, gently shoving my chest as I laughed. "It's a horse tail, you doof."

"Show me?"

She turned and bent over, shaking her plump ass. The rainbow tail around her waist swayed, and I was mesmerized, making out the shape of her under that fabric, feeling my cock swell in my jeans.

I didn't realize Mia hadn't taken her eyes off me.

She cleared her throat, snapping my focus. "Lilly makes a great Rainbow Dash, doesn't she?"

My mouth went dry as Mia's stare turned smug.

"Yeah. You both look great."

She tsked at me. "Well, thank you, but Lilly looks stunning, don't you think? Look at those blue legs. I bet Trevor's going to spend the entire night drooling over her."

I was instantly jealous.

As Lilly turned back around and leaned over the counter, picking out a few pastries, Mia inched closer.

"The boy is obsessed. But I guess that's obvious, since he wants a spot at South Bronx. I'd be surprised if he doesn't keep her all to himself tonight."

The idea of Trevor *keeping her to himself* boiled my fucking blood.

I tried to ask Lilly calmly, "Shouldn't you be studying?" but it came out harsh. I sounded like an asshole and I knew it.

My tone surprised her enough that it took her a moment to say, "I have been. All day. And anyway, Trevor's waiting for me."

Mia planted an elbow on the counter. "Which means we have to go," she teased, "because we both know he'd be all twisted up if he thought you weren't coming. It's too bad though. You could've used the sleep."

Lilly lifted a shoulder. "I know but... he wants me there."

The blue paint on her face couldn't hide a damn thing. I could tell from looking that Mia was right. Lilly should've been in bed, not on her way to a party.

And now I was frustrated for a different reason.

I looked away and tried to push all this anger into a neat little box. But apparently, I couldn't find one big enough.

Did Trevor know she'd been studying all day?

This test made the difference between whether or not Lilly would graduate. He had to know what this meant for her.

Which meant that he didn't care that she needed rest.

And what kind of boyfriend didn't give a shit about what she needed?

I went back to working the machine so I could get them out the door as soon as possible, but Lilly could tell something was wrong.

"Shawn, what's going on with you?" she asked, putting her hand on my bicep.

"Nothing."

I wanted to shrug off her touch as much as I wanted to jump over this counter and kiss her.

Fuck this.

Fuck this *feeling*.

I shut my eyes as Mia's sing-song teasing wormed into my ears. "You could come with us."

I clenched my teeth and shook my head.

"Oh, come on. It'll be fun. We'll just strip off your shirt and paint you." Mia clapped. "Now that would be fun." She turned to Lilly and pretended to whisper, "Do you think he's a big boy under those jeans? I'd skip this party just to find out."

Lilly gave Mia a look like she couldn't believe she'd just heard what her friend said.

"*Mia*. Okay, I think you need to get laid more than I do. Leave Shawn alone."

As Mia laughed, Lilly's fingertips brushed mine, and I lifted my stare to meet hers.

"Are you okay?" she whispered.

I shrugged. "I'm fine. Just tired."

She wasn't convinced.

I'd made her coffee the way she liked it and held it out to her, trying to make up for snapping earlier. "You deserve a break. Go have fun."

She gave my hand a squeeze, and I studied the counter as they picked up their food.

As they left, Mia sang, "Bye, Shawn," taunting me, making it obvious.

But if Mia knew how I felt about Lilly, I didn't care. I cared that Lilly was doing it again–hurting herself to make someone else happy.

And Trevor should've known better than to let her.

CHAPTER 14
SHAWN
MONDAY AFTERNOON

Tristy's Coffee Shop

LILLY TOLD me about the costume party, and how she'd been roped into planning it alongside Stacey. I wasn't surprised. No matter how tired Lilly was, the sorority president was great at getting Lilly to do whatever she wanted.

And so was Trevor. I heard all about how he pinned her to a wall and stuck his fucking tongue in her mouth.

"What's wrong? You don't like Trevor?" she asked, looking up at me.

I almost didn't hear her. I was too busy thinking about slicing Trevor's tongue with a cheese knife.

"Nothing's wrong."

"Are you sure? You look kind of angry."

"I'm not angry."

I tried to leave. It wasn't her fault, or Trevor's, that I

felt like this. But if I didn't get out of here, I knew I'd say something I'd regret.

Her hand wrapped around my arm. "Shawn–"

"I'm fine, Lilly," I said, faking a calm I didn't feel as I eased out of her grip. "I just... want to get back to work."

"But we're on break," she blurted at my back, "and I've been holding this in all day."

I turned to face her. "Then talk to Mia about it. We both know she lives for this shit."

Lilly looked like she was close to begging. "But I already know what she'll say. She'll tell me to break up with him."

I raised a brow at her. The thought of her dumping Trevor lifted my mood, and just like that, I wanted to know the rest.

"Why would she do that?"

Lilly made a face, like she'd sucked on a lemon. Her freckles bunched around her nose, and it was so adorable, I almost forgot why I was mad in the first place.

"Because... the kissing isn't great."

Well, I loved hearing that.

"But you've kissed before, right?"

"Yes, but–" she pulled another face "–it's not getting any better."

My smile was instant, and at seeing it, she groaned. "You're going to make fun of me, aren't you?"

I folded my arms and shrugged. "No, I get it. Bad kisses don't get your panties wet."

She smothered a shocked smile, gave me an unconvincing, "*Shawn*," and I laughed.

"What is it that you don't like?" I asked.

She lifted a shoulder and I moved closer. The sound of the coffee grinder hummed through the walls, loud enough to remind me that no one could hear us.

We were alone in the back room while Tristan and Uncle Henry managed the front, which, I knew, wasn't a smart move. I shouldn't have been alone with her.

"He always grabs my chin, and... he's so tall. It's like this." She held her jaw and jerked it up. Her neck was hinged at a ninety-degree angle, and judging from the look on her face, the position wasn't her favorite.

"Ouch," I said, my smile growing by the second.

"Then he just shoves his tongue in, and I can't even move."

"Or breathe, I bet."

I was getting way too much out of this.

What a fucking kick. To know Trevor wasn't satisfying Lilly the way she deserved. And with something as basic as a kiss, too.

It was like all my Christmases came at once.

She let go of her chin and looked at me. "Exactly. What am I supposed to do? Do I just pretend it isn't bad?"

I snorted. If Lilly wanted me to give her advice on

how to kiss her boyfriend, she was looking in the wrong place.

"I'm with Mia on this one."

"But it's just kissing," she grumbled. "I can't break up with him over that."

I shrugged. "You can do whatever you want. If you're not feeling it, you're not feeling it."

"But I don't know if that's what this is. I don't know what 'feeling it' looks like."

I shook my head, willing myself not to say—

"I could show you."

And there it was.

I should've left when I had the chance. I knew I'd do something stupid if I stayed. But I was a moron, and now here we were.

She frowned, confused. "How?"

I grunted, taking a moment, and I needed it because just the thought of teaching her what it meant to enjoy a kiss was making me so hard, I couldn't think straight.

But, it didn't take long before I said, "Take out your hair."

Her frown deepened, but she lifted her hands to her topknot. As her long, brown strands unraveled, she started to work her fingers through it.

"Don't," I told her, gripping her wrist and pulling her closer.

She stumbled into me, surprised. "Don't what? Touch my hair? Why—?"

"This is why." I let go of her wrist and threaded my hand through the soft hair at the nape of her neck.

Whatever she was about to say faded into a low moan. I pressed into her, moving slowly, letting her drop her head back into my palm as her eyes fluttered shut.

"You like that, don't you?"

She murmured a slight, "Mhm. But Trevor wouldn't just..."

My thumb grazed her chin as her voice trailed off, smoothing the spot she'd roughly gripped earlier. The noise she made was soft, but it went straight to my gut.

One eye opened, and she looked up at me, put a hand on my chest and smiled. "This is nice, but it isn't the same as–"

Her voice slipped into another moan as I cupped her chin with my other hand. We were so close that if she shifted just an inch closer, she'd feel how hard she'd made me through my jeans.

But she stayed where she was, with my fingers tangled in her hair, letting me stroke her soft skin.

Having her here like this made it easy to forget. All the reasons I knew I shouldn't touch her–gone, just like that.

The way I held her took the pressure off her neck, and, from the look of her soft smile and half-closed lids, she trusted me enough to relax.

I wished I could've said the same for myself.

She smelled so sweet, so good, that it wiped every

other thought from my head. I bet she'd taste even better, and fuck me, I wanted to find out.

I dropped my mouth to her ear.

"This is when I'd kiss you. I'd take it slow, just like this, then I'd–"

"Hey, have you guys seen–" Tristan rushed into the room, stopping just inside the doorway.

I let go of Lilly and stepped back, but it was too late. He saw us.

He looked from Lilly to me with a growing smile.

Lilly's eyes opened, and she murmured a little, "Hmm?" as she noticed Tristan. She gathered her hair and twisted it around her head as she dreamily asked him, "What did you need?"

"Uh." He put his hands on his hips. "The takeout cups. I need a new sleeve."

She blinked a few times, like she was waking herself up. "Oh. I'll get them for you. Are Karim and Dean here?"

The trainees were rostered on for the afternoon shift, which was about to start any minute now. Tristan nodded.

"Great. I'll show them where they are."

As Lilly drifted off, I realized she had no idea that I was a second away from kissing her. If Tristan hadn't walked in, my control would've snapped.

I was on edge, instantly frustrated. I knew it was a good thing that nothing had happened, but I couldn't just... switch off this fucking *need* to touch her.

I needed to be alone. To calm down and think.

But judging from the look Tristan gave me, I wasn't going to get that.

"What was that?"

"Nothing."

I drifted to the loaded shelf of coffee beans and picked up the inventory ledger, pretending to study it.

"That didn't look like nothing. It looked like you were about to–"

"We don't have time to talk about this. Lunch rush is about to start."

"Shawn, come on. You can tell me."

"I don't have anything to say."

He rolled his eyes at me. "Yeah, right. Because you weren't about to kiss Lilly."

"That's not what that was."

"Then what was it? Because I've caught you staring at her for months now. And a crush was one thing, but I think it's a little more serious than that now, isn't it?"

I stared at him for a few seconds, not sure of what to do or say. Tristan just blindsided me.

"I don't... we're just friends. That's it."

He grinned then, probably thinking about his wife.

"So were Nikki and I. For years." As quickly as it came, his smile faded. "For too long. I should've told her how I felt sooner."

I shrugged. "You've got her now, and that's what matters, right? Anyway–"

"You should tell Lilly," he said, cutting me off.

I scoffed, trying to come up with something to say. "Tristan, it's really not like that."

"Why not? Did you already talk to her?"

He sounded so sure, like he knew what he'd seen and nothing I could say would convince him otherwise.

And, well... shit. Between him and Mia, I must've been pretty bad at hiding how I felt.

Was there even a point to denying it? With Tristan, at least I knew I could trust him.

So I lowered my voice and admitted, "I can't. She's dating another guy."

Tristan paused, frowning like he'd just remembered that Lilly was already with someone else.

"Okay yes, there's... Trevor. But if she knew how you felt, maybe she'd–"

This time, I cut him off. "I'm not doing that."

He instantly deflated. "Why not?"

I gave him a look. "Maybe because it'd be a shitty thing to do?"

"I think not telling her is worse. She should know."

I shook my head, then tried to explain it in a way I knew he'd understand.

"Tristan, if I told her, she'd try to fix it for me. Because she'd hate knowing she was the reason I felt like this." I couldn't put how I felt into words, but I didn't need to. Tristan got it. He'd been here before. "I'm not doing that to her."

I could see it on his face. He was about to argue with

me. He might've understood, but that didn't mean he agreed with how I was handling it.

But I'd had enough.

"We're not you and Nikki. We don't have what you guys have."

My boss put a hand on my shoulder and squeezed.

"I don't think you're right about that. I think if you tell her how you feel, things will change."

I was done talking about this. I stepped out of Tristan's grip, still holding the inventory ledger.

If I told Lilly, things would change. That was true. But it wouldn't be for the better.

I knew Lilly well enough to know how she'd react. She'd be torn between Trevor and me. She'd twist herself in knots trying to figure out how to please the both of us.

It would hurt her to know this was hurting me, and she didn't deserve that kind of pain.

If I was going to do anything, I'd do it knowing we'd both be better off by the time I was done.

And that meant letting her move on without me.

CHAPTER 15
SHAWN
FRIDAY AFTERNOON

Tristy's Coffee Shop

THE DOOR tinkled open and shut, and I pushed my mood aside, ready to lose myself in today's lunch rush, when the sight of a familiar blonde surprised me.

Stacey?

Stacey never came to the shop. Why would she? There was a Starbucks right next to campus.

She had to be here for Lilly.

Tristan didn't seem to notice the pretty blonde at our counter, despite her standing there in a thin satin sundress.

It was March in Manhattan. It was freezing. And she wore that on the subway?

She seemed totally unaffected by the cold. Her glossed lips curved as she glanced around the shop.

Lilly came out of the back room then, stealing my

attention. She almost did a double-take when she noticed her sorority president, but instead, she frowned at me. So this was a surprise for her too.

"Sorry, ma'am, what can I get you?" Tristan smiled as he leaned on the counter.

Stacey popped a hip, tilted her chin, and smirked. "Actually, I'm here to see Shawn." Looking me up and down, she added, "He can take my order."

Tristan shot me a confused glance before stepping aside so I could slide in front of the register.

Raising a brow, I said, "I thought you were here for Lilly."

I could pinpoint the exact moment Stacey wanted to roll her eyes but didn't. Her smile locked in place as she focused on Lilly.

"Hey, there you are." She lifted her hand, almost like she meant to wave, then awkwardly said, "I wanted to check this place out for myself. The other girls rave about it."

There were no other girls. The only sorority sister who came here was Mia.

But Lilly didn't correct her. Instead, she bit her bottom lip, nodded, and went back to restocking the pastries behind our glass display.

"You didn't come all the way here for a cup of coffee, did you?" I asked, stepping behind the machine and flaring it to life.

She leaned on the counter, her smile teasing. "Oh, Shawn, you know I came to see you."

Tristan shot me another glance. Stacey's flirting must've somehow wormed into his dense, I-only-see-Nikki brain.

I ignored him and went back to serving my customer.

"And... what can I help you with?"

Her eyes were hooded and lazy as she looked me over again, slower this time. It made my muscles tighten, like some kind of survival-mode response, and I wondered if this was how Lilly felt when her anxiety made her want to throw up.

"I think you know what you can help me with." She flicked her hair back and leaned on the countertop, chin in hand, fingers curled around her sharp jaw, eyes fixed on mine. "But I'll take a mocha for now."

In the time it took to make her order, she tried flirting at least three more times. I didn't bite.

Instead, I set the cup in front of her and forced a brightness to my voice, the same way Lilly would.

"Here's your order, ma'am." I smiled wider as her expression dropped. "Have a great day."

She straightened, and just like that, she was done playing with me.

"Oh for fuck's sake, Shawn. Will you just take me on a date?"

I fought the urge to laugh. "Whoa. Where'd that come from?"

Then Lilly's hand was on my shoulder, pulling me back just enough so she could wedge into the space between my hip and the counter. Without thinking, I pressed into her from behind, and heat flooded me. I shifted, moving my hardening cock away before it could push into her.

"Stacey, is this about Trevor?"

The blonde's blue eyes narrowed. "Why would this be about my cousin?"

And now I was just confused. I had no idea what was going on.

"I don't... then why are you here?" Lilly asked.

Stacey scoffed. "Believe it or not, I'm just here to see him."

Lilly looked at me over her shoulder. "He already said he doesn't want to... date you."

"I heard him," Stacey snapped. "I have ears, you know. What I want to know is *why*."

Lilly went stiff against me. I wanted to squeeze her shoulders, help her relax, make her see that Stacey's tantrum wasn't our problem. But I kept my hands to myself as she turned her beautiful face up to mine.

She looked torn, like she didn't know what to do. And that made me desperate to fix this for her.

Like it or not, Stacey was her sorority president. She could make Lilly's life hell until graduation, and I couldn't ignore that.

"Fine. We can talk." I pointed at an empty booth. "Wait there. I'll be a minute."

Stacey turned to go, and Lilly let out a sound of relief before wrapping her arms around my neck.

She whispered, "Thank you," into the curve of my shoulder, and I had to shift again. That was all it took to set me off—her, this close. So fucking close, and still not mine.

I swallowed hard. "It's nothing."

She let me go with a soft, apologetic smile. "It's not nothing, Shawn. But maybe if you talk to her, she'll back off a little."

Back off a little? From me, or from her?

But before I could ask, Lilly turned to the register and served another customer.

I went to the booth, watching Stacey's face pinch as I sat across from her.

She folded her arms and asked, "Okay, just tell me. Why don't you want to sleep with me? Everyone wants to sleep with me."

Trying not to laugh, I bit my lip and lifted a shoulder. Poking the blonde's ego didn't seem like the smartest move here.

"It's not you, I just don't..." I sighed, trying to decide on the excuse I'd give her. But between Mia's teasing and Tristan's pushing, I was tired.

As I sat there, not sure of what to say, my gaze drifted to Lilly, like it always did. She was a fucking magnet.

I couldn't have been staring at her for long, but Stacey's gasp pulled my focus back just in time to see her eyes widen.

"Oh my god. It's Lilly, isn't it?"

And that was enough for me. I almost stood to leave, but she leaned over the table, grabbed my arm, and held me in place.

"You don't want me because you want her," Stacey said, and I tried to scoff, ease my arm from her, and shake my head, but she steamrolled right over me.

"It makes sense. You two spend, like, every second together."

Stunned yet satisfied, she let me go and relaxed into the booth.

I took a breath and tried again. "We're just friends. And I'm not interested in dating anyone this close to graduation."

She shot me a look of disbelief. "Yeah, right. You think I'm dumb enough to believe that? You were staring at her."

Ah, shit.

Well... Stacey could believe whatever she wanted. I didn't have to admit it.

"Look, I'm not interested in seeing anyone right now."

"What about after graduation?" she asked.

"I'm teaching at Classical."

She raised a brow. "With Lilly? She's dating my cousin, you know."

The reminder irritated the hell out of me. "I know. I'm not going to South Bronx. I got an offer from their Brooklyn campus, and I'm... accepting it."

"Me too." Her eyes narrowed. "So, you're not following Lilly to her dream job then?"

I dropped my eyes to the table. "It's like you said. She's with Trevor. She'd be better off with him there."

She smirked. "Wow. Poor Shawn can't chase after the girl he wants. That's tragic."

Yeah, I wasn't sticking around for this. "If you're done, I've got work—"

"You're not my type anyway."

A laugh burst out of me, fast and sharp. "Okay... that's great, then. See you at graduation."

I rapped my knuckles on the table and started to leave when she said, "We should probably talk, though."

I paused. "About what?"

She rolled her eyes. "Brooklyn, obviously. We'll be working at the same school. It might be nice to... I don't know, get to know each other? Before we start teaching?"

She cringed, like it was the most awkward thing she could've said. And it probably was. She'd been a pain in Lilly's ass for years, and the last thing I wanted was to spend more time with her.

But... she was right. We'd have to work together at some point. And soon.

"I guess we could do that," I said, flicking my glance to Lilly, glad she couldn't hear any of this. "As long as you don't give Lilly shit about... me."

That was as close as I was going to get to admitting

Stacey was right, and she was smart enough to read between the lines.

"Don't worry, I won't," she said. "Trevor hasn't nagged me since they started dating, and I'd like to keep it that way."

My fists clenched so hard I felt my nails cutting into my palms. Ever since that costume party, I hated hearing his name.

Fucking Trevor.

She noticed my hands and opened her mouth, but didn't call attention to it.

Instead, she said, "So, we'll be working at Brooklyn together. That's exciting. Oh." She sat up and planted her elbows on the table. "I wanted to ask about this guy. Jacob."

And once again, I was thrown. I hadn't heard that name in a while. "Jacob?"

"Yep." She bobbed her head. "He said something about you tutoring him in high school?"

A minute ago, I was desperate to get off this table and get back to work. But with that one question, she kept me there.

As I told her about Jacob, the reason I wanted to teach, and my plans for the next few years, Stacey just... listened. Actually listened. Which wasn't something I was prepared for.

I couldn't figure this girl out.

Who was Stacey Atkins? Just a pain-in-the-ass sorority president? Or something deeper?

Whoever she was, I wasn't going to figure it out in one afternoon. Besides, no matter how much time she'd spent listening to me just now, I couldn't ignore how shitty she'd been to Lilly for the past few years.

I didn't like Stacey, but maybe I didn't have to.

Maybe I just had to put up with her. And if it meant she'd give Lilly some breathing room, it'd be worth it.

On her way out, she stopped by the counter. I went to the back room, ignoring Tristan's damn judgy face while Stacey bent to whisper something in Lilly's ear.

NOW

CHAPTER 16

LILLY

Verra Convention Centre

MIA STARED AT ME, skeptical. Usually, that would've been enough to make me lose focus, but after more than a week without progress, I couldn't afford to look away from my monitor.

"So, he did what you wanted? After you bawled your eyes out in front of him?"

I lifted a shoulder. "I guess so? I don't–it's fine. I finally have a working computer, and that's all I wanted anyway."

"Okay, fair enough. I'll leave you alone then. Call me if you need me."

I nodded, eyes still glued to the screen as she left.

I typed and typed and typed.

Email after email landed in my Sent folder, and I double-checked each attachment before hitting send.

It felt so good to finally do something.

To be able to tick jobs, tasks, duties off my list.

With every email and phone call, I updated the project plan and savored the sight of things falling into place.

People passed by my desk. The elevator dinged faintly, muted by the clack of my fingers racing across the keyboard.

I lost track of time, only pausing to swat Mia's probing, tickling touch away from my ribs. The fluorescent lights beat down on me as I squinted at my screen, relaxing in the quiet of the now-empty office.

I sighed, sinking into my chair. I was finally alone, and I liked it that way.

The sun dipped behind the Manhattan skyline as the noise of the city filtered through the windows.

I glanced behind me at the other desks.

Some were messy, some were tidy.

Teachers. We were a mixed bag. You never knew what you were going to get.

I stood, stretching as my stomach grumbled. I felt better than I had in days. I finally felt in control. But I was hungry. Maybe I could knock out one more task and order takeout.

Humming to myself, I scrolled through food options on my phone, trying not to think about Mrs Hernandez or the stack of module work waiting for me. I was here, being productive. That's what I had to focus on. And I'd order some tacos while I was at it.

"Lilly?" a deep voice said behind me, making me squeal.

"*Shawn.*" I turned to him with my hand to my chest, gulping in a breath.

He held out his hands, apologetic. "I wasn't trying to scare you."

"It's okay." I held up my phone. "I was just ordering takeout. Want something?"

He frowned, and I noticed the blazer draped over his arm, the first two undone buttons of his shirt, and his missing tie. His big hands gripped his jacket as his shirt stretched tight across his chest.

My own hand drifted to my waist, remembering what it felt like to have those hands wrapped around me, lifting me.

Wait. Earlier today, I hated him. And now I was... ogling him? Oh, god. Not again. Mia would *not* approve.

"But... maybe Nikki would?"

I let out a surprised laugh, mortified I'd said that out loud.

Shawn stepped closer, and I'd forgotten the way he did that, the way he took up space. With him this close, staring at him felt like my only option.

Magnetic wasn't a strong enough word to describe him.

And then I realized that, since I'd asked him about dinner, I'd ogled him, embarrassed myself, and now I was just flat-out staring. All in the space of a few seconds. My cheeks burned.

I was hopeless.

"Nikki wants takeout? Is she on the phone now?" Shawn asked, confused.

Another nervous laugh slipped out. "No, I meant... I could definitely go for a taco. What about you? Interested?"

He kept frowning as he said, "I don't think it's a good idea for you to be here this late."

I waved my phone. "We used to pull late nights at the coffee shop all the time. This is nothing."

He stared a moment longer before dropping his laptop bag and blazer onto a nearby desk.

"If you're staying, so am I." He ran a hand down his face and dragged out a chair. "What're you working on?"

I shook my head. "Uh-uh. No. You're not staying here, Mister Jackson–"

"Shawn." He shot me a look. "I think we're past that now."

"Why's that?"

"Because you cried in my meeting room."

I bristled at the edge in his voice. "So?"

"So if someone else walked in, it could've ended... badly."

I knew what he meant, even if he didn't say it. It wasn't professional, and if someone had caught him comforting me, it could've caused more problems for both of us.

Still, I folded my arms and dug my heels in. "Well, I

wouldn't have gotten upset if I had a decent computer in the first place."

He let out a dry laugh. It seemed like it didn't take much to frustrate him these days. Not when it came to me.

"I should've known this wouldn't work. You and me together like this—"

"Let me guess," I cut in. "It's torture."

"Lilly."

"You're the one who said it, not me."

He stood and came closer, and I backed into my desk on instinct. My breath caught as he studied my face.

"It's been years. I thought you'd be over that."

I scoffed. "Maybe I would be if you actually spoke to me."

"We were at work events," he said softly. "I didn't want to make a scene."

The way he looked at me then was almost gentle, and it lit me up from the inside out.

"I wouldn't have made a scene."

But then he raised a brow, and just like that, I wanted to push him away.

"You know what? You were right. We don't need to talk. You should pretend I'm not here, like you always do."

He squeezed his eyes shut and let out a breath. When he opened them again, it was like he'd flipped a switch. Back to bland, professional Shawn.

"Have you ordered your food yet?"

A strangled groan gurgled out of me, and I stomped my foot like a toddler. "No. And I'm not ordering anything until you leave."

"I'm not leaving until you do."

I growled, frustrated. This was why I'd been so confused five years ago. He'd confused me back then, and he was doing it now.

"Why do you care if I work late?"

He gave me a look that was so familiar that I suddenly felt like I was in the back room of *Tristy's*, trying not to panic as Shawn offered to help me study.

"Why wouldn't I care?"

"Because you hate me," I shot back, exasperated.

He gave me a dark look then, like what I'd just said crossed a line. He took another step, and I was practically sitting on my desk. A few more inches and my ass would be on my keyboard.

He was so close, but it still surprised me when he planted his hands on either side of me, caging me in.

Nerves tightened my stomach, and I swallowed, waiting. His voice was low, but clear.

"You're wrong. I never hated you."

His eyes dropped to my mouth as he licked his bottom lip. My gasp was soft, but the throb between my thighs was sharp and sudden. He leaned in, just an inch.

I made a noise and squeezed my knees together, bracing for... whatever Shawn was about to do to me.

But nothing happened.

I looked up to find him backing away from the desk.

While I was still trying to process what I'd just felt, he put his hands in his pockets and shifted back to unbothered and professional. Again.

I could've screamed.

"I want to get through this fundraiser without any more problems. Do you think we can do that?"

Still flustered, I stared at the ground and nodded.

"Good. What did you want to finish tonight?"

Still sitting on the desk, I pointed at my monitor, which had gone into sleep mode.

"Let's get your list done so we can go home and eat something," he said as I slid off the desk, bent over my chair, and shook my mouse.

My computer woke, and there was my desktop, just as I'd left it. I could feel Shawn's eyes on me as I worked.

"I just have to send the approved logo to the coffee cup distributor, order the T-shirts, and confirm our storage facility," I told him.

"We don't have enough space for the cups."

I eyed him over my shoulder. "What do you mean?"

"I met with the Board yesterday, and they pulled one of the storage units. I don't have anywhere to put them."

I straightened. "Then what am I supposed to do with thirty thousand takeout cups?"

He shrugged. "I know a guy who can help."

Rolling my eyes, I said, "Of course you have a guy. But we're on a tight budget. Is this going to cost us anything?"

He smiled, and those damn dimples made my insides melt. Mia was right. He was a ridiculously good-looking asshole.

"It shouldn't. Not if we ask nicely and promise to go to his next gallery showing."

And then it clicked. "Your guy is Tristan?"

"Well, yeah. He has enough space."

"So I can order them?"

He nodded. "We should check with him first, but I doubt he'll say no."

I rubbed my chin, aware of Shawn watching me. "Maybe I should offer to babysit the girls again. As payment."

He gave me a small smile, and for a second, he almost looked like the Shawn I used to know. Almost.

Then his smile slipped. "You're not still doing that, are you?"

I pulled out my seat and sat, my fingers already tapping against the keyboard. "Doing what?"

I could feel him behind me.

Was he staring at my neck? I almost wanted to turn around just to check.

Earlier, he'd been so close... I'd honestly thought he was going to kiss me.

Did he want to?

Probably not. God, was I becoming Mia-level

horny? I needed to stop thinking of him like he wasn't an asshole who blocked me out of his life for five years.

"Overextending yourself."

"Over... what?"

"Lilly, you know what I'm talking about."

I gave in and glanced at him over my shoulder. His grip was tight on my chair. He was tense. But why? What did I do to make him feel like this?

He might've denied hating me, but after everything he'd done to keep me away from him, I found that hard to believe. And the way he was speaking to me now didn't help either.

"No, I don't."

"So you haven't been taking on too much at work?"

The edge in his tone was back. And I didn't like it.

"It's my job to help my students."

"Even if it means losing your job in the process?"

Well, this lecture sounded familiar. I could almost hear the exact words he'd say next: *Every time you're dragged into someone else's problems, it ends up stressing you out.*

Ever since he said that, I couldn't do something for someone else without hearing his voice in my head, and I was tired of it. He thought he knew better, and that wasn't fair.

I stood, and as I did, the chair collapsed under his grip. He caught it before it hit the floor, and I huffed as I spun on him, wishing he'd embarrass himself for once.

"What're you talking about?"

He stood at his full height, almost like he was ready for a fight.

"Mia told me about Mrs Hernandez. And Trevor. Lilly, you know you're not supposed to give your personal number to parents. Trevor can hold that over you, even if you do well here."

I was too frustrated to notice the way Shawn was looking at me.

I was too tired, too irritated, to feel anything else as I snapped, "Why would you care about what I do? You spent the last five years treating me like I meant *nothing*, Shawn. You don't get to give me advice anymore."

He jerked back like I'd slapped him.

"Fine. Then finish what you're doing so we can get out of here." He shook his head and muttered under his breath, "Torture was fucking right."

I pulled my chair back and went to work as he stood behind me and ran a hand through his hair.

Breathing in and out, slowly, I tried to loosen up and look at this from another angle.

Technically, I'd gotten what I wanted. We were... talking.

And I was making progress. Now if I could just finish the module and get a new tutor lined up, my job would be safe, and I could put all of this behind me.

CHAPTER 17
LILLY
THURSDAY AFTERNOON

Verra Convention Centre

IT WAS THURSDAY. The day after Wednesday. The day before Friday.

Oh, how I hated Thursday.

Normally, Thursday was fine. Thursday came before the final day of work. Thursday meant duties, responsibilities, and worries were starting to die down.

Thursday meant planning all the fun things I could do with Mia over the weekend.

But this Thursday wasn't exactly a pleasant one.

Mrs Hernandez was on a mission to find the best possible tutor for her daughter, and I was the one thing standing in her way.

I was the incompetent employee who couldn't do the job. I was the piece of metaphorical gum on her otherwise pristine designer shoe.

And the only way to get her to stop seeing me that way was to give her what she wanted.

So I posted ads on a few websites and signed up for others, searching the web for someone who fit.

The tutor had to be:

- Female
- An adult
- Knowledgeable about literature
- Willing to take twenty dollars per hour

I searched and searched until my eyes hurt. When my focus wasn't on Trevor's teach-to-the-test module, it was on my hunt for a tutor.

Now, as I sat in my desk chair—the one Shawn threatened to crush under his weight two nights ago—I switched on my monitor and fixed my worn-out eyeballs on the website in front of me.

"That doesn't look like work, Lilly."

I blinked up at Stacey.

"Hi to you too," I mumbled.

Stacey stood to the side of my desk with one hand on her hip and the other wrapped around her notebook. What was in that notebook?

Was it a plan for the fundraiser? A list of all the outstanding duties? Or a letter to Trevor about all the things I'd done wrong over the last two weeks?

And there I went, my mind wandering as whatever Stacey had just said went right over my head.

"Sorry, I missed that."

"I asked you for an update. Have you finished tweaking the logo to fit the keyrings?"

I hesitated. I didn't want to give Stacey the satisfaction... but then I shook my head. She let out a frustrated noise, but her eyes twinkled.

I bet she was loving this.

Me. Failing.

It only made her look better.

It probably made Shawn happy too. That he'd chosen to work with her at Brooklyn instead of with me at South Bronx. This whole experience probably proved something for him, that he'd made the right decision after graduation.

I turned my head, found him studying a handful of papers, and bit my bottom lip.

I knew I wasn't here for him. I was here for me, and for my students. I was here to earn my place at South Bronx.

But it would've been really nice if I could've just... set a better standard from day one instead of floundering like I had.

I shook my head, trying to clear it. My thoughts were taking weirder and sadder turns than usual. I must've been more tired than I thought.

"Can you fix it today?" Stacey pushed, bringing me back to attention.

"I'll get them finalized this week. I just have to get this done first."

She stared down at me, at my takeout coffee, at my

half-eaten chocolate croissant, at the picture I had of Tristan, Nikki, and their two adorable girls: Kelly, and my namesake, Lilly.

"What exactly are you getting done? Are you that behind on your work for next semester?"

God, that was scary. She sounded exactly like the Stacey I remembered and avoided.

"No, actually. I'm trying to find a tutor for one of my students. Her mother wants her to go to an Ivy League school, and–"

Stacey pointed her notebook at me. "I don't care. While you're here, your job is to help us get this fundraiser up and running."

"I know that, and I'm doing my job. I spent the last two days catching up on my work, which I wouldn't have had to do if my computer worked from the start."

I folded my arms and tried to keep my voice even, but my face burned. "I've been getting the work done, so will you just... cut me some slack? We aren't in a sorority anymore, and I don't need you to keep checking on me."

She let out a noise, turned on her heel, and left.

Standing up to Stacey just felt... like a big deal. Like something that put my body on high alert, almost like I'd been convinced she was about to yell at me. I put a hand to my chest, counted my heartbeats, and started to calm down.

But as the morning turned into evening, and my search results came to nothing, my heart sped up again.

I was going to fail at this.

I might've finally gotten the fundraiser back on track, but this? There was no way I could fix this.

Because no self-respecting woman who spent years studying literature would take twenty dollars an hour at the last minute just to help me please a demanding parent whose head was too stuffed full of unrealistic expectations to listen to what her daughter actually wanted.

After all my years dealing with panic attacks, I thought I'd be smart enough to see them coming. But I wasn't.

Still, I took a breath and tried.

I tried to calm down, but I'd lost control. My mind was racing, and I couldn't stop it.

I could see it as if it'd just happened. Mrs Hernandez telling Trevor about me, Trevor asking how she'd gotten my number in the first place, him asking everyone to leave so he could tell me how useless I was right before he fired me.

I could see myself packing my desk, putting the framed picture of my mother in a box, riding the subway home to an empty apartment. Alone. With no job, no mother, no one left to tell me I'd be okay.

My stomach tightened, funneling until I could feel acid burn the back of my throat. And I couldn't breathe.

I couldn't *breathe*.

My wheezing sounded far away, like it came from

someone else, and I tried to ignore it as I looked for one, two, three things I could recognize.

Then large hands wrapped around my shoulders, squeezing them, and I heard a soft but deep voice repeat the one thing that always helped.

"Jump up, make a sound, hey, stomp your boots, turn around. Start now... make a change, gonna make that sound. Come on, Lil, sing with me. Jump up, make a sound, that's it, you got it. Start now, make a change, gonna make that sound. Yeah, that's it. You're okay. I've got you."

He kept singing, and his voice turned into hands that pressed against my cheeks, brushed my bangs back, smoothed the stress from my skin.

I looked up at him as my breathing slowed, watching his shoulders drop with relief.

"You remembered the song," was all I could think to say.

The set of his jaw told me he was at least a little insulted. "As if I could forget it. You made me listen to it so many times, it's burned into my brain."

My laugh was shaky; my toes were still a little numb, but I managed, "I should probably apologize for that."

Shawn shook his head and frowned, annoyed. Or... maybe he wasn't really annoyed? Maybe he was just scared. Shawn had gone a full five years without seeing one of my panic attacks. Maybe he forgot what they were like.

"Where's Mia?" he asked, his voice gentle.

I looked around the almost empty office, and noticed Stacey standing by the elevator. She was waiting for Shawn. And by the tap of her foot against the floor, she wasn't waiting patiently.

"She went home an hour ago. I told her I had to stay late," I said, my eyes still on Stacey.

He cupped my chin and turned my face until I was looking at him. Despite what my gut had just gone through, he still made my stomach flip.

"Eyes on me, Fares. What happened? Why did you have an attack?"

My eyes dropped to his lips. His full, perfect lips.

"I've been trying to find a tutor for Mrs Hernandez. If I don't have someone lined up by tomorrow, she's going to submit a formal complaint to Trevor."

Shawn's brows shot up and he scoffed. "Some parents..."

He let go and stood, and I instantly missed the feel of his hands on me. Which was just... so frustrating. Between the panic attack and wanting Shawn to touch me, clearly I had zero control over myself.

"Stacey, could you come here, please?" he asked.

She came without question, but shot him an exasperated look all the same. Shawn didn't notice. His focus was on me.

"What kind of tutor is she looking for?"

I answered, giving him her list of demands, and Shawn rolled his eyes.

"It's amazing, isn't it? The sense of entitlement some people have." He looked at the blonde by his elbow. "Do you think one of your Kappa sisters can step in here?"

It clicked for me then, in an instant.

Shawn had just asked Stacey to find a student from Pace. A legacy of Kappa Delta.

Why didn't I think of that? I was part of the alumni. I could've searched the student board for someone who was willing to take a low-paying tutoring job.

I facepalmed and groaned as Stacey put her phone to her ear. She stared at me, as icy as ever, before turning her back on us. She walked behind a load-bearing column as Shawn knelt by my chair.

"Are you all right?" he asked, softly.

I nodded, and he murmured, "You scared the shit out of me."

Oddly enough, knowing I'd scared him made me laugh. But it was cut short as he stood, pulled me from my chair, and wrapped his arms around me.

As he hauled me into him, my pulse skipped. I couldn't remember the last time he'd held me like this. He was warm and solid, and he smelled incredible. Musk and wood mixed with ruffled papers and roasted coffee. My body felt like lead against his, finally relaxed, even if it was just for that moment.

"I wasn't trying to. It just happened," I said, discreetly burying my face in his chest.

His voice felt like a deep rumble, vibrating through

me. "I know. But what if I wasn't here?" He swore under his breath, then his hand came to rest on the back of my neck. He gently stroked me, and I instantly melted.

"I would've been okay on my own," I breathed out. "But I... definitely like this better."

I leaned into his touch, but he tensed, backing away before I could get comfortable.

"Sorry, I–shit, Lilly, I can't be... I shouldn't do... this."

I blinked up at him, still feeling a little touch-drunk. "Uh..."

"A lot's riding on this fundraiser for me," he said, his voice quiet. "My Maslow initiative is getting thirty percent of the money raised."

I had no idea what that had to do with... whatever we were just doing.

I gave him a look, and he could tell I was confused, but before he explained, he looked over my head at Stacey, like he didn't want her to hear what he said next.

But she was still talking on her phone behind us, so he said, "Look, I know things between us haven't been easy. But I need them to be. Just until this thing gets off the ground."

"What... does that mean?"

"It means I can't have you yelling at me one minute, then hugging me the next," he whispered, and I understood what he meant. My fuzzy brain was finally picking up speed.

This was his whole career. This fundraiser, and the initiative he'd been working on. His reputation as a thought leader was on the line, and that meant he couldn't do or say anything to screw it up.

And all I'd been doing was pushing him, in one way or another, to do and say all the things he shouldn't to a fellow teacher.

No matter what we might've meant to each other once, it wasn't a good look for him now.

"Oh... uh, you're right. Maybe... maybe we could have a... a truce?"

One thing I could never forget, ever, was how devastating Shawn's smiles were.

They were sexy, slow, deliciously dimpled things that made me feel like I'd won, really won, something special. They fizzled my mind, cooked me from the inside out, and I adored them.

But after five years believing he'd hated me, I never expected to see one again. So, imagine my surprise when he gave me a full, genuine smile as he said, "Truce," and held out his hand.

My throat ached as I swallowed and slid my palm into his.

"You're off the hook," Stacey interrupted, walking back toward us. "One of our legacies needed a tutoring job. I gave her your number."

Then she looked down at our hands, paused mid-shake, like Shawn and I were doing something disgusting. I let go as my phone vibrated, scooping it from my desk as the screen lit with a text from someone named Kya.

Her message was full of emojis and exclamation points, but she said she wanted the job.

I put my phone to my chest and breathed out, "Thank you."

I was so relieved.

But all Stacey did was tighten her lips and ask Shawn, "Can we go now?"

He looked out the window, probably checking to see whether it was dark outside. I answered his question before he could ask it. "I'm leaving now anyway."

As I picked up my handbag, I started thinking over how I could make this up to Stacey.

Shawn might've asked for the favor, but she could've said no or come up with an excuse. And I'd still be tutor-less, about to land a formal complaint that would definitely get me fired.

She stopped it from happening. *She* did that.

Maybe this was a first step. Maybe we could brush things under the rug and start fresh.

But as Shawn said, "Good. You can leave with us," the look on her face told me the last thing Stacey wanted from me was gratitude.

She was going to get it anyway.

FIVE YEARS AGO

CHAPTER 18

SHAWN

FRIDAY EVENING

Tristy's Coffee Shop

"You're not going to tell me who it is?" Lilly asked, disappointed.

I thought Stacey and I were on the same page. She wasn't supposed to say anything. Even hinting at how I felt wasn't okay.

Maybe it was her ego. Maybe Stacey needed Lilly to know that I wasn't interested in her because there was someone else.

But still. I didn't expect her to tell Lilly on her way out of the shop earlier today.

Fuck me. How was I going to get out of this one?

"I think is easy guess," Uncle Henry muttered.

Great. So he knew too? Shit.

And now he was teasing me right behind Lilly's back.

"Is she a teacher?" Nikki asked, folding her arms over her pregnant belly. From the corner of my eye, I could see the wicked smile curving her lips. "Maybe she's in your class."

I stepped back from Lilly and stumbled onto the sofa. As soon as we were done closing, Lilly cornered me in the back room, and the rest followed.

There was no point denying that every person here knew how I felt about Lilly, which meant that if I didn't handle this, it was only a matter of minutes before she found out.

I panicked. "Guys, I didn't mean it. I was just trying to get Stacey off my back."

Lilly came to stand in front of me. "You mean there's no one you're into right now?"

I looked away. "No. There's no one. But... you know how Stacey is. It's easier if she thinks there's someone else."

My gut twisted. I hated lying to her like this.

Mia piped up from the corner of the room. "That's probably true. She's not exactly reasonable, is she?"

Tristan blinked. "She did seem a little... aggressive when she came in before."

"Aggressive is putting it nicely," Mia muttered.

Lilly turned and looked around the room. "Why are you all here? He's never going to tell all of us who it is. Will you guys get out?"

Waving her hands, she ushered everyone out the

door, and they went, all of them getting way too many kicks out of this.

Lilly turned back to me with her hands on her hips, feet planted a shoulder's width apart. I knew that pose. She'd practiced it in class. It was meant to show she meant business, but all it made me do was drag my eyes up and down her small, curvy frame and laugh.

"What?" she asked, dropping her hands by her side.

"That was pretty good. The way you were standing, I mean."

She eyed me, and I guess she thought that maybe I was about to tease her. And usually, I would. But not this time. I was just happy she let me change the subject.

"You're going to manage the hell out of a class one day, Lil."

"Thanks. I hope so." Her smile was grateful, but it disappeared as quickly as it came.

She sank into the sofa next to me and sighed.

"Trevor's been offered a spot at South Bronx." Her fingers found the hem of my shirt and tugged. "But I still want you there with me."

I leaned over, resting my elbows on my knees as I looked into her face. "Why would you want me there instead of him?" Then, because I couldn't resist, I added, "Is it because he still hasn't figured out how to kiss you?"

She laughed and lifted a shoulder, her cheeks

flushing as her eyes dropped to her hands. "It's not that... but it's just–what if it ends badly, you know? And then we'd still have to work together. I don't want that to happen."

She wasn't wrong. Working with an ex wasn't fun.

"It's probably a good thing you and I never hooked up then."

The morning shift might've gotten awkward if we'd ever crossed that line.

Still. I would've taken that risk if Lilly was single. I understood why Trevor wanted to take that risk now.

Lilly's eyes flicked to mine. "Is it?"

She asked so softly that it took me a second to process what her question meant.

Is it a good thing that nothing ever happened between us?

And I wanted to beat myself over the head then, because... shit. Now I was hoping for something that wouldn't happen all over again. And I wanted to tell her.

I wanted to *tell her*.

Instead, I shook my head. Even though it was killing me not to say it out loud, I knew I couldn't do that to her.

"I don't know. All I know is you're dating Trevor and... we'll be leaving this place soon."

She gave the hem of my shirt another tug as she said, "If I knew you had feelings for someone, maybe I could've done something. If you tell me who she is, I could... talk to her."

So, she didn't believe me then. She thought there was someone else, and she was apologetic about it, like it was her fault that I'd never gone after the girl I wanted.

And I knew what that meant.

"You know why I don't tell you these things?"

Her eyes narrowed. From the tone of my voice, she could tell I was done talking about this.

"Because I want you to leave it alone. I don't want your help."

She shot me a look, like she was hurt, then let go of my shirt. "I was just... you didn't tell me, and I thought maybe I could try and make up for what happened with Stacey."

I sighed and pinched the bridge of my nose.

I couldn't even pretend to be mad at her anymore. She meant well. She always meant well. I just wanted it to mean more than that.

"You don't have to do that kind of thing for me. I see what it does to you."

"What what does?"

"You know what I mean. Every time you're dragged into someone else's problems, it ends up stressing you out."

She frowned, confused. "It hasn't been that bad. I can handle it."

Yeah, I didn't agree. That sorority was taking too

much out of her. It left her with just enough time to pull a shift here, then run back to her dorm to help someone else study for something her degree had nothing to do with.

"What I'm saying is, I just want you to focus on yourself. And let everyone take care of themselves for once."

"It's not like I have a choice, Shawn." Something crept out of her tone, and I could tell she was getting defensive. "I can't say no."

Maybe I was touching a nerve here, which was the last thing I wanted to do.

I just wanted to take care of her. I wanted to show her that she didn't have to do all this shit alone.

And the urge to do *more* than that was so fucking strong, that I had to get off this sofa and get away from her. Which left her to stare up at me from where she sat, still frowning.

I tried again.

"It's just that you've got this exam coming up, and you've already failed it once. If you don't pass, you won't graduate, and then what? Taking some time to study couldn't hurt."

She looked away from me with her jaw locked tight. "I'm going to pass, Shawn. I have to."

"If you keep going like this... you might not."

It might have been true, but as soon as the words left my lips, I knew that saying something like that was pure stupidity. I was just making her feel worse.

Her expression shut down, and I knew her anxiety was stirring through what I'd said, adding layers that weren't there, making her believe the worst about something I never should've brought up in the first place.

"You don't think I can do it?" she mumbled, not waiting for an answer before her eyes squeezed shut. She bent over her stomach and sang, "Jump up, make a sound, hey, stomp your boots, turn around, start now, make a change, gonna make that sound."

Shit.

In an instant, I was by her side, trying to do the shoulder-squeeze thing that calmed her down, but she pushed my hands away.

"Lilly, of course I think you can do it, I just meant you need time to study–"

"What is this?" Uncle Henry's thickly accented voice entered the room before he did. "What you do?"

"I think she's going to be sick," I told him as I looked around for anything that could help her.

"Why she sick? What you do?" he repeated, not waiting for an answer as he shuffled back out.

"You fix it," he yelled over his shoulder, and I quickly took a bucket from a nearby shelf, knelt in front of her, and held it to her chin.

As her breathing slowed, I growled at myself, so frustrated that I'd made her this upset. I couldn't believe I'd been too much of an asshat to realize that her exam was a real problem for her.

She didn't need someone to remind her to study. She needed help.

Uncle Henry was right. I had to fix it.

So even if it meant putting myself through fucking torture, that was exactly what I was going to do.

CHAPTER 19

SHAWN

MONDAY EVENING

One Month Until Graduation
Tristy's Coffee Shop

CLOSING TIME FINALLY CAME AROUND. Lilly finished mopping as I stacked the last of the chairs, and Tristan wrapped our uneaten pastries in a bag. It wasn't long before it was just the three of us alone in the back room again.

Tristan and I were counting shelves of coffee bags, bread, and condiments while Lilly collapsed on the sofa behind us. Then the door opened and shut with the sound of a woman groaning.

As she walked into the back room, a heavily pregnant Nikki grumbled, "I can't believe I have another two months of this to go. I can't actually get any bigger, can I?"

Tristan's eyes lit up as his wife shuffled closer for a kiss.

"You definitely can," I told her. "But if you two keep going at it the way you do, that baby might shake loose before we're ready."

Nikki laughed. "If I could help it, I would. But I'm so hormonal right now, and–" she gestured to Tristan "–my husband looks like this."

Yeah, I could see that. I'd heard customers call Tristan a thirst trap before. Not that he cared. He only had eyes for Nikki.

Even now, he ran a finger across her cheek and said, "I can't wait until you start maternity leave. I'm never letting you out of our bed."

Then they did what they always do. They made out like no one else was in the room.

I rolled my eyes. "I can't believe I'm used to watching you two grope each other. It should make me gag."

Nikki's honey-brown hair swished around her shoulders as Tristan broke their kiss.

Chuckling, he asked, "Are you saying you're not going to miss this when you go?"

"Ohhh don't remind me," Nikki groaned. "I can't believe you guys are leaving. Have you decided where you're teaching yet?"

Yes, but I still hadn't told Lilly. I dreaded just the thought of telling her.

But that wasn't today's problem, so I shrugged it off and said, "You know where Lilly's going."

"I have to go to South Bronx," Lilly muttered in a voice so small that I barely heard it.

The shift in the room was instant. Nikki pulled away from her husband, looking as worried as I felt.

"Hey, you okay?" she asked Lilly.

"It's just graduation, you know? It's a big deal," she said, strained.

Nikki and Tristan swapped glances.

"Did something happen?" Tristan asked, folding his arms.

Lilly shook her head slowly, but neither of them looked like they believed her.

"I'm going to South Bronx Classical. I'm going to teach at my mom's school."

"You are," Nikki said, probably as confused as the rest of us.

Something was off with Lilly, and I was pretty sure I knew what it was.

"And nothing's going to stop that from happening, right?" Nikki asked.

Lilly nodded. "Nothing. Except, my final exam is in a week and I haven't... studied enough."

Nikki didn't miss a beat. "Why not?"

"I've been so busy." She held up her hand and lowered fingers as she listed all the things she'd been doing. "I had to teach another Kappa about merchandising, and then there was this study group I had to manage, and I created a lesson plan with–"

"Lilly, what happens if you don't pass this exam?" Tristan interrupted.

She paused, looked at our older boss, then her eyes landed on me. Her voice dropped as she admitted, "I might not graduate."

As Nikki plopped on the couch and wrapped an arm around Lilly, I couldn't just stand there and let her think that was true.

"Yes, you will. I'll help you."

I didn't want to bring this up now–I almost gave her a panic attack just mentioning the exam last week–but I'd been thinking about it all weekend. I was going to pick a quiet moment to talk to her, then make my offer.

But this was as good a time as any.

Lilly blinked, and I took in the surprise on her face. "You don't have to help me... I just need to get organized, you know? And then I'll be okay."

"But I already have everything you need," I argued. "Index cards, highlighted texts, study sets. You might as well use it. Just give me one night to walk you through my notes, and that's it. Guaranteed pass."

I was aware of Nikki and Tristan trading stares to my left, but all I could see was the way Lilly relaxed. The gratitude she looked up at me with–fuck. It felt good.

I knew what I was signing myself up for. Being

alone with her somewhere private, knowing I couldn't touch her. It'd hurt.

But I couldn't walk away when she needed me. I couldn't live with myself if I did that. Even if I planned to teach somewhere else after graduation, I could at least say that I helped her with this.

Tristan took my shoulder and tugged. I turned to him as he whispered, "Are you sure you can handle that?"

"Huh?"

Nikki and Lilly fell into a conversation of their own, distracted, but Tristan kept his voice low anyway.

"Look, I get it. I know how you feel. People keep taking from her and she doesn't know how to say no—you're tired of watching her go through that and you don't want her to fail. But studying with her means being alone with her."

He paused, then repeated, "Can you handle that?"

I suppressed a groan, but it wasn't easy. "I work with her almost every day. I'll be okay."

It was a lie and we both knew it.

He softened. "It's killing you. Isn't it?"

My jaw locked up on its own. "I'm fine."

I knew nothing was going to happen between us. That wasn't why I was doing this.

"We'll study here. Tomorrow," I told my boss, loud enough for Nikki and Lilly to hear.

There was more space in the coffee shop than in our

cramped dorm rooms… less clutter for me to deal with. And less Mia, which was always a plus.

Tristan lifted a brow at me, then shrugged, letting my shoulder go. "If that's what you want, then sure. You can take the back room."

Lilly sounded more like herself as she said, "Okay. Just me and you after work, and we'll lock up when we're done. Thank you, Shawn."

I looked at her, met her eyes, watched her smile, and tried to ignore the lift in my chest. The way my skin went hot and cold all at once.

Tristan let out an amused huff, like he knew how truly fucked I was, and honestly, he wasn't wrong.

"Great," I told her. "One night with me, and you'll get what you need."

I winked before I could stop myself.

CHAPTER 20
SHAWN
TUESDAY MORNING

Tristy's Coffee Shop

WHAT THE SHIT was I thinking?

I winked at Lilly.

After all the months I spent holding it together, I winked at her like an idiot.

I thought I could handle this. I'd been alone with her more than once over the years. But on my way to work this morning, I pictured all the ways the study session I volunteered for could go wrong. Or right, if she—

Fuck no. I wasn't supposed to want something to happen. I'd accepted that nothing would.

I was supposed to keep my shit locked down until graduation. That was the plan.

But as I stepped inside and heard Tristan say

goodbye to Nikki, my eyes snagged on the back room, and it was like I couldn't control my thoughts.

Even now, I was picturing Lilly bent over the sofa with her leggings wrapped around her ankles. Her peachy ass in the air, looking over her shoulder at me, waiting for me to spread her perfect thighs.

She'd be dripping wet, begging, and I'd take my time. I'd run my fingers along her soft, warm slit, and trace tight, slow circles around her clit. She'd moan in her husky, cocktease voice, and I'd drag it out, teasing her.

Damn, what would it feel like to have her underneath me like–

"Hey, you've been staring at the sofa for a while. You okay?" Tristan's voice pulled me back to our busy shop.

No. I wasn't okay. I was so hard-up, I could've drilled a hole in the countertop.

"Yeah, I just didn't... sleep," I told him. "I'm probably going to need one of those double-shot lattes you make for Nikki. Actually, can you make it a triple?"

He gave me a smile. "I'll make you a double. A triple and you'd be too jittery to do anything."

"Ha. Says the man who burned himself last month."

He chuckled and shrugged. "I'd take the burn over what you're doing tonight."

Yeah. I would too.

Tristan stepped behind the coffee machine while I

stared into the back room. At the throw blanket, the sofa cushions, the overhead heaters.

I didn't know what was going on with me.

I knew Lilly wasn't interested. She was with someone else.

But I couldn't stop thinking about it—all the things I wanted to do to her in there.

Fuck.

This was supposed to be about helping her. She was in trouble, she needed help, I offered. That was all this was supposed to be. Why couldn't I–

"Hey, can you grab a muffin?" Tristan repeated.

"Uh... oh. Yeah. Sorry."

He eyed me, handed me my coffee, and said, "Come on, Shawn, you can't help Lilly if you can't get your head on straight."

Well, that was probably true.

The problem, though, was that I wasn't thinking with my head.

NOW

CHAPTER 21
LILLY
WEDNESDAY AFTERNOON

Verra Convention Center

"HIPPOS CAN SLEEP UNDERWATER," I said while watching Shawn fight a smile. "They can't breathe, but they do this thing where they bob up, get some air, and sink back down, all without waking up. I always thought that was pretty... cool."

My voice trailed off, getting quieter and quieter as everyone around the table stared at me.

We were in the meeting room, having our weekly staff update. Three weeks in, halfway done with the fundraiser, and I'd finally gotten a handle on most of it.

Well, except for the whole talking-to-people thing.

Fun facts usually helped me hold a conversation, but it looked like this one was ending it.

"Well, that's definitely something I didn't already

know. Thank you... Miss Fares?" Shawn had to bite his bottom lip to stop himself from laughing, and it felt good to know I'd at least gotten a chuckle out of him. The heat in my cheeks cooled a little.

From the corner of my eye, I noticed Stacey's clenched jaw, and assumed, judging by the way she stared down at her notes, that she still wasn't happy with me.

I wasn't sure why. I was trying. I really was.

Whenever I bought Mia a batch of crullers, I made sure to put a few on Stacey's desk too. I started handing in my reports early. I asked her how she was every morning. I even listened to her complain about the guy she stood next to on the subway yesterday.

He was picking his teeth an inch away from her face, and no matter how far back she leaned, it didn't matter. A bit of chewed food landed on her blouse and instantly made her sick.

Stories like that usually made Mia roll her eyes, but not me. If Stacey needed a sounding board, I was more than willing to be that for her. Because even though it was pretty clear that she didn't like me, she'd solved my tutor problems anyway.

Mrs Hernandez was happy with Kya. I'd had no complaints so far from either of them. Which was such a relief.

Last week, my job was hanging by a thread. And now? It wasn't. But not just because of Stacey.

I was nailing my tasks at the fundraiser, and was almost done with Trevor's module. It seemed like everything was finally coming together, and it made me feel like maybe I wasn't completely useless after all.

"So, I'd say we're on track. Well done, everyone."

A handful of teachers started clapping. Then Mia side-eyed me as she put her hands together. So I... joined in too. By then, I guess it was weird not to?

Shawn looked at me, raised a brow, and I fought the urge to giggle.

He was probably used to it by now, but the fact that he was Shawn Jackson—thought leader, initiative driver, educational standard setter—wasn't something I'd come to terms with yet.

And I definitely hadn't come to terms with the amount of applause the man received on an almost daily basis.

As the clapping died off, and chairs groaned as people stood to leave, I dragged a pink cake box across the table.

"Guys, before we all go, is it okay if I steal a bit of your time?" I asked, reminding myself that these were just people. I stood in front of entire classrooms full of people every day. My students were half my age, sure, but still. They were definitely people.

I could do this.

I looked at Shawn and he nodded, letting me know that I could keep going. Everyone sat back down as I cleared my throat.

"I know we've been working hard, but, without our project manager, I think we can all agree the fundraiser would've been a mess by now."

I stole a peek at Stacey, who was completely thrown. She probably didn't know what to think as I slid the pink box in front of her.

She met my eyes and gave me a look, like she was confused and panicked. I'd seen that expression enough times in the mirror to know it when I saw it, and it made my cheeks heat all over again.

Was this a bad idea? Was I trying to fix something that couldn't be fixed?

I kept going, almost speaking on autopilot.

"Personally, she's been a big help to me these past few weeks, and even though I've given her every reason not to be, she's been pretty patient too. Stacey, this is just a small thank-you from us, for being a great project manager."

I flipped back the box lid and showed her a red velvet cake that had the words *Thank you, Stacey* written in delicious, white cursive.

The teachers around me cheered. Well, except for Mia.

I started to feel a little surer about this whole cake-appreciation thing as I watched Stacey's eyes glass over.

Staring at the cake, she said, "You remembered my favorite flavor."

I shrugged. "I might have the memory of an elephant."

As Stacey laughed, Mia grumbled, "Oh, for cripes' sake." Shawn shot her a warning glance.

But Mia ignored him. She stood, pushing her chair into the table hard enough to shake it.

Rolling her eyes, she asked on her way out, "Do you really think she deserves a cake just for doing her bloody job?"

Her question was just mean enough that the room went quiet.

The shift was instant. Stacey's expression dropped, and I didn't know what to do.

But I had to fix it. I was the one who put Stacey on the spot, so I should—

Stacey stood and clapped her hands, interrupting my thoughts. She didn't look any less insulted by what Mia had done, but she definitely seemed ready to move past it.

"Thank you all for this. I think we should put it in the kitchen so everyone can have a slice."

"Oooh, I'll take it," said a teacher with a wild mess of curly hair. I was pretty sure her name was Sharon. "I can cut the slices." She took the box, winked at me, and led the way to the kitchen as she told everyone, "I love cakes—I bake, too. Mostly cupcakes. Maybe I'll bring a few in next week."

As they all funneled out, Shawn leaned over. His

breath brushed the shell of my ear as he asked, "Can we talk for a minute?"

As I looked up at him, I tried not to shiver. "Is it about Mia?"

I wished I could say the truce we'd set was messing with my head–and it really could've been–but I couldn't stop myself from reacting this way.

Shivering, flushing, sweating–Oh, I was especially tired of sweating every time he looked at me.

"No, but if you could talk to her about this... thing she has going with Stacey, that'd help. I need a non-hostile work environment to keep this project on track."

"I get it. I'll talk to her."

"Thanks. And I wanted to thank you for trying to smooth things over with Stacey, too."

"Oh?" I put my hands behind my back and resisted the urge to bounce on my toes.

God, why was I like this?

"Yeah. She's been under a lot of pressure lately, and I know you two haven't been getting along. It was pretty great of you to be the bigger person."

I lifted a shoulder. "I just wanted to thank her. You asked her to do it, but because of her, I've got a happy Mrs Hernandez. She saved my job."

He gave me a smile, and suddenly he was closer, and it was harder to breathe. But not in a panic-attack way. In a forget-how-to-use-bodily-functions way.

My pulse thudded in my ears as Shawn did that

sexy thing where he chewed one side of his bottom lip before speaking, and I hated that I liked it so much.

"About that. I was thinking about putting in a call to Trevor. To ask him to back off. Professionally, I mean. Would you... be okay with that?"

Oh, be still my ovaries. He was *not* my knight in shining armor.

"Thanks, but no. I should handle Trevor myself. Besides—" I dared to give him that light, friendly punch-to-the-chest thing I'd seen people do, and felt awkward all over again. "I'm doing everything he wanted me to do. He can't fire me now."

Ignoring the fist I still had pressed to his hard chest, he frowned. "Lilly, I don't want to sound like I don't believe you're a good teacher. I do. It's hard to believe you could be bad at anything—"

"Math. You know I'm awful at math."

His low laugh felt like a small victory. Some things really never changed, like how good it felt to make him smile. At this point, there was no denying that I really was hopeless when it came to him.

"You passed the basic Praxis requirements, so you're not that bad."

"But that was six years ago. If you don't use it, you lose it. I can honestly tell you I haven't had to use algebra in my classroom once," I admitted.

His smile widened, and I could feel my chest expanding to match the size of it.

"My point was about the test scores. You might be

able to kill it at this fundraiser and finish that... module he signed you up for, but raising your class grades could be a problem. Do you have a plan for that?"

And just like that, my smile slipped. "I don't have a plan... exactly."

"It's okay. You have time. I'll help."

I ruffled my bangs just to have something else to do. "No. You shouldn't have to help me. I can do it myself."

It was like I could sense his next reaction, and it made me nervous. And just like I thought he would, he scowled at me.

"But I want to. I know what your job means to you, and I want to help you keep it."

I put my hands on my hips and started pacing. This felt too familiar, and I wasn't sure how to handle it.

"My job is my problem. And you're busy. I don't want to waste your time."

"Lilly," he growled, a warning. "Just accept the help."

I shook my head, my heel caught on the carpet, and I stumbled. I yelped as Shawn caught me, and my hands squeezed his firm forearms.

And now I was ogling his forearms? This was getting sad.

But I didn't have any more time to think about it, because Shawn turned me, sat me on the table, and pressed his palms against either side of me.

I suddenly felt like a naughty student who needed to be pinned down and given a lecture.

He was so close that I felt almost forced to breathe him in. His scent was heady enough that, when I glanced up to see the look on his face, I was almost surprised by how frustrated he was.

"One thing that's never changed is how fucking stubborn you are. I've spent years working on this exact thing—you know I have. And you still don't want my help? Tell me why."

"I just..." I didn't know how to finish that sentence.

And I couldn't focus on what he was saying because I was too busy focusing on what he was doing.

He towered over me, cornering me against the tabletop. He seemed so irritated with me, and that tell-tale throb was back, pulsing between my thighs.

I was wet.

I was wet.

Oh, if I thought I was mad at myself before, I was definitely mad now.

Flushed from head to toe, I muttered, "I just... don't want to make things harder for you. You have so much to do already."

He clenched his teeth so tight that the muscle in his jaw twitched. As he moved away from me, I clamped my legs shut. It barely dulled the pounding, but I'd take it.

"You don't like the idea of putting me out because you let people put you out, and you know how shitty that feels. Right?"

He watched me, waiting for the nod of my head, but

I was only half-listening, so all I did was stare. He let out a breath and ran his hand through his hair, exasperated.

"Lilly, trust me when I say that helping you wouldn't bother me. If you won't let me call Trevor, at least let me do this for you."

I crossed my legs and squeezed my thighs together, rolling my hips on the wooden surface. I was turned on, and I was so used to giving myself immediate attention when I needed it that I did it without thinking.

But I didn't think he'd noticed. He was too busy staring daggers at the wall above my head. So I rolled my hips again. Just as his gaze dropped.

And he definitely noticed this time.

His eyes turned an inky black as he watched me, and within a second, I stopped moving. But it didn't seem to matter. He stepped closer.

His voice was low, and god, I loved the way he said my name.

"Lilly." He was close enough to touch me now. "Are you—"

"Cake's ready. Come grab a slice."

Sharon's head popped in and out so quickly, it made both of us jolt.

Then Shawn shut his eyes. He breathed in slowly and let it out, as if he needed a second to calm down. Judging by the way his nostrils flared, maybe he did.

I'd probably never know what he was going to ask me. Because instead of shutting the door and trailing his hand up my thigh, like I wanted him to, he nudged his chin toward the exit.

"Come on. We better get you a piece before it's gone."

I bit my lip as he took my hand and lifted me from the table.

I wasn't hungry for cake. But I couldn't bring myself to ask for what I really wanted.

CHAPTER 22
LILLY
SATURDAY NIGHT

Lilly's Apartment

LYING ON MY BED, I slipped my hands under the covers. Naked, I skimmed my fingers across my skin, touching the crease where my ribs met my breasts, tracing circles until I found my nipple. I sucked in a breath as I pinched it, and slid my other hand down my stomach, between my legs.

In my mind, it was Shawn's hand. He was between my legs. He was sliding his thumb over my nipple.

"Are you wet?" he'd ask, finishing that question I never got to hear. "Is your pretty little pussy soaked for me?"

I bit my lip as I sent a finger inside, imagining the satisfied sound Shawn would make if he could feel what he'd done to me.

"Good girl," he'd tell me, pushing his finger deeper.

"Look how tight and wet you are. You want me to fuck you, don't you?"

I slid my bare legs along the soft sheets and moaned as I added another finger. It felt so good. I was so ready to come.

Taking my hand from my breast, I reached for my nightstand, picking up my pocket-sized vibrator and flicking it on. It hummed as I put it to my clit.

Letting out another moan, I threw my head to the side and kept going. My fingers slid in and out, again and again.

"Do you know how fucking sexy you are?" Shawn's voice, still just a fantasy, vibrated through me, and I almost came right then and there.

I curled my toes, rolled my hips, and then there it was, uncoiling low and warm, shooting through me like electricity.

I rode out my orgasm, biting back a scream. When it was done, I pulled everything away, turning off the vibrator as I enjoyed the afterglow.

My body felt heavy, tingly, and throbby. It felt nice. Until I started to feel a nagging guilt in the back of my head.

"Why am I still thinking of him?" I asked my ceiling. "Of all the men I could be thinking about, why him?"

My ceiling wasn't exactly the chattiest area of my apartment, so naturally, it didn't answer me back.

"One of these days, I might have to replace you with a therapist," I mumbled, still staring at it.

Some people thought attraction wasn't something you could help. They thought of it as a mix of chemicals and pheromones. And maybe it was. But I was starting to think that my attraction to Shawn was rooted in something deeper. Something I really wanted to resist, but couldn't.

I let out a deep breath and stood, putting on a lightweight robe as I padded back out to my kitchen. A box of cold, half-eaten pizza sat on the counter, and I washed my hands before I picked up a slice. The cheese was hard, and it was amazing.

I needed it too, after the week I'd just had. But then, if I put aside all these weird, unwanted feelings for Shawn, things weren't too bad.

In fact, they were almost good. So good, that I could make a list out of it.

1. **The fundraiser was going well.**

I was on track with my tasks, and all that was left to do was coordinate the delivery of my merch next week, which was beyond exciting.

In fact, while I was sitting at my desk on Friday afternoon, my phone rang.

"Hi, Trevor," I answered, too happy with my progress to be upset with seeing his name on my screen.

"Hi." He sounded put off. "I was calling to check in. How are things going?"

I wasn't surprised. After that first call, Trevor called during my second week too. It was the end of week three, and he was consistent. I'd give him that much.

"Good, actually. Everything is on track."

"On track? That's... great. How, uh, how exactly did you manage that? Mia mentioned that you were having some technical issues last week."

"I was, but as soon as they were fixed, I worked late for a few nights."

"You did?"

I nodded, forgetting he couldn't see me. "Yep."

"Right. You're all caught up then," he muttered, and oddly enough, it didn't sound like he was happy.

So I gave him another bit of news.

2. **The module was almost done.**

"I'm up to date on the module too. And I've got a plan to raise my student exam scores."

"You... have?"

Oof, he sounded more disappointed than ever.

"Shawn helped me with it. He gave me some resources too, and walked me through how the module could fit into my teaching style, which is great, because I didn't want to overhaul everything just to–"

I must've been rambling, because Trevor felt the need to cut me off.

"Shawn helped you? Shawn Jackson?"

"Uh... yes?"

I peeked at Shawn over my cubicle wall, and there he was, clapping another teacher on the shoulder for a job well done. It did things to my chest to see him like that.

"I thought you hated each other."

"We did, but we called a truce, and now I think we're maybe friends again?"

"Really? After what he did to you?"

"Um… I guess."

"Did he at least tell you why he did it?"

I stiffened a little. "Trevor, you know why."

"No. All I know is what you and Mia told me. But that doesn't explain why he went out of his way to avoid you for so long."

And that made me grind my teeth. I ended the call with a frown, which didn't seem fair after finally telling the head teacher of my faculty about how hard I'd been working.

I should've felt great. Instead, I was feeling pretty low. Even though:

3. **Stacey was treating me like a regular human being.**

Stacey came by my desk to thank me for the cake, and we talked a little.

It felt nice. It felt like a clean slate.

That was until Mia walked over, holding her nose.

Stacey warily asked, "Does something smell?"

Mia leaned in and whispered, "I didn't want to say anything, but your pit stains are a bit hard to ignore. You might want to do something about them before Shawn notices."

Stacey's eyes went wide. She turned and almost ran to the elevator, her arms rigid by her sides. Mia cackled.

"Mia, that was low."

She held her stomach, like she hadn't laughed that hard in weeks. "Oh, I know, isn't it great? One of my freshmen gave me the idea."

"Well, that makes sense. Only you would take advice from a freshman."

She laughed harder, which wasn't the reaction I was hoping for.

"Do you think maybe we could try being nicer to her?" I asked. "She really saved my ass with the whole tutor thing. Maybe she's changed."

Mia rolled her eyes. "The only thing that's changed about her is her bra size."

"You don't know that."

Mia scoffed. "Yes. I do. She's been riding your ass since you got here. Just because she's lightened up for one bloody hour since you gave her that cake, doesn't mean she's changed. In fact, that tutor she lined up for you? She's probably thought of a way to hold it over your head later."

"Mia, come on."

"No, you come on. You can't ignore everything she's done to you."

"But she works with Shawn now—"

"That doesn't mean anything. She could have him as wrapped around her finger now as she had you back then. He probably jumps through hoops to keep her happy just like you did."

"Mia."

"I just want you to be careful." She gave me a soft look then, like she'd been worried about me. Then she held up a paper bag. "And will you stop buying me crullers? You don't need to thank me. I'm doing this with you because I want to."

I pouted. "Okay... but what about coffee?"

She told me she could get her own coffee, then wrangled a promise out of me that I wouldn't start blindly trusting our ex-sorority president again. And I couldn't blame Mia for feeling the way she did.

Stacey had only ever looked out for herself.

So overall, things were going well. I mean, if I didn't scratch the surface, I could believe things were the way they were supposed to be.

But... "Who am I kidding?" I mumbled around my mouthful of stale pizza. "Stacey and Mia can't stand each other, Trevor's still looking for ways to fire me, and I just made myself come while thinking about Shawn. I'm a train wreck."

But, then again, when was I not?

CHAPTER 23
LILLY
MONDAY MORNING

Verra Convention Center

I HEARD Mia's voice from down the hall, and ran into the small kitchen. It took half a second to realize who she was yelling at.

"God, you are such an asshole. Admit you were wrong. Apologize." Mia wasn't handling this argument quietly, and it wasn't long before everyone else filtered out of the room.

"You both need to get over it, okay? Just move on. It was five fucking years ago."

Stacey's screech was louder than Mia's yell by a long shot. Sharon, the baker of the buttercream cupcakes resting on the small table between them, snuck by me as I hurried in.

Mia huffed. "But we're still dealing with it. Lilly is still dealing with it. How do you not see that?"

Stacey's eyes went wide as she noticed me trying to catch my breath. She looked prepared to take down the both of us. But I wasn't there to fight. I was there to stop it.

"It's not my fault you two don't know how to handle your shit. It's not like I forced her into anything. She didn't have to date Trevor. She could've said no."

"If she didn't date him, you would've kicked her out of the sorority, you evil bitch." Mia's voice grew louder, and then it all happened so quickly.

She lifted a cupcake and threw it at Stacey.

There was a choked cry, and then Stacey leaned over the table, shoving a cupcake in Mia's face.

Which kicked me into action.

I grabbed Mia's shoulders and tried to pull her away from Stacey. But then I was dragged into it somehow, and they were reaching over me to get to each other.

"Stop, please, this isn't okay," I yelled, but they weren't listening.

Their manicured nails raked down my wrists, and I ended up covered in frosting.

"What are you *doing*?" I heard Shawn's low growl before I saw him, and when I did, it was almost like he'd appeared out of nowhere.

He forced himself into the middle, separating Mia from Stacey without having to touch either of them. Stacey stepped away as Mia glared at Shawn's back, while I collapsed against the sink, very aware of the icing on my cheek, my neck, and my new pastel pink blouse.

Mia had her hands on her hips and started shifting her weight on her feet. She had cake in her hair and all over her corporate dress. She looked like she still wanted to fight.

Stacey didn't. She'd given up. She was all soft doe eyes and hunched shoulders, looking up at Shawn like he was her hero.

And Shawn just looked pissed. Like we were three students caught scratching the side of his car.

"What the hell was that about?"

Punishment was in his voice, and a thrill slid from my toes to my fingertips.

Oh. My. God. What was wrong with me?

This wasn't the time to get hot and bothered.

Mia glared, lips pursed tight, as she whittled her movements down to nothing. "Why should I tell you? You're just going to take her side."

He shook his head, exasperated. "Mia, this is the second time I've had to pull you off of Stacey since you got here."

Mia pointed at him. "See? That right there. You blame me and Lilly every time."

He rolled his shoulders, trying to calm himself. "Will you please just tell me why you two were fighting?"

"All right, fine," she ground out. "We were having a

chat about how your little lapdog here used to bully Lilly."

"His... lapdog?" A look of confused disgust passed over Stacey's face, and then it was gone in an instant as she turned to Shawn. "I didn't bully her. I couldn't make her do anything."

Shawn's eyes flicked from Mia to Stacey to me. He had no idea what was going on.

And why would he? The only person he hadn't cut ties with was Stacey. And she had no reason to tell him about all the things she'd forced me into.

"Okay, there's a story here, and as much as I'd love to hear it, we aren't here to talk," he said. "We're here to work. Is that clear?"

All this authority pulled a shiver up my spine.

"Get a grip, Lilly," I muttered.

My muttering didn't go unnoticed. As Mia and Stacey left to clean themselves up, Shawn's attention landed on me, and I found myself straightening as I wiped at a patch of icing.

"Were you a part of that?" he asked. "Or were you just trying to break them up?"

He drifted closer, and without thinking, I leaned back against the sink. "I was trying to stop it, but I wasn't very helpful, I guess."

"Yeah, well, at least you tried," he sighed.

I held my breath as he reached out to scoop icing from my shoulder.

"It's in your hair too." His voice was soft, and it made me squirm a little. This felt too familiar, too comfortable, and it shouldn't have.

"It was probably a given that I'd end up covered in frosting at some point," I muttered.

He licked his fingers and broke into his classic smile, the kind that made my chest ache.

"Probably."

"Is it okay if I clean myself up?" I asked.

"No."

My mouth dropped open. "What? Why?"

He shrugged, then teased me with, "You're sweeter like this."

I huffed and pushed off the sink. "No, what I am is sticky, and I'm going to shower whether you give me permission or not."

A laugh poured out of him as I stomped to the door, and I looked back to watch his face shift with it. With warmth, with joy. Those dimples, those eyes, those lips.

"I don't think so, Miss Fares. There's no frosting on that ass of yours. You can sit down and work."

I put my hands on my hips. He was joking, I knew he was, but I wasn't going to be swayed that easily. For once, Trevor was right about something. Shawn had five years to make up for.

"So not only are you looking at my ass, but I'm 'Miss Fares' again?"

He lifted a shoulder, laughter gone, but his smile was still there.

Ignoring the comment about my ass, he said, "You could go back to being Miss Fares, if that's what you want."

I dropped my arms and went back to him. I needed to know why he'd cut me out for so long. He owed me that much.

"What I want is to know why you ended things the way you did. I thought we were closer than that."

His gaze lifted over my head, back to the doorway, as if Stacey or Mia could walk in any second now. "If we were so close, why don't I know what's going on between those two?"

"Stacey and Mia?" I asked, absently wiping more cream from my blouse. He nodded as his eyes followed my fingers. "Mia never really got over what Stacey did to me back then."

He shook his head. "That's the part I'm not getting. I know she gave you shit sometimes, but that's it. What else did Stacey do?"

I folded my arms and shifted on my feet, not sure if I should tell him.

"Lilly?" he pushed, and I gave in.

"Remember our last few months before graduation?"

He put his hands in his pockets and nodded.

"Stacey used to be upset with me because I... brought the grade average down in our sorority. Because of the first time I failed my final exam. And, um, it made me pretty anxious."

"I remember that part."

"Oh. I thought I hid it well."

He gave me a small laugh, and I bumped my shoulder against his, grateful at how easy it was to slip into this.

"She was going to kick me out of the sorority. Unless I did what she wanted," I explained. "And you know what being there meant to me. My mom was a Kappa."

He nodded, understanding. I didn't have to explain it. Shawn knew all the reasons it was important to me. Which was why the way he treated me before this fundraiser was so confusing. And hurtful. He knew me so well. He was one of my closest friends. I spent the past five years wondering if all that was just... in my head. If it was a lie. If he was pretending the whole time we worked together at *Tristy's*.

But looking at him now, I didn't think so. It seemed like he genuinely had no idea what Stacey put me through back then. But if he knew, would it have changed anything?

I'd probably never know the answer to that.

"So, Stacey gave me work to do for the sorority, and I had to date Trevor because he was Stacey's cousin—"

"Wait," Shawn interrupted. "Stacey forced you to date Trevor?"

I nodded, and he frowned.

"Why would she do that?" he asked.

I shrugged. She never told me.

I asked Trevor once, and he didn't seem to know what I was talking about. He told me all he'd asked for was an introduction, and instead, Stacey arranged a date with me.

She never explicitly said I had to keep dating him, but with all the threats she had hanging over my head, I felt like I didn't have much of a choice.

Shawn's gaze searched mine. "Why didn't you tell me?"

"You were so protective of me back then. If I said anything, you would've tried to fix it."

His hand found his hair and ran through it. My knees weakened.

Nurgh, hold it together, Lilly.

"I... might've," he admitted. "If there wasn't another way around it."

"And I didn't want you to do that," I sighed, leaning against the table. "I made the mess; I had to dig myself out of it. And I tried to make things work with Trevor, but there just wasn't any... chemistry, I guess."

"Then you broke up after graduation?"

"It took another year, but yes."

His frown deepened. "So when you were struggling to pass your final exam, she set you up with Trevor and gave you extra work for the sorority?"

"Yes, but, to be fair," I reasoned, "I don't think she cared about my exam. I think she cared that the sorority ran smoothly."

That only made Shawn scowl even more. "And she knew you wouldn't say no when she asked."

"I would've done anything to stay there," I agreed, shrugging. "Mia always told me not to trust Stacey. If I didn't tell her about my mom, none of it would've happened."

"Mia was right." He swore under his breath. "I had no idea it was that bad. And I didn't do a thing to help you."

I looked up at him, surprised by the frustration lining his face.

"It wasn't your fault." I reached out and tugged on his shirt, twisting my fingers into the fabric like I used to. "I wasn't exactly honest about everything I was going through."

"But I didn't see it, and I should have. I should've been there when you needed it."

"You were," I told him. "You helped me study, remember?"

His big, warm palm was suddenly on my cheek, and I watched as he wiped away the frosting there.

He stared at his thumb, his voice low as he said, "Yeah, we... studied. But if I knew you didn't have feelings for Trevor, maybe I would've–" He ran his thumb against my lips, shocking me.

My stomach erupted. Nerves sped through me so fast they were almost paralyzing. I just stood there, licking the pad of his thumb, tasting the sugary icing on his skin.

His groan was so quiet, I almost didn't hear it over the roaring in my ears.

"Fuck," he whispered, his eyes on my mouth. "Do you know how badly I wanted you back then?"

I was stunned.

So stunned, that I barely managed to ask, "You... wanted me?"

My fist clenched in his shirt as I told myself how little sense that actually made. There was no way he'd spend so long avoiding me if that was how he felt.

But then, his fingers were in my hair. He pulled me closer, and, god, his touch was rough, a drug.

Maybe... maybe I was wrong.

"I still want you," he rasped, cornering me against the table, wrapping my hair around his fist, tipping my chin up.

It was another shock when his mouth brushed against mine; so soft at first. Then his fingers tightened in my hair, and I let out a breath as he stepped between my thighs, parting them in a way that made my skirt ride up.

He licked my bottom lip, groaning into my mouth, and my tongue slid against his before I could stop myself.

Oh god, it felt so good. Warm, deep and heavy, settling low in my stomach.

As his fingertip traced the nape of my neck, he pressed into me, and I moaned.

For the first time in a long time, I wasn't thinking.

There was no nagging voice in the back of my head. Nothing to remind me of what a bad idea this was. Of where we were, what we were doing, or how confusing my feelings for Shawn had become.

Reaching between us, I ran my palm along his length, surprised by just how thick and hard he felt. He pushed into my hand, groaning like he wanted more, and I was so ready to give it to him.

His other hand was on my thigh, slowly sliding up, and I held my breath, so lost in his touch, so drunk in it, that I wanted him to feel how wet he'd made me.

Just a little more, just a tiny graze, just a small taste of relief.

His tongue was driving me crazy, and his fingers were so close. Almost there. God, I wanted him inside me—

"Oh, now that's what I'm talking about."

Mia's outburst made Shawn and me jolt apart. My eyes flew from Mia to Shawn, and back again as I took in the stunned, then tense look on his face.

He backed away, swearing under his breath. Then, before I could think of anything to say, Shawn turned and walked out, his voice rough as he said, "I have to go."

And I was left standing there, trying to breathe, pressing my fingers to my lips, then running them to the back of my hair, as if I needed to remind myself of what he'd just done to me.

They were small movements. They lasted only a few seconds before Mia started whooping.

She grabbed my hand and squeezed it, smiling at me as if Shawn didn't just leave me feeling as confused as I'd felt all those years ago.

FIVE YEARS AGO

SHAWN

TUESDAY

Tristy's Coffee Shop

THE MORNING TURNED INTO NOON, and I kept looking up each time the door opened, hoping to see Lilly. And every time it ended up being another customer, my gut dropped.

Damn. I was in deep.

But why?

What did I even *like* about Lilly?

Sure, she made me laugh sometimes. She was the only person to make coffee shoot out of my nose because of something she said.

But then, there was the way she liked what she liked and did what she did.

Any other woman might've been embarrassed about watching movies meant for girls half her age, but not her. For a woman with social anxiety, she didn't seem to give a fuck about what other people thought.

Even now, whenever she threw on one of those films, her face lit up with this ridiculous, beautiful joy that was impossible to look away from.

And as much as I didn't like how she burned herself out for other people, I had to admit, the way she cared was rare.

She was fun, smart, and probably kinder than most people deserved. Maybe that's why I–*fuck, fuck, fuck.* I couldn't keep thinking about her like this.

Eventually, Lilly rushed in, wearing her usual black tee, leggings, and an oversized cardigan, carrying a tote bag full of heavy textbooks and loose papers.

At the sight of her, my stomach climbed into my throat. I swallowed it down as she joined me behind the counter.

"Oh... this stuff is heavy. One sec."

She was breathless, and I mentally filed away the sound of her voice as she hid her things in the back room. I glanced up just in time to watch her bend over her bag, and had to stop myself from groaning over the way her ass looked.

This was fucking agony, and we hadn't even started studying yet.

Lucky for me, it didn't last long. She stood and slid her apron over her head, leaving her completely covered and shapeless.

But then, there was her face. Her flushed cheeks, her freckles, her eyes–I couldn't look away.

If she noticed I was staring, she didn't call me on it. Instead, she asked, "Are you still okay for tonight?"

I swallowed again, nodded, and tried to give her a smile, but I was so ready for closing time, so desperate to be alone with this girl.

Shit. I was so fucked.

❧

Tristy's Coffee Shop: Closed

Lilly's bangs brushed her knuckles as she rubbed her temple and said, "Okay, I need a break."

We were alone in the back room sitting on the pile of blankets and cushions I'd propped on the ground. At the last minute, I brought in a tray of leftover cupcakes, and set them down next to us.

When we first walked in here after closing, she looked around, then up at me, and I could tell she was confused.

I told her, "We might as well be comfortable, right?" to try and put her at ease, but I couldn't shake this feeling.

This felt like a date.

I tried to ignore it, and as we studied, we fell into an easy enough rhythm. But now that we'd stopped, I had to rein that feeling in all over again.

"Why is it always so cold in here?" she grumbled, reaching over the cushion behind her to get to her tote bag.

I made a small noise as I watched the hem of her shirt ride up. It stretched around the soft curve of her waist, showing me a slice of her smooth navel, and my hands flexed on instinct.

What would she do if I just... touched her there? Just reached out and slid a finger over her skin.

Would she like it?

Would she want–Shit... Tristan was right. I couldn't handle this.

I was already hard just sitting here thinking about touching her. I had to get a grip.

So, for the sake of what was left of my sanity, I managed to stop eye-fucking her bellybutton as she put on a sweater.

And... okay. I couldn't let this slide.

"Lilly... what is that?"

"What?" she asked, looking around the room.

I shut the textbook I was holding and dropped it on the ground.

"That pink and blue thing you're wearing. What is that?"

She looked down at her chest and shrugged. "What? You squirted sauce on my cardigan."

Okay, yes, I squirted sauce on her cardigan earlier today, and it was hard to regret doing it after it earned me a laugh from her. Even if it meant ignoring the voice in the back of my head that told me I only did it because I wanted one less layer on her body.

But for her to replace it with that?

I couldn't ignore it. I had to tease her. There wasn't another choice here.

"It looks like a rainbow puked on you."

She grabbed her pink sweater and pulled it tight so I could get a better look. There was a picture plastered across the middle: a blue pony with a rainbow mane galloping across a white cloud, and it was so Lilly that I had to admit—I loved it.

"What's wrong, Shawn? Does Rainbow Dash's awesomeness offend you?"

She stood on her knees, shuffled closer, and wiggled her sweater in my face.

I bit back a laugh.

"That sweater doesn't belong to you. It belongs to a five-year-old with a doll-collecting obsession."

She pretended to gasp. "How dare you. My Little Pony is timeless."

"It's a ridiculous money-grab for kids."

She put her hands on her hips. "No, it's magical and amazing, and I know you like it."

My brows shot up as she waved her sweater in my face again and sang, "I'm awesome, it's a warnin', watch out for me, I'm as awesome as I oughta be."

I smiled as she rocked back on her heels.

"Hey, I got one. I almost forgot what that looked like on you."

She leaned back on a cushion, stretching, as I asked, "What what looks like?"

"You, smiling. You've been kinda grumpy lately. I can't remember the last time you laughed."

I frowned. "I sure as hell got a laugh out of spilling sauce on you today."

She sat up and scowled. "You told me that was an accident."

I held up my hands. "I did you a favor. That cardigan was so old, even Uncle Henry would've thrown it out."

A giggle burst out of her, and she leaned back again, relaxing.

We were both quiet for a while, and I just sat there, listening to her breathe. She shut her eyes and sighed, and it was nice. Us, quiet like this. It was comfortable. And after everything I'd been putting myself through, it was a welcome change of pace.

Quiet was never really Lilly's thing, though.

"Did you know fish can get seasick?" she asked, and I couldn't control the laugh that came out of me. I almost snorted.

Which seemed to satisfy her. She nodded and nestled deeper into the cushions.

"I've been wanting to tell you that for days."

"Oh yeah? I've got one for you too. Did you know male monkeys go bald the same way men do?"

I could tell I'd surprised her by the noise she made.

"Really? I can't believe I didn't know that. But it

kind of makes sense. Maybe men evolved from monkeys after all."

I squinted at her. "It's... scientifically proven that we did, Lil."

She shook her head. "Nope. Women evolved from mermaids. I can feel it in my fish bones. It's why I get seasick, you know."

The image of Lilly barfing over the side of a boat with a fishtail growing out of her ass was funnier than I wanted it to be, and I laughed again.

This was so easy. Right here and now, just the two of us. I loved being around her like this. Hearing her laugh, making her smile... I couldn't imagine a time or a place where seeing those things didn't make waking up every day feel worth it.

"Shawn?"

"Lilly?"

"Do you think I'll pass this time?"

I stretched out next to her, taking in the way she looked up at me, like she was starting to feel anxious.

"You'll pass. If I could do it, so can you."

She raised a brow. "Shawn, just because you–of all people–passed, doesn't mean I will."

"Why not?"

"Because you have the highest grades in our program. This exam was easy for you. But I failed. Again. Maybe I'm just not cut out for this."

She let out a frustrated noise. "I just really want it,

you know? Mom made it look like–" her voice caught, and she clamped her mouth shut.

I'd been trying not to touch her all night, but even though she was doing her best to hide it, I could tell she was upset. I couldn't lie there and ignore it. I reached for her and pulled her into me.

"Lilly, no. You'll pass. I know you will."

I spoke into her hair and traced small circles on her back, but as she settled against my chest and buried her fingers in my shirt, I knew holding her like this was a mistake.

We were too close.

Her body was on mine, pressed so tight I almost couldn't breathe.

All I had to do was lift her chin, and that'd be it. I could finally kiss her–taste her.

And, god, the way she smelled. Like toasted cinnamon and honey. I didn't realize how badly I'd missed it until now.

Yeah. This was definitely a mistake.

I moved away, forcing myself to let go of her, and the blankets gathered underneath me. She pulled back, following my lead, and my chest wound up at her eyeline.

Her glance dropped to my pecs, and she let out a giggle.

"What?" My voice sounded like I'd swallowed gravel.

"Nothing. Just thinking about how insane your chest looks in that shirt."

And even though it just took everything in me to fight the urge to kiss her, I had to laugh.

"Like what you see, Fares?"

She screwed up her cute little nose, but couldn't hide the blush creeping across her cheeks.

"Maybe a little. But you know what would make this—" she waved her hand at me "—even better?"

"What?"

With lightning-quick reflexes, she reached back, scooped up a cupcake, and squished it into my shirt.

"Holy—"

She laughed as I jerked up and stared at the pink frosting splattered all over my chest.

"Consider it payback for my cardigan." She winked and took a bite of what was left in her hand.

I gave her a look and reached behind her, taking a cupcake from the tray. She squealed, jumped up, and ran around the room as I chased her. Her laugh was contagious, and as I caught her with one arm wrapped around her waist, I mashed the cake into her stomach.

She looked down at the mess on her sweater and playfully grumbled, "This was my backup. Now I need to find another one."

Still laughing, I slid my hands down her hips, not wanting to let her go. But as she lifted the hem of her top, eventually, I had to.

Stepping aside to give her space, I looked over my

shoulder at the cluttered heap of cushions, cakes, and textbooks on the ground, and was about to rearrange it all when Lilly's muffled, panicked squeak made me turn back to her.

And then I froze, stunned.

Lilly's arms were in the air. Her black tee was stuck to her sweater. And both were bundled around her head.

And I saw everything.

From the waistband of her leggings to her flimsy, pink cotton bra.

Holy shit...

She tugged, trying to take it all off, and her perky breasts bounced a little as she moved.

I groaned. If I thought I was struggling before, the sight of her now, half-naked like this, was enough to drive me insane.

I should've looked away, but I was already struggling not to touch her.

God, and I wanted to. So fucking badly.

I wanted to take off her bra and find out what her nipples tasted like. I wanted to slide off her leggings, lay her over the arm of the sofa, and strip her down to nothing.

But I wasn't going to do any of that, because what I wanted didn't matter.

So I grabbed her sweater and pulled it off slowly, trying not to hurt her. It wasn't long before she was free.

I swallowed, handed over her clothes, and turned around as she separated her black tee from the bundle of pink fabric.

"Oh my god," she muttered, and I ground my teeth. She wasn't the only uncomfortable one here.

"Are you... decent yet?" I asked, looking down at my trapped cock. It twitched in my jeans.

Fuck me... The things she did to me. I could barely think straight.

"Yes," she said, still breathless. "I can't believe that happened."

I turned to face her. Her voice was shaky, her eyes were glassy, and her flushed cheeks had pink frosting spread across them. I reached out and wiped some of it away.

"You've got a little something here."

She didn't move. Instead, she stared as I licked it off my hand.

"How's it taste?" she asked quietly, probably trying to sound like what'd just happened didn't have to mean anything.

But I wasn't thinking. I couldn't think. Not anymore. Not after seeing her like that.

I ran my thumb across the icing on her cheek and put it to her mouth.

"You tell me."

My whole body went rigid as her soft lips wrapped around my finger.

Fuck.

I tried to tell myself that this wasn't what I thought it was, that Lilly didn't know what she was doing. But as her tongue swirled around my thumb, my pulse thudded, pounding in my ears.

I was fucked. Completely fucked.

I wanted her spread out, naked, wet, and ready for me.

It took every inch of willpower not to push her against the wall and just... *take* her.

She looked up, meeting my eyes as she sucked. There was something dark there, almost swallowing her green eyes.

Did she... want me?

My cock ached. And she was flushed from head to toe; I could see it.

I pulled my thumb out of her mouth and dragged it down her bottom lip. I was a second away from losing control, and the way she gasped didn't make it any easier.

She was so tempting like this.

Just one more step. That was all it would take, and I was so tired of fighting it.

But just as I bent to kiss her, the bell near the front door chimed.

"Lilly? Are you ready to go?"

I knew that voice.

Trevor.

Fucking *Trevor*.

This had to be a joke.

NOW

CHAPTER 25
LILLY
MONDAY MORNING

Verra Convention Center

MIA STARED after me as I left the kitchen, muttering, "I can't believe him."

This wasn't *Tristy's*, we weren't college graduates, and I wasn't going to let him get away with walking away after touching me like that.

Who did that?

Who kissed someone and just... left?

Shawn Jackson, apparently.

I opened the meeting room door to find him behind it. His suit jacket was gone, his tie was loosened, his sleeves were rolled up, and I hated it.

I hated how good he looked.

I hated that it was so easy for him to walk away from me.

And I hated how he made me feel.

I mean, my thighs were still shaking.

But I was hurt too, and it wasn't fair. The way he treated me wasn't fair.

Without looking up, he muttered, "Please. Not now, Lilly."

"Not now?" I stepped in and shut the door behind me. "Are you kidding me?"

He turned away from me, running his hands down his face, then through his hair. "I can't do this again. I can't."

"You can't do what?"

He shook his head. "It shouldn't be this hard."

"What shouldn't be?"

He finally looked at me, and I could see that he was frustrated. But so was I.

So I stood there and waited for him to answer my question.

How could he treat me the way he did after all these years, then kiss me?

I deserved to know.

But clearly, he didn't think so, because instead, he said, "It's our fourth week on this fundraiser. We're almost done. I need to get through this without any more issues. That means no more fights between you, Stacey, or Mia. I want professionalism from the three of you from now on. Do you think that's something you can manage?"

He spoke to me like I was... nothing. Like what we just did meant nothing. I was stunned.

"Are you really asking me that?"

He started to walk away, and–No. We weren't doing this again.

He had to talk to me.

I reached out and took his arm.

"You kissed me."

He looked down at my hand, gently easing it from his arm and holding it. "I know. And if it wasn't Mia who walked in, that could've been–Lilly, it was a mistake. It won't happen again."

He smoothed his thumb against my knuckles before letting me go.

But I wasn't ready to let *this* go. "You can't just pretend we didn't–"

Shawn's phone vibrated in his pocket, and I made a noise as he reached for it and said, "I can't do this right now."

I shook my head, so upset that he thought he could just sweep this under the rug like it never happened.

"Yeah, well, neither can I," I muttered, walking out and shutting the door on him as he answered his phone.

When I made it back to my desk, I dropped my forehead to my keyboard. I laid there and stewed before I remembered I was still covered in buttercream frosting.

I gathered my things and went home to shower.

Wednesday Morning
Verra Convention Center
Lilly

MY FOURTH WEEK was mostly spent avoiding Shawn, finalizing Trevor's module, and arranging the delivery of merch from one place to another.

I had one last thing to deal with: the reusable coffee cups. I couldn't find someone to take them to *Tristy's* for storage.

And that was how I ended up knocking on Shawn's door, watching as he lifted his head. As soon as he realized it was me, his shoulders stiffened, his jaw clenched, and his brows drew together.

All the progress we'd made—gone, just like that.

Holding in a sigh, I said, "Sorry to interrupt, but I've got a problem."

He stood, walked past me, and shut the door. "What is it?"

"It's the coffee cups. My last truck driver, uh, his wife's water broke, and I haven't been able to find anyone else. We need the cups delivered and stacked in *Tristy's* by tomorrow, so... what do you think I should do?"

Shawn's shoulders dropped a notch, and I guessed it was with relief.

Did he think I was here to pick a fight?

"I can pick up a truck from a friend of mine, if he isn't using it."

"Wouldn't you need a license to drive it?"

"I have the right license."

I rolled my eyes. Of course he did. Why wouldn't the great Shawn Jackson know how to drive a truck?

"If your friend isn't using his truck, could we ask him to do the job?"

"He runs the business," he said, as if it answered my question.

"Which company is it?"

"TLC."

"I called them. They said all their drivers were busy."

"Right, but he might have a spare truck we can borrow. I'll call him."

I mumbled, "Okay, then... I'll leave it with you," as I walked out.

And sure enough, half an hour later, he was back, towering over my desk.

"The truck is booked for tomorrow, and Tristan agreed to help me unload them. If you can print the invoice for me, I'll take care of the delivery."

I straightened in my seat. "I need to be there. They need my ID to release them."

He hesitated. "You have to be there?"

"Yes. I've had to be at every other pickup."

We stared at each other. He raised a brow, and I frowned.

He probably knew what was going on here as much

as I did. He didn't want to spend time alone with me if he could help it.

He broke first, looking at a spot on the wall above my head and giving it a stiff nod.

"Okay. Be ready at seven tomorrow morning. I'll pick you up, and we'll go from there."

He turned to leave as I squeaked, "Seven in the morning?"

When he didn't answer, I stood and raised my voice. "All the other deliveries were scheduled for the afternoon."

He didn't slow down. Instead, he looked over his shoulder and said, "Well, I'm busy, Miss Fares. It's one morning. You can handle it."

Ugh. Stuck in a truck at an ungodly hour with Shawn Jackson. Perfect. Just what I needed.

~

Thursday Morning
Outside Lilly's Apartment
Lilly

I STUMBLED out of my apartment building wearing a tight pencil skirt and purple blouse, clutching one of my reusable to-go cups.

It had a picture of Ursula, my favorite cartoon villain, and a quote that read, '*You poor uncaffeinated soul*', which was exactly how I felt this morning.

Poor and uncaffeinated.

Armed with my coffee and handbag, I managed to get to the curb without tripping over myself, and looked for Shawn. He was already there.

I grumbled, picking up the pace. I should've known he'd be here early. He was always early.

He stood on the sidewalk, wearing a snug V-neck tee and gray jeans, and opened the passenger door once he spotted me.

Shawn was as thoughtful and reliable as ever. He offered me a soft, "Good morning," as he held out his hand.

And I was as stubborn as ever.

I ignored him and found my own way into the truck, which definitely wasn't made for anyone under five foot eight.

Once I finally made it in, I had to catch my breath. That was not an easy climb, especially this early in the morning.

Without another word, Shawn sat next to me. We drove in silence for most of the way, until I finally gave in.

"Tell me why you did it, Shawn."

The warehouse was a few miles away, but we were stuck in traffic, trapped inside a big steel rectangle with wheels. He had nowhere to go this time.

This time, he had to talk it out with me.

"Lilly, I don't want to go over this."

Or not.

"But you kissed me. The least you could do is talk to me about it."

He shook his head. "Déjà vu."

"This whole thing is déjà vu," I muttered.

He let out a sigh. "It was years ago."

"So?"

"So, why does it matter now?"

I growled, frustrated. "It matters because... you were my friend, and it hurt when you cut me out like that. It felt like I never really mattered to you."

He almost sounded offended. "You mattered."

I scoffed. "Yeah, sure I did."

"You did. It just... wasn't easy to be around you back then. It still isn't."

"But why? What did I do?"

"You didn't do anything. You didn't have to."

He sighed, as if trying to decide what to say. But, despite all my pushing, I wasn't ready for what came next.

"I think it's pretty clear I was... attracted to you back then."

A laugh burst out of me. Of all the things he could've said, I wasn't expecting that.

"Clear? It wasn't clear, Shawn."

He glanced at me, then back at the road before I could blink. "Trying to kiss you in the back room while we were supposed to be studying for your exam wasn't clear enough?"

"You didn't try to kiss me."

He didn't. I was sure about that.

He freed me from the sweater wrapped around my head, saw me half-naked, and put his thumb in my mouth... but he didn't try to kiss me.

He clenched his jaw and tightened his grip on the wheel. His biceps flexed, veins popped, and my thighs?

They squeezed. Against my better judgment too, the traitors.

"I thought I made it obvious," he admitted, looking uncomfortable.

I leaned forward and searched his tight, tense expression.

"You think it was obvious? Shawn, you're so... I have no idea what you're thinking. I don't know what you think happened that night, but I know what we did last week. You kissed me. But then you said it was a mistake. And every time I ask you why you cut me out, you just ignore it, like it isn't worth talking about. I told you why Mia was angry with Stacey when you asked, but you can't seem to do the same thing for me. I just want answers, Shawn. Not having them is frustrating. I am *frustrated*. Will you please just talk to me?"

He glared at the road, and it kicked into action, as if he willed the cars to part.

"The great Shawn Jackson, everybody," I muttered, folding my arms and staring out my window.

"I don't see the point."

"In what?" I asked, watching the Manhattanites walk along the street. It felt odd not being one of them.

To be in a truck instead of on the sidewalk. The crowd jostled side by side until they eventually filtered into the subway.

"In talking about it."

I groaned, tempted to kick the glove box. "Just tell me why you did it. Was it because I was a total mess back then?"

"You weren't a mess. You passed, and you graduated. I was proud of you."

"Then what was it?"

He sighed as we turned into the warehouse driveway. "I wanted... more, I guess. And you didn't."

My ears couldn't have been working properly. There was no way he said what I thought he'd said.

"What are you talking about? Why would you think–? You never asked–"

I cut myself off because I wasn't making sense. None of this made sense. The kiss in the kitchen last week didn't even make sense.

He turned his head toward me, just a fraction. "That night when we studied, you left with Trevor."

"Shawn," I sighed. "I had to."

Workers sidled up next to the truck, wheeling pallets of plastic-covered coffee cups.

Shawn watched them for a moment, then said, "No, you had a choice. You could've stayed. With me."

Then he popped his door open, climbed out, and shut it. Leaving me to sit there alone.

There wasn't any reason to hide how I felt now. Not

when there wasn't anyone who could see or hear me in this truck.

So I squeezed my eyes shut, and screamed.

I screamed loud and long, until my throat started to ache.

Why was I doing this to myself?

Why couldn't I just accept it?

My dad left when I was a kid, my mom died when I was a teen, and Shawn avoided me for five years.

Shouldn't I have been used to this by now?

My scream faded, and honestly, I felt better. Until I opened my eyes and noticed a small crowd of workers staring at me.

They heard. Oh, god, they *heard*.

But how could they hear me?

I groaned and slapped my hand to my mouth.

I must've looked insane to them.

A head-to-toe flush broke across my skin like a rash, and I slouched lower in my seat, until Shawn yanked my passenger door open.

He looked up at me like the fact that I'd screamed in this truck was a perfectly normal thing to do, and said, "Lilly, we've got a problem."

FIVE YEARS AGO

CHAPTER 26
SHAWN
TUESDAY NIGHT

Tristy's Coffee Shop - Closed

LILLY'S SPINE SNAPPED STRAIGHT.

Her forehead smashed into my chin, and she pushed my chest before slapping her hands against her mouth. She was retching.

"Lilly?"

She shook her head, still gagging. Her hands were on her mouth and stomach, shoulders heaving. Rubbing my jaw, I stepped back and looked for something she could throw up in.

But I was too late.

She lurched, bent over, and emptied whatever was in her stomach. Her fingers didn't stop any of it, and soon there was a wet pile on the floor between us.

I found a bucket, handed it to her, then stripped off my shirt, using it to mop up the mess.

While staring at the bucket in her hands, she called out, "Uh, Trevor, stay there, okay? I'll be out in a minute."

He asked, "Can I come back there?" like he was trying to flirt. He had no idea that Lilly felt so anxious that she'd made herself sick.

But as she looked from the open doorway and back to me, squatting shirtless on the ground, I could tell she was panicked.

"No, no, I'm almost done," she yelled at Trevor.

Then she bent down to me and whispered, "Put something on. No. Hide in the studio. Quick. *Quick*."

Trevor called out, "I'm coming back there," and the color drained from Lilly's face.

I opened my mouth to speak, but... what was the point?

It was obvious that she was worried about Trevor seeing me here in the back room, alone and shirtless, with her. And if I ever needed a reminder that she was taken, the look on her face just now was as good as any.

But if I'd actually kissed her... shit. How much worse would her reaction have been?

The least I could do for her now, after fucking things up the way I already had, was to stay out of sight.

Still holding my filthy shirt, I hid in the doorway of the connected studio apartment, the one Tristan used to live in before he married Nikki, watching Trevor walk in as Lilly pulled something black out of her giant bag of textbooks.

"What's all this? Where's Mia?" Trevor asked, waving at the blankets, cushions, and cupcakes on the ground.

"Just, um, Mia had to go, so I was about to clean all this up."

Ah. That made sense. Trevor thought she'd spent the night studying back here with Mia. Not with me.

That was probably for the best. If Lilly's boyfriend knew how I felt about her, he'd have every reason to feel jealous. Like I did now.

My fist tightened around the shirt in my hand. I hated standing here, hiding like this. But if this was easier for her–

"Can you leave it for tomorrow?" Trevor asked, wrinkling his nose at the mess we'd made together.

Lilly bit her bottom lip, nodded, then disappeared into the bathroom. When she came out, she was in a tight, black, strapless dress.

It looked painted on, ending high on her thigh and hugging the curve of her ass. Her hair was down, flowing past her shoulders in a wave that framed her face. Her eyes were outlined with mascara, her lips re-glossed, the puke gone.

She was gorgeous.

But I would've taken her exactly as she was earlier tonight. In her pink pony sweater.

"Can you pick one of the pastries for me while I pack my bag?" she asked Trevor. "I'm starved."

He smirked as he put his hands around her waist, and in that moment, I saw red.

I wanted to rip his fingers off. One by one.

Fuck, I hated feeling like this. I thought I was better than this.

"But we're going out to eat."

"Please? I'm so hungry."

He looked down at the tray of cupcakes, shrugged, and did what she asked.

Once he was gone, her heels tapped against the floorboards as she hurried to me and whispered, "I'm so sorry."

"Are you okay?" I asked. She might not have looked like it now, but she was sick only a handful of minutes ago.

Her mouth dropped open in a soft 'o' like she was surprised that anyone cared enough to ask. "I think so."

"What's he doing here?"

"He wanted to take me out after I finished studying."

I shook my head. "You told him I was Mia? Why didn't you–fuck it. Just go. I'll clean all this."

"But–"

"Go. It's okay."

She grimaced like she was in pain, and I wished I could kiss that look from her face.

"But I can't just leave you to clean up after me, not after I–"

"Lilly, I swear, it's fine."

"Lilly?" Trevor called through the doorway. "We have to leave now if we're going to make it in time."

She cringed, then turned and yelled out, "I'm coming," as she stepped away from the door.

She mouthed, "I'm so sorry," to me again, then left.

I pinched the bridge of my nose and took a breath as the front door tinkled shut.

It looked like our study session was over. And maybe... everything else was too.

~

ALMOST TWO WEEKS LATER
Thursday Afternoon
Tristy's Coffee Shop
Shawn

WHAT THE FUCK was I thinking?

I never should've been alone with her.

I never should've touched her.

I definitely shouldn't have put my finger in her mouth–who does that?

When Lilly came to work the next day, she could barely look at me as she said, "I'm so sorry, Shawn. I can't believe that happened. Oh god, I can't believe I left you to clean up."

And at the time, as she hid her flushed face in her hands, I tried to make it seem like it didn't bother me. Which was a pretty obvious lie.

I couldn't stop thinking about that night, and I hated the way it ended.

And now, here I was, over a week later, grunting as I slammed a bag of coffee beans onto the countertop.

I couldn't believe how close I came to losing control. But the feel of her tongue as she sucked on my finger?

It was... holy shit.

If I just pushed her against that wall and kissed her, maybe she would've–my cock twitched, and I dropped the thought. I didn't need to be turned on right now, and I definitely didn't need to go over this again.

Lilly didn't want me. She was with Trevor, and I had to accept that.

The door tinkled open and shut. A brunette smiled shyly at me on her way to the counter, and I wracked my brain, trying to place her. She'd definitely been here before.

I lifted a finger. "Hey, Rosie, right?"

She nodded, her face lighting up. From the corner of my eye, I watched Lilly straighten. She was cleaning tables with our trainee, Karim, across the shop, and I could feel her watching me.

"Caramel macchiato, am I right?"

Rosie beamed, nodding again, and I stepped behind the machine, firing it up.

Lilly said something to Karim before leaving him to finish clearing plates. She walked behind the counter, set down her tray, and didn't look up as she quietly said, "She's pretty. Is she your type?"

"Don't know," I muttered. "I'll have to find out if she likes pink frosting first."

Lilly's cheeks blushed pink as she mumbled back, "I said I was sorry. You don't have to rub it in my face."

Rosie's expression fell as the hiss of the coffee machine drowned out our voices. I handed the hot drink over the counter, taking in her disappointment at the lack of digits scrawled on her cup.

As Rosie turned to leave, so did Lilly, both giving me their own version of a confused look. But to me, it was pretty simple.

Rosie was cute, but she wasn't Lilly. And I didn't have the energy to pretend I wanted someone else.

But it wasn't long until graduation. Just a few more weeks, and it would be over.

I rolled my head, trying to get rid of some of the tension in my neck, when my phone vibrated in my pocket.

I pulled it out, surprised to find a text from Mia.

M: *Will you and Lilly kiss and makeup already? You're going to South Bronx whether you like it or not.*

I rolled my eyes, and replied with:

S: *She doesn't want me there anymore.*

M: *What on earth makes you think that?*

S: *She's barely spoken to me all week.*

M: *Oh, she's just embarrassed. You know what happened, you were there. Pink frosting can make a person do crazy things. I should know ;).*

Well, fuck.

S: *Of course you know what happened.*

M: *Yes, of course I do. Now get over yourself and talk to her.*

S: **Groaning emoji**

M: *Pull up your big boy pants and fix this. She doesn't need to worry about you AND South Bronx. She's already got that lanky fucker to deal with.*

I snorted. At least Mia and I could agree on Trevor.

S: *I don't think so. She doesn't need me there.*

M: *Oh, you dense, fit, sexy, sexy man. She does need you.*

M: *She was anxious that night, and you know she was desperate to get through her exam. It was just a misunderstanding.*

M: *But she's passed now, and you both need to talk it out.*

This time, I didn't hold in my groan.

S: *Okay. I'll figure something out.*

M: **Horned smiling emoji* Good. By the way, I've heard the sight of you shirtless is quite breathtaking. Send pics?*

～

Thursday Afternoon

Tristy's Coffee Shop
Shawn

WALKING INTO THE BACK ROOM, I caught Lilly's attention and asked, "Can we talk?"

She bit her bottom lip, but nodded.

I rubbed my neck as she walked ahead of me, stepping into the empty studio.

My neck, shoulders, back—everything—ached. Doing this was mentally and physically draining.

But Mia was right. We needed to talk. And now that Lilly was done with her exam, I had no reason to hold back.

But a big part of me couldn't believe I was really about to do this.

I rubbed a hand over my face as Lilly did a quick turn around the room, maybe to prepare herself for what she thought was coming, I didn't know. But I knew if I didn't get this out now, I never would.

She turned back and asked, "What did you want to talk about?"

I swallowed around the thickness in my throat, but my voice didn't sound right to me as I told her, "I have to talk to you about South."

Her shoulders dropped. "South Bronx?"

"Yeah. I'm not taking the job."

She frowned, drifting closer. "But wait. Why not?"

"I got another offer. A better one. From Brooklyn."

"A better one." Her voice hitched. "What does that mean?"

"It means they're giving me the chance to do more than just manage a classroom."

She started fidgeting, voice straining as she said, "And you don't think South has those kinds of opportunities? Because they do. When my mom worked there—"

"Lilly, it's too late," I interrupted, wanting to get this over with. "I've already called both schools."

"But then—" she paused, her eyes growing wide as she realized "—Trevor's going to take your spot."

I shook my head at her, frustrated. Why was she getting so upset?

It was true that Trevor irritated the shit out of me, that I didn't think he knew how to give her what she needed.

But she wanted to be with him. She left with Trevor that night.

"Isn't that a good thing?"

She worried her bottom lip, then told me, "Trevor wasn't the one who helped me pass my exam, Shawn. You did."

It hit me then—what she was really upset about. "Lilly, you don't need me there. You can do this on your own."

"What if I can't?" She reached out, grabbed the hem of my shirt, and tugged on it. "The only reason I'm even graduating is because of you, and if you're not there with me—"

"I can't base all my decisions on you, Lilly," I snapped. "You're not mine to worry about. You've got Trevor for that. He should be there with you, not me."

Saying it out loud hurt more than I wanted to admit. But I couldn't follow her to her dream school hoping that things would be different one day.

Lilly's confusion melted into something wounded, and I could swear that just seeing that look on her face made my chest close in on itself.

"But… is this because I did something? What did I do?" She straightened then, as if she'd just figured out the answer to her questions. "This is about last week, when we studied, isn't it? I know leaving you to clean up after me wasn't okay, but I won't do it again."

I shook my head and looked away. I couldn't take having her eyes on me. Not while she sounded like this.

"It's not about that," I ground out, voice rough, hoping she'd just let this drop. "Brooklyn is the better choice for me."

"So that's it then? You don't want to work with me anymore?"

I scrubbed my palm across my mouth, muttering into it. "Honestly, yes. Working with you is torture."

Her mouth went slack. "Working with me is torture?"

"Yes. And I can't fucking take it anymore."

I said it without thinking, and in an instant, I regretted it.

Her reaction was... devastating. I never wanted to see that look on her face again.

The way her eyes welled up. The line that formed between her brows. The way her lips opened as if she were in pain.

Her voice trembled as she said, "Well, then... fine. You won't have to."

I wanted to grab her, pull her back, and tell her I didn't mean it.

Instead, I let her walk out, listening to the catch in her throat as she told Uncle Henry, "I'm taking a half day."

She wiped her cheeks as she left, and knowing I was the one who put them there made me feel like an absolute piece of shit. My throat felt rough, like I'd swallowed sandpaper. I threaded my fingers through my hair and tugged.

Tristan was wrong before. Being alone with her, knowing I couldn't touch her–that didn't kill me. This did.

I hated this. Letting her think that I didn't care.

But Mia was right.

Lilly needed to know where I stood. I was never going to take that job at South Bronx Classical.

She was better off without me.

NOW

CHAPTER 27
LILLY
THURSDAY MORNING

Inside the truck

I WAS NUMB.

Stunned.

Completely and totally dead inside.

I was back in the truck. Shawn was next to me. The truck was full of beautifully branded coffee cups. He drove, and I stayed quiet.

Sixty thousand cups sat behind me, jostling in their pallets. They bumped against the metal wall, but I could barely hear them move over the pounding in my head.

I screwed up. And it was over.

Everything I'd been working for. Gone.

Trevor was going to fire me the second he found out.

"What are we going to do with thirty thousand extra cups?" I squeaked.

Shawn looked like he wanted to strangle the steering wheel. "We'll figure it out. Don't worry."

"It came from my email address. But I didn't send it."

"I believe you."

I looked down at the piece of paper in my hands. I held it so tight that my knuckles were turning white, and I knew I should've tried to calm down, but I couldn't.

The vendor gave me this paper.

It was a printed copy of the email requesting the order, and it came from my address, along with a copy of the updated invoice.

He'd given this to me to prove that I'd asked for double the amount of coffee cups, and the paperwork was signed off by both Shawn and me.

Shawn shook his head when he saw it, telling the vendor it was a mistake.

But the rep just stood there and shrugged, telling us, "The order's already been paid for. If you don't take them, you won't get a refund."

What happened? What actually happened?

I checked my sent items, and there the email sat–a digital copy of the version I had in my hands now.

I was in so much trouble.

I turned to Shawn and asked, "How are Tristan and Nikki going to store all these?"

"We'll figure it out," he repeated. Without taking his eyes off the road, he reached over and squeezed my knee. "I'm not letting anything happen to you, okay? I'll take the blame for this."

My heart cracked, just a little, and a hint of feeling came back. "You shouldn't do that."

He forced a smile. "Yeah, well, I was told my career can take a hit like this and keep going. I'm the great Shawn Jackson, right?"

I didn't laugh. Because this wasn't funny.

I didn't write that email. Shawn didn't sign off on the order.

And I didn't forge his signature.

I know I didn't.

God, I wished my mom were here. If she was, I could've talked to her about this.

But with her gone, there was only one other person who would understand what this meant for me.

I pulled out my phone and wrote a message to Mia.

L: *Something happened. I have twice the amount of coffee cups loaded in the truck right now. That's $30k taken from the budget instead of $15k.*

L: *I mean, did I black out at my desk, or something? How could I have ordered this many cups and not remember it?*

M: *You couldn't have. Shawn would've had to sign off on the order. I know we don't like the asshole, but we both know he wouldn't make a mistake like that.*

L: *He says the order papers were signed with a fake signature. Someone forged it.*

M: *Why would you forge his signature for extra cups?*

L: *I wouldn't. I didn't. But the order came from my email.*

M: *Then it had to be that asshole.*

M: *Trevor.*

My stomach dropped.

L: *???*

L: *What???*

M: *I went to the school last week to pick up some unit revisions.*

M: *And caught Trevor sitting at your desk.*

I held my breath and waited for Mia's next message.

M: *I told the principal about it because I didn't want to worry you, and she said she gave him permission to log into your computer to check on report grades, but I wouldn't put it past that bastard to send a fake order using your email address.*

Did I... did I read that right?

I reread Mia's text. And then I read it again.

And again.

Until it finally hit me that, if what Mia said was true, if Trevor was the reason for–

"That-that-that *asshole*," I stuttered, gripping my phone so tight I could've shattered the screen. "He's the villain!"

"What?" Shawn asked, surprised.

"Trevor. Mia told me she caught him sitting at my computer. I think he's trying to, to–"

"You think he sent that email?" Shawn's glance flicked from me to the road and back again. "Why would he do that? Stacey told me Trevor's still pretty obsessed with you."

"Are you kidding? He hates me."

"No one could hate you."

"Except you," I shot back.

"Lilly." The way he said my name sounded like a warning. "I've already told you. I never hated you."

"But you said working with me was torture."

"Because being around you was torture."

I laughed then, because I didn't know how else to feel.

This didn't make sense–what was happening right now didn't seem like a real thing that could happen.

Was my boss–my ex-boyfriend–really trying to get me fired?

While I sat in a truck with a man who kissed me years after cutting me out of his life?

Who still said working with me was torture?

"Yeah. It must've been," I told him, thinking about Trevor, about how he'd changed after we broke up.

How Shawn spoke to me the week after he'd helped me pass my final exam.

"What's wrong with me?" I asked before throwing my phone in my handbag. "What did I do to make the both of you treat me like this?"

Honestly, I was hoping for an answer. A real one, this time.

But instead, Shawn just shook his head, turned the wheel, and parked the truck in the loading dock behind Tristan's shop.

∿

Thursday Morning
Tristy's Coffee Shop
Lilly

Nikki held me tight. I didn't realize how upset I was until she'd wrapped her arms around me. Before I knew it, I was crying into her blouse.

Little Lilly, Nikki's daughter, pulled on my skirt. "Can you play with us?"

Her older sister, Kelly, bounced on her toes to my left. "Yeah. I want to play."

I could hear Tristan's footsteps behind me. His voice was low and gentle as he told them, "Aunt Lilly's here to work, girls, not play. Come with me. Uncle Henry needs another cuddle."

He gently untangled the girls from my legs, and I mumbled an apology into Nikki's shirt.

"No, don't worry about them," she said. "We need to find a way to prove you didn't do this."

Pulling back from Nikki, I wiped my eyes on my

wrists. "Mia said she saw him sitting at my desk. She might write a statement if I asked her to?"

Nikki folded her arms and tapped her chin. "That won't be enough. Not if he already cleared it with the principal."

She thought for a moment, then asked, "What about security cameras? Do you have any in your staffroom?"

I shook my head. "Nothing like that."

"Well... is there a chance you could get him to confess?"

"I'll get that fucker to confess," Shawn muttered from behind her. "As soon as this fundraiser is done."

She gave him a weak smile. "You're not planning to get physical with him, are you? Because that's probably not the best way to handle this. And I really don't want to represent you in court."

"Yeah, well, you might have to."

Nikki turned back to me, jerking a thumb in Shawn's direction as she asked, "Are teachers usually this violent?"

While frowning at him, I told Nikki, "Don't worry. He won't do anything to Trevor. His career has more riding on it than mine."

Shawn stood across from Nikki and me with his arms folded. Now that he didn't have a steering wheel to strangle, he looked more furious than... I didn't think I'd ever seen him this angry.

"Lilly, your career is just as important," he ground out. "And he can't get away with treating you like this."

Nikki looked from me to him and back again. "I know this is bad, I really do. But the fact that you two are finally talking? It's kind of nice."

"I don't think we should get used to it," I said. "As soon as this fundraiser is over, Shawn will probably go back to forgetting I exist."

He shook his head. "I should. You're fucking impossible sometimes."

I wrapped my arms around myself and muttered, "See what I mean?" as Nikki tsked at Shawn and gave him a look I wasn't sure I recognized.

~

Thursday Evening
Tristy's Coffee Shop
Lilly

"Put that one over here," Karim told Dean.

"But I think we should stack this corner first," Dean answered.

"Guys, how about we finish the pile we're working on?" Tristan suggested, as gentle with them as ever.

"And when you're done over there, we can fill this space here," Shawn said.

It was still hard to believe how different Karim and Dean were now.

They were only kids when they replaced Shawn and me five years ago, and back then they were adorably tall and gangly, a lot like Shawn at that age. And—also like Shawn—I didn't think they knew what to do with themselves most of the time.

But, because he probably couldn't help himself, Tristan took care of them. And he also taught them how to get the most out of all their teen energy.

Over the years, they joined Tristan in the gym before opening the shop together each morning. And now, those tall, gangly boys rivaled both Tristan and Shawn in size alone.

It was kind of them to help us move all these boxes into the studio. And doing something physical together like this felt like a welcome distraction. With everything going on with Trevor and my job, I had to admit, this was what I really needed right now. To feel like I was doing something useful.

"We should start a moving company," I whispered to Nikki as she helped me clear out some of the junk from the back room. "Four guys, one truck—think of the money we'd rake in."

She raised a brow at me. "You're not giving up on teaching just like that, are you?"

Ah, Nikki. So blunt, like always.

"No," I said, looking down at the box of paintbrushes in my hands, trying to ignore the twist in my chest. "But I might not have a choice."

"You have a choice," Shawn called out as he wiped sweat from his forehead. "We'll fix this."

I looked away from him and noticed the smirk on Nikki's face. "What?"

"You're blushing," she teased.

I quietly went back to organizing paintbrushes.

Hours later, Karim and Dean were the first to drop off.

Once it was time to close the shop, the two exhausted twenty-three-year-olds left to shower. Tristan and Shawn kept going well after the closing routine was done.

When the cups overflowed from the studio to the back room, cramping the space, all I could do was stare at all of it as Tristan tossed Shawn a set of keys.

"You guys remember how to lock up when you're done?" Tristan asked. He waited for Shawn to nod, then looked at me. "Lilly, it'll be okay. We'll help you sort this out."

Then they were gone, and now it was just Shawn and me.

Alone. In the back room. Together.

He stood next to me and lifted the hem of his shirt to wipe his face. Sweat traced the defined lines of his chest and abs, and I had to look away before he caught me staring.

"We're almost finished," he said, maybe to reassure me that we wouldn't be alone for long.

Following him back out to the loading dock, I looked up at the sunset. This had taken all day. Did we have an entire day to waste on stacking boxes like this?

We would have been done sooner, probably in half the time, if we had fewer cups. Did this set Shawn back on his goals for the fundraiser? Was he worried?

He didn't seem like he was. He just kept walking down the short alleyway, examining the back of the truck like it was the only thing on his mind.

Then he surprised me by bending and lifting the ramp. My hands flew to my mouth as I watched him push the steel sheet back into place.

His thick arms strained under the weight, but he was patient as he nudged his chin at the side of the truck.

He grunted out, "Lock it for me?" and I lurched into action, rounding him and putting locks into place.

I nodded when I was done, and he let go, taking the lead as we both went back inside.

"That's done," he said, nodding at the mountain of cups in front of us.

I sighed and hugged my arms to myself. "This is definitely my fault."

"It's Trevor's. Didn't we already decide that?"

"But maybe if I handled things better with him, this never would've happened."

"It's okay. We'll just... deal with it."

The edge in his tone made me wince. "Shawn, I'm sorry. I can't believe I–"

"Will you stop trying to take the blame for shit like this?" he snapped, glaring at me. "This didn't happen because you did something wrong. This happened because whoever did this is an asshole."

I looked away from him. "And you think it was Trevor."

"If Mia thinks it was him, then that's good enough for me." He cursed under his breath, put his hands on his hips, and shook his head. "I can't believe you dated him. Of all the men you could've—"

"Hey, it wasn't easy, you know," I blurted, annoyed with the way Shawn was speaking to me. "Stacey was about to kick me out of the sorority. It wasn't exactly fun for me."

With his arms folded across his chest, he came to stand in front of me. He was so close that I had to crane my neck to look up at him as he said, "And how do you think it was for me? I had to watch you with him."

I shook my head, instantly confused. "I don't—how was that—why did you care? It wasn't like who I dated mattered to you."

"You think—Fuck," he swore, running a hand through his hair. "Why am I still doing this? Why are we still arguing about this?"

"Because you won't talk to me," I told him, desperate for him to finally deal with this. "Because you pushed me away, pulled me back, pushed again, and won't give me a reason for any of it."

"I thought you wanted to be with him," he said

roughly, like having to say it frustrated him. "And that meant you didn't want me."

I scoffed and dug a finger into his chest. "Oh, come on. *You* didn't want *me*. You're the one who pushed me away, Shawn."

"You think I didn't want you?" he asked, his voice low, almost as if he couldn't believe I thought that.

I let out a strangled noise. "Of course you didn't. I'm torture. Right?"

"That doesn't mean what you think it does."

"Oh, sure it doesn't."

I turned to leave. I didn't know why I thought he'd give me a straight answer for once.

I didn't matter to him.

No matter what he said or what he did, the fact was that he cut me out of his life, and he never would've done that if he had feelings for me.

I was ready to end this night and deal with Trevor alone. But Shawn gripped my wrist and spun me back to face him.

"Lilly, I wanted you so bad—you drove me fucking crazy. And I didn't know how to handle it."

I drove him crazy? What did that even mean? God, I was so tired of this.

For years I'd wondered what I'd done wrong, why he'd said those things to me that day in the studio. But even now, after weeks of working with him at this fundraiser, I wasn't any closer to getting what I wanted from him.

He kissed me. He called what we did a mistake.

He said he wanted me. He called me torture.

He pulled. He pushed. He made no sense.

And I'd had enough.

I jerked my wrist out of his grip, lifted onto my toes, and put my face in his.

"You didn't—are you kidding?" I pushed his chest, trying to get him to back off, but he trapped my hand beneath his. "If you wanted me, you should've told me."

He spoke slowly, deliberately, through gritted teeth. "You were with someone else. What was I supposed to do?"

"*Anything,*" I yelled, trying to tug my hand free. "I was embarrassed, Shawn. That night, when we studied, when I got sick and left you to clean up after me—I thought that was why you didn't want to be around me anymore."

My throat started to ache, and there was a hot prickle in the back of my eyes, but I'd been holding this in for years. I couldn't stop now.

"I didn't know how you felt. Maybe if you kissed me—if you did something—maybe this would be different. Anything else would've been better than you cutting me out of your life."

"You would've wanted that?"

He let go of my hand and without thinking, I admitted, "Yes. I've always wanted that."

I saw the shift in the way he looked at me then, but

the last thing I expected was the feel of his hand around my waist, pushing me into the wall, trapping me against it.

"What are you doing?" I asked, breathless, not sure I really wanted an answer.

"Lilly, I never stopped wanting you," he told me, his voice low and hard. "But if you tell me to stop now, I will."

It happened so fast that it pulled a gasp out of me.

He gripped my ass, lifting me. My legs wrapped around him on their own, my hands came to rest on his biceps. And I just... stared at him, so stunned by the thrill that shot from my toes to navel.

He held me, pinning me in place, until he was suddenly so close that the tip of his nose grazed mine. He moved slowly, waiting for me to push him away, to tell him to stop like he'd asked me to.

But I didn't. Instead, I tilted my chin up, just a little. Just enough to brush my lips against his.

He groaned out a soft, "Finally," against me, as if he'd been waiting for this.

Then his mouth was on my neck, warm, rough, and urgent. He ran his teeth along my skin, making me shiver. He tugged my skirt up around my thighs, and I didn't even care that the seams were tearing.

My hips moved on their own, rocking into him on instinct, and he bit my bottom lip, slipping his tongue in my mouth. I made a small sound, quiet and frustrated, already throbbing.

He felt so hard between my legs, so good, right there, right where I needed it.

Where I'd needed it for weeks.

He broke our kiss, and his lips brushed my earlobe as he growled, "Tell me this is what you want. Say it. Because I'm not stopping now."

CHAPTER 28
SHAWN
THURSDAY EVENING

Tristy's Coffee Shop - Closed

Somewhere, in the back of my mind, I knew we shouldn't be doing this.

There was a reason I shouldn't have kissed her.

But Lilly was here, with her legs wrapped around me, her fingers digging into my hair. Her body moved on top of mine like she couldn't get close enough, and god help me, after so long, the last thing I wanted to do was stop.

She broke our kiss long enough to unbutton her blouse and take off her bra, and—holy shit, her tits. They were perky, soft, and so fucking perfect I forgot how to breathe.

"Fuck me," I muttered, then dragged my tongue across her nipple.

After years away from her, I thought I had this under control. But I was wrong.

Groaning into her skin, I dug my fingers into her ass and guided her up and down my length. The quiet, breathy noises she made were my new favorite sounds. She tugged at my shirt, silently asking me to take it off.

I paused, but not because I didn't want to. I wanted to feel her skin on mine. So fucking badly. Just her toasted cinnamon and honey scent alone made me rabid.

But I had to know that she wanted this.

Her hips slowed as she looked down at me.

"I need to hear you say it. Do you want this?"

She tugged on my shirt again. "I do," she whispered. "Please."

That was all I needed to hear.

Bending to lick her breast, I pulled her nipple back into my mouth and sucked hard.

She gasped, fingers twisting in my shirt. A small, strained sound vibrated in her throat, and I needed to know how wet she was.

I slid my finger along her inner thigh, stopping just out of reach.

"Oh god, Shawn," she moaned. "Please. You're just... please?"

"Tell me what you want, and I'll do it."

She bit her lip, hesitating.

I smiled against her breast and inched my finger

closer. Her breath hitched as I brushed her wet, swollen skin.

She flushed, wriggling in my hands.

"Please, Shawn."

"You want me to touch you?"

She nodded. "Yes. And…"

I turned and eased her onto the sofa.

"And what?" I asked, looking at her flushed cheeks and wide, green eyes. "What else do you want me to do to you?"

As she hesitated, I stood, took off my shirt, and loosened my jeans, loving the way she gasped when I pulled myself out. She stared at it, licking her lips like she wanted to taste the liquid on my tip, and that drove me so insane that the urge to fuck her pretty face made me reach out and cup her chin.

Her flush deepened, and her words came out in a rush. "I want you inside me. Please?"

With her eyes still on my erection, she licked her lips, and I shook my head, muttering, "You've got no idea what you do to me, do you?"

Her eyes flicked up to meet mine, just a second before I gripped her ankle and dragged her to the edge of the sofa. She let out a soft squeal, but didn't stop me from ripping off her skirt and sliding her underwear down her legs.

She spread her knees for me as I ran my hand up her thigh, her hips twitching when my thumb found her clit. Her eyes fluttered shut, her lips dropped open with a small sigh.

All those nights in this shop, alone, picturing her here on this couch, and still, nothing could've prepared me for this.

I'd never seen anything this perfect before. Her, naked, spread out in front of me. Ready to be fucked.

Circling her entrance, I watched her writhe around my finger as it disappeared inside her. She threw her head back against the cushions, panting as it slid in and out.

Another finger eased in, and she gripped the edge of the sofa. I knelt in front of her with my head between her legs, and sucked hard. She lifted her hips and squealed.

My tongue teased her clit as my fingers moved in and out, and the taste of her was so sweet that my cock throbbed as she rode my face. Her fingers twisted around my hair as she moaned, begging me to keep going–like I'd ever fucking stop.

It wasn't until she drove her feet into the sofa, lifted her hips again, screaming and shaking, that I decided she'd had enough.

"Oh my god," she sighed. "That was... oh my god."

"I'm not done with you yet," I told her, pulling away long enough to find a condom.

I rolled it down myself as she stared up at me, dazed, like she wasn't sure that what I'd just done to her was real. And fuck, I couldn't wait anymore.

Her back arched as I eased the tip in, pulled out, and ran it along her slit. She let out a sharp gasp as I pressed the weight of it into her sensitive core, then wrapped her legs around me, dragging me deeper with her ankles, pushing me into her.

"Fuck..." I groaned.

She felt so snug and warm, like she was made for this. It was so good, I couldn't move. Not yet. Not until I had control over myself.

I pressed my thumb to her clit, making her back arch again, and it was easily my favorite thing to watch. Her head thrown back, hips rolling, breasts bouncing, nipples nice and tight, like they needed to be licked.

But then, every muscle I had tensed as she writhed around me, and I couldn't wait anymore.

She felt better than anything I could've hoped for, so fucking good—so hot and sweet—that it took everything in me not to drive into her. Starting slow, I inched deeper.

And I wouldn't stop until I had her screaming for me again.

Lilly

HE WAS INSIDE ME.

Shawn was inside me.

Thick and hard, stretching me until I fit around him.

But I already came on his tongue, and I wasn't sure I could take any more. Having something this big inside me... it burned.

But as he kept moving–harder, deeper, faster–a deep, warm kind of pleasure, one I hadn't felt in a long time, uncoiled low in my stomach, drowning out the pain.

He kept playing with my sensitive clit, and I started to roll my hips, already close. Then he pressed his fingers into me–hard–and my insides melted. Exploded.

Holding a cushion to my mouth, I screamed and shook underneath him, pulling more of him into me. I came so hard that heavy pulses thrummed under my skin, stunning me, but I still didn't want him to stop.

I told him to keep going, keep going, please. I never wanted it to end.

His fingers were firm and fast, almost punishing my clit, and I was delirious from the feel of it.

He grunted low and deep, going still, with only his cock twitching inside me, sending aftershocks through my belly until he slowed and pulled out. With shaky hands, he pulled off the condom, knotted it, and sat on the hardwood floor.

For a few moments, there was nothing except the sound of our breathing as it filled the back room of our old workplace.

Shawn's low curse was the next thing I heard as he pushed a soft piece of fabric between my thighs. Then he whispered, "You're soaked," and I surprised us both by laughing.

CHAPTER 29

SHAWN

THURSDAY NIGHT

Tristy's Coffee Shop - Closed

LILLY WAS naked on the sofa, her legs still splayed open as she laughed. I was on the ground in front of her, covered in sweat, but I found a clean rag and pressed it to her.

Her laughter faded, and she shook her head at the ceiling. "This is crazy."

I stared up at her. "Yeah. Maybe it is."

This was the last thing I thought would happen. I thought, when I volunteered to drive that truck, that we'd spend the day stacking boxes and I'd see her at work tomorrow.

After the way I'd handled that kiss in our staffroom kitchen, I thought she'd want nothing to do with me.

Fuck, I'd never been happier to be wrong in my life.

But my voice seemed to snap her out of whatever

post-sex fog she was in. She sat up and hugged her clothes to her chest, watching me like I was a second away from doing something to hurt her.

I probably should've expected it. Her, looking at me like that.

But, for a minute there, I forgot all of it. The fight we had years ago. Trevor. The fact that I'd been trying to stop this exact thing from happening.

"Lilly, that was–"

"Don't say it was a mistake," she warned, upset.

We sat and stared at each other.

Her shoulders were tense, her jaw set, her eyes wide and lips pinched. The grip on her clothes was so strong that her knuckles were starting to turn white. Even her toes were curled. She looked like she was waiting for a fight.

But I didn't have it in me anymore.

In the last five years, not once did I stop thinking about her.

And I tried. I really did.

I threw myself into work, giving it everything I had because I wanted to move on.

That was the plan. I pushed her away so I could finally get over her.

But it didn't work. No matter how hard I tried, what I did, or who I dated.

Lilly Fares was the only woman I wanted, and I'd fucked it up years ago.

I thought I'd accepted it—until she showed up at my fundraiser, under that stack of chairs.

"I wasn't going to," I told her, looking away.

It was a long day. I was physically wrecked from stacking those boxes, and it was late. I needed sleep. We both needed sleep.

But right now, what I really needed was to fix this.

She was slow to relax, like she didn't want to trust me. But her shoulders started to drop, and she loosened her grip on her clothes.

"Lilly." I reached up, wrapped an arm around her, and dragged her onto the floor with me. She gave me a half-hearted grunt and pushed against me a little, but once she was settled in my lap, she curled into my chest. I breathed in the smell of her hair and said, "I don't want to fight anymore."

"You don't?" she asked, like she wasn't ready to believe me, but when I shook my head, she started tracing circles on my skin.

"I'm tired of it. And it hasn't helped either of us."

"So... what does that mean?" she asked softly.

I sighed and dropped my head back against the wall.

There was so much to explain. My feelings then, my feelings now. Why I tried to stay as far away from her as possible.

Where did I start? Where could I start?

"Remember when you and Mia showed up here, dressed for that costume party?"

"Hmm?" she asked, and I could tell she was thinking, trying to place it. Then she made a noise and said, "You mean the one where I went as Rainbow Dash, and Mia was Ariel?"

"That's the one." My fingers flexed on her waist. It felt so good to have her so close. The sex we'd had was... incredible. But I dreamed of just holding her like this. "I was so jealous."

She looked up at me, and there was her anxiety, as easy to pick up on as ever. It reminded me to go slowly, gently.

But she wanted to know everything, so that's what I'd give her.

"But... why?" she asked.

I breathed out a laugh. "You still don't get it, do you?"

She blinked up at me and shook her head.

"I was... I was so. It was like... I wanted you like I'd never wanted anything else, and I couldn't get it to stop. The way I felt about you? I've never felt like that before."

She frowned, not quite convinced yet. "But we were friends. I didn't think you thought of me like that."

"I didn't always," I admitted. "But one day, it just hit me. I couldn't stop looking at you. Then I couldn't stop thinking about you. When I was alone, you were all I..." I trailed off, shifting her in my arms, showing her what I meant.

Her clothes dropped to the ground, and I had her

naked again, straddling me on the floor of our old coffee shop.

I was already hard again. A little raw after what we'd just done, but hard.

With my hands on her hips, I pulled her close, squeezing into that tight little space between her thighs. Her breath came in sharp, then she held my shoulders and slid her still-wet core along my cock. I groaned low in my throat and kissed her neck, taking her earlobe between my teeth as she shivered.

"Do you know how many times I thought of doing this?" I asked her.

She let out a soft little moan as I cupped her ass. "Why didn't you tell me?"

She surprised me then. She lifted, angled her hips, and sank down on me. The noise she made was almost like a whimper as I sucked her nipple into my mouth.

She was still warm and tight, still pulsing and shivering around me. I leaned back against the wall and let her set the pace. She put both hands on my chest and started rocking up and down.

"Shawn?" she asked, her hips slowing.

We didn't have another condom. This wasn't smart. But I couldn't think with her wrapped around me like this.

I shook my head, eyes half-closed as I gripped her tighter and made her move faster.

"After." I couldn't talk now. Not like this. Not until she was done.

She swiveled her hips around my tip, teasing, until I pulled her down, filling her.

She gasped, her breasts jiggling with the impact. But then she was angling her hips again, eyelids heavy as she rode me.

"You like feeling full like this?"

"Yes," she breathed. "I really like it. But I never thought you'd–" her breath caught in her throat, then she moaned again "–ah, want me like this."

I squeezed her ass, spreading her, then touched the base of my cock from behind, finding where I slid in and out. She made another soft noise, her pink nipples tightening as her breasts bounced in my face. I grunted, already close.

"I always wanted you. I still want you. Like this, naked, on top of me, every fucking day."

She bit her bottom lip and rocked faster. Was she coming again?

Moving from her ass to her pussy, I played with her clit.

There was no more talk after that.

The only sounds that filled the room were the wet, hot, slippery sounds of my cock sliding in and out of her as she came, trembling around me. She dropped back onto my chest, and I pulled out, still throbbing.

She laid there, sleepy and satisfied on top of me, her breath warm on my skin, as I reached around her and wrapped a hand around my cock. I worked it until I came, letting my cum drip on her ass.

She lifted her chin and kissed me with a small, lazy smile on her lips. "I could do that. Maybe. If you feed me cupcakes first."

I laughed then, wrapping my arms around her like I'd never let her go.

~

Shawn

WHEN SHE STARTED TO DRESS, it felt like something was over. Like fingers had snapped, and the spell was broken, leaving us in a quiet shop in the middle of the night.

I pulled my shirt on slowly, watching her step into the skirt I'd ripped. I made a face at the tear along the seam. It was worth it, but Lilly couldn't leave the shop like that.

"Wait."

She paused, looked around the room, then up at me. "What is it?"

"You've got a... uh, this—" I put a finger to the split I'd made "–here."

She looked down and grumbled, "Oh, great. This is the only skirt that fits me right now."

"Take it off."

Her eyes snapped to mine. "Shawn, you can't be serious."

"Look, don't get me wrong. I'd love to do that to you

again," I told her, grinning. "But right now, I need you to take that off so I can sew it for you."

She paused and clamped her mouth shut before quietly muttering, "Oh."

I laughed, leaning down to pinch her thigh, then laughed harder when she squealed and slapped my chest.

"Tristan probably still keeps a kit here, under the counter," I explained, taking her hand and leading her from the back room to the shop.

The front was dimly lit, but warm and familiar. I felt underneath the counter and pulled out the kit Tristan kept for emergencies.

Putting the small red case on the counter, I found the needle tucked into a black spool of thread, and gestured for Lilly to take off her skirt and hand it over.

She did what I wanted, and the look on her face made it seem like she didn't know whether to kiss me or tease me. I was fine with both.

It was probably a good thing my hands were busy. She needed a break.

But when she crossed her still-bare feet over each other, squeezed her thighs, and sighed out a happy little, "I can still feel you," I fought the urge to drop her skirt and throw her over my shoulder.

"Lilly," I warned. "If you keep going like that, I'm going to drag you back to that sofa. And this skirt might not survive a third time."

She padded closer, lifting onto her toes so she could put her arms around my shoulders.

"But you can fix it for me, right?"

I bit my lip, fighting a smile. "You wanted to talk, remember?"

"I do." She dropped back on her feet as I knotted the string. "You still haven't told me why."

"Why what?" I cut the thread and held out her skirt, checking it before handing it to her.

She took it, sliding it up her legs without looking away. "Why didn't you tell me how you felt?"

I shrugged. "You had an exam to worry about, and a boyfriend. You were dealing with enough and I didn't want to add to it."

She zipped the skirt with a small pink flush on her cheeks. "You thought it'd make me feel anxious. Because I was with Trevor and couldn't give you what you wanted."

I could always trust Lilly to read between the lines.

"Exactly. I thought I was doing the right thing."

She slumped against the doorframe, a little sad. "And if there was no Trevor?"

I raised a brow. "Then I would've done more than just stick my thumb in your mouth."

She laughed, and hearing that sound felt like warm soup on a cold day. Then she came close enough to slide a hand up my chest, which made me groan as I pinned her arms to her sides.

"If you start touching me, I'm going to touch you,

and then we're never going to leave. Do you want Tristan and Nikki to open this place with us still here?"

She looked up at the ceiling and tilted her chin, like she was considering it. I bent to her ear and whispered, "Do you want them to see you naked, moaning, while I hold your waist, bend you over, and fuck you?"

She shivered, but shook her head.

"So... what would you have changed? Back then?" she asked, routing the conversation back to semi-safe territory. "If you could, I mean."

I frowned. "I don't know. I wanted you, but you were with someone else, and I thought the smart thing to do was to... take that job with Brooklyn."

I let her go, folding my arms so I wouldn't be tempted.

"It was killing me. To be around you like that, you know? I could make you laugh, I could make you smile, I could be there for you and talk to you, but I couldn't have you. I thought I could handle it, but that night, when we studied together—you had to know I made a move on you."

While making a face at me, she asked, "When did you make 'a move'?"

I smirked at her air quotes. "How many friends do you know who stick their finger in someone's mouth, and watch them suck it?"

Her flush deepened. "I didn't think that meant anything."

I shook my head, amazed that she really had no idea.

"Lilly, you're beautiful. And that night you were half-naked, covered in frosting, and I got to feel your tongue on my skin. It drove me crazy–I was about to kiss you."

"But you didn't."

"Because you left with Trevor. And that made the whole thing real for me. You were with someone else, and I had to move on."

She shook her head. "You know it wasn't my choice, Shawn."

"Now I do. And I'm going to talk to Stacey about it."

She bit her bottom lip and nodded. God, all I wanted to do was kiss her.

But instead, I told her, "You know the rest. I told you I couldn't work with you anymore. And it was true. I couldn't. I was... in love with you. And if I had to watch you be with him at South Bronx–that wasn't something I could do."

Her mouth dropped open, just a little, before she asked, "You loved me?"

I nodded, and... there was a small part of me that, after holding it in for so long, didn't want to admit the rest. But she deserved to know. And after everything I'd already put us through, the last thing I wanted to do was hide it from her now.

"I still do."

Her eyes flared with surprise. That was probably the last thing she expected me to say.

I shrugged. "It was why I couldn't just pick up where we left off. Five years full of educational conferences, and every time I saw you... Lilly, I tried. I wanted to get over you, and sometimes, I thought it worked. But then I'd see you and it was just..." I broke off and shook my head.

"Torture," she finished, understanding.

Her flush faded, and the way she frowned made me want to smooth her bangs back from her forehead. But I knew that if I touched her again, this conversation would be over, and it was important for both of us that we have it.

"I thought you hated me," she said, quiet and sad. "And I didn't know why. The only thing I could think was that maybe you were tired of dealing with my anxiety."

I smiled, because it was such a Lilly thing. To get caught up on the idea of me being put out by her.

"No. I mean, I wish you didn't have to deal with it, but it had nothing to do with why I decided to... do what I did."

It was because of Trevor. Even now—the coffee cup issue, Lilly's job security—all of it was still because of Trevor.

If I was ever in the same room with him, I'd—

"But... god, Shawn. I can't believe you."

Lilly's voice was so low, I almost didn't hear her.

But now, looking at her, I could see that there were... tears in her eyes?

Shit.

The panic I felt was instant.

I reached for her, wanting to do something. Touch her. Hug her, maybe. Anything to keep her from crying. But she stepped back. Away from me.

"You wouldn't talk to me, and this was why? I broke up with Trevor, you know. Four years ago. You could've talked to me then. But no. Instead, you made me feel like... like *shit*, Shawn. I thought you hated me. And now... what? I'm supposed to forgive you just because we had sex?"

She glared up at me, her cheeks wet. They weren't sad tears. They were angry ones.

She was mad... and she had every right to be.

I cleared my throat. "I'm sorry, Lilly. Really, I am. Tristan was right, I should've told you–"

"Tristan knew?" she squeaked, her voice so high it made me wince.

"I'm sorry," I repeated, hoping that this time, maybe, she'd accept it. "I never wanted to make you feel that way. I never hated you. I loved you, and I still do. But I was an idiot, I know that. And if you want nothing to do with me, I–"

"Oh, no. Don't do that," she sniffed, wiping her tears on her wrist, her eyes puffy and wet. "You're not going to give me some speech about how you were an idiot and you don't deserve me and if I want nothing to do with you, then you understand, and we can go back to the way things were—No. You're going to stay this time and make it up to me."

I rocked back on my heels, stunned. I'd never seen Lilly this angry before.

"If... that's what you want," I told her, slowly, not sure of what else to say, "then I'll do anything."

She looked at me squarely and said, "Good. Because I love you too, you asshole."

I... what?

Did she just—?

I stood there, dumbstruck, as her fists wound into my shirt. "But if you ever do that to me again..." she warned me, "*don't* do that to me again. Ever."

My chest burned. In a way I'd never felt before.

She said she loved me.

Lilly loved me.

And she was waiting for me to say something, but my tongue felt too big for my mouth. Eventually, I managed, "I won't," and she sniffed again, nodding.

"Okay. Then take me home. You can start by giving me a real apology tonight."

As she threw her arms around my neck and put her head on my chest, I hid my face in her hair, still not sure that this was real.

But I was ready to take her home and find out.

CHAPTER 30
LILLY
THE SAME NIGHT

Lilly's Apartment

HE WAS STILL INSIDE ME.

Thrusting short, sharp movements that made my back arch. In between saying things like *more, please, oh god, don't stop*, other... more embarrassing sounds slipped out of my mouth.

But I couldn't control it. I really couldn't. Because his thick cock had found the one spot that melted me into a puddle of warm, satisfied goo.

He was between my legs, sitting on his knees with my thighs resting on his, spreading me out in front of him. Only my head and shoulders touched the mattress. His grip on my hips was almost bruising—and I liked it.

Almost as much as every other thing he'd done to me tonight.

"So fucking good," he grunted through his teeth. "But if I don't stop, I'm going to come inside you."

I made a small whimpering noise that sounded a lot like disappointment. I didn't want this to end.

But, my eyelids were heavy, and I was exhausted. It was four in the morning. He'd made me come with his cock, his fingers, and his mouth. I was sensitive and raw, and we'd just run out of condoms.

But I couldn't explain it. I just wanted more.

He pulled out, gripped the back of my knees, and flipped me. I laid on my belly, not able to do much of anything as he smoothed his hands over my ass.

He ground out a low, "So perfect," before he spread me apart.

The air in my apartment was too cold to be bared like this, and I shivered, wondering what I looked like to Shawn. Braced on my knees, my face in my mattress, my hips twitching. I was sore, but I was wet and trembling.

He made a low, deep, primal noise, and then his warm breath brushed the back of my thighs.

I squeaked.

He was so close, still holding me open, and then there was his tongue, sliding from my clit to my entrance and back again with slow, deliberate strokes.

I almost died.

"You taste so sweet. I could lick your pussy for days."

He sucked and teased me, gentle yet somehow

rough. My hips moved on their own, chasing the feel of his tongue as he pulled back and grunted, "I've wanted to do this to you for so fucking long."

He skimmed my clit, making me groan into the sheets as he did it again and again, a little harder each time. I was shaking, barely able to keep my legs braced. But I was lost. Completely drunk on the way he touched me.

I came hard.

The mattress muffled my screams as my back arched, feet kicked, and toes curled. I was still coming when he stopped, lifted my ass, and pushed his cock back into me. It was instant. Another orgasm made me buck into him, forcing me to take him deeper as he held my hips, and I could feel my insides pulse around him.

"Good girl... that's it. I love it when you come for me," he murmured as I bit into the sheets. "The way you squeeze my cock—fuck. It's like you're made for this."

My eyes rolled back as he let me ride it out, his fingers digging into my hips even harder than before.

But I didn't care.

And it felt so good not to care for once.

He pulled out for the second time, and I crumpled underneath him. My skin felt like it was humming. The space between my thighs was so sensitive that if he touched me there again, I didn't know if I could take it.

I let out a high-pitched noise as he cupped my ass cheek and grunted. The next thing I felt was something warm and sticky. It wasn't the first time tonight that he'd come on me, and I was starting to think it was his new favorite hobby.

"I think... we might be done. For tonight," Shawn decided, letting me go.

"Uh-huh," I sighed as he picked up the small washcloth from my nightstand and cleaned the mess he'd made on me.

Lifting the covers, he settled in beside me, and tucked them around us. Snuggling into him already felt like the most natural thing I could do, and though putting logical thoughts together felt like too much effort just then, I knew that I was happy in a way I hadn't felt in so long.

But he was right. We were definitely done for tonight.

"I don't think I can handle anymore," I agreed.

He ran one hand through my hair as the other slid down my back. "But you took me so well. I think you could take it again."

I smiled into his chest. "I'm sore, Shawn. I need a break."

I looked up in time to watch a smirk play out across his face, and I just... it was so perfect. He was so perfect. This was so perfect. The best night of my life.

Trevor, the email, and the fundraiser budget were still there, taking up space in the back of my mind. But right now, in this moment, even my anxiety couldn't reach me.

"So, what now?" he asked while checking our phones side by side on my nightstand. "If we fall asleep, we'll be worse off in the morning."

"You think we should stay up?"

I felt him nod into my hair. "Probably. But if I'm not allowed to touch you... what do you want to do instead?"

I leaned over him, picked up the remote, and turned on my small TV.

Shawn groaned. He knew what was coming. "Which one are you going to make me watch?"

I gave him a toothy, sneaky grin as I flicked through my saved shows, and chose an episode.

The phrase, "*Well excuuuuuse me, Your Highness,*" filtered into the room, and Shawn groaned again as I nestled into him.

"You know I hate this."

He was right. I knew he hated this show. I could still remember the day I found this animated series based on his favorite childhood video game, and the last thing I expected was for him to complain about how the show had gotten everything wrong.

I shrugged. "I just felt like watching it."

He lifted a brow. "You felt like watching it? It had nothing to do with me?"

I shook my head. "Nope."

"Really?"

"Yep."

I burst out laughing as his fingers prodded my ribs,

tickling me until I couldn't breathe. "Stop, stop, please! You win! You were right!"

In an instant, the tickling was over. He made a grunting noise that sounded a lot like vindication mixed with annoyance, and rearranged me until I was sitting between his legs with my head tucked under his chin.

"I knew you chose this to punish me," he muttered, and I giggled.

He said he'd do anything to make up the last five years to me, but a night of sex followed by a show he hated didn't seem like that big a punishment. I'd like to think that I could've come up with something nastier than this.

"It isn't the worst thing," I told him.

"Lilly," he drawled. "This show is the worst thing you could've chosen, and you know it."

"Well, it's already on, so... too bad."

He wrapped a hand around my waist and pulled me into him. My back was to his chest, my legs splayed open across his thighs. His hands were on my nipples, rolling them between his thumb and finger until I squeaked.

Letting a breast go, he slid his hand down my stomach and muttered, "Then it looks like I'll have to find something else to play with."

His fingers were rough against my clit.

My voice came out a little high, and a little desperate. "I thought you said we were done."

His lips brushed my shoulder before he gently bit my neck. "You want me to stop?"

"No," I breathed. "But, I'm not used to this. I don't think I'll ever get used to this."

"You will," he promised, his breath warm on my skin. "We've got a lot of catching up to do. And I will never get tired of making you come."

The episode played, sending bright colors across my walls. The volume was low enough that it became just another noise in the background.

It seemed like there wasn't a single thing that could compete with what Shawn was doing to me.

"Please," I begged, not sure of what I wanted, because as sensitive as it felt, something familiar was building inside me, and my hips rolled at the feel of it.

His chuckle was low and warm against my earlobe. "Look at you, riding my fingers." He slipped one inside and my breath hitched. "How many times have you come? Six? Seven? You want more, don't you?"

I couldn't answer. I couldn't think. All I knew was that this wasn't like anything I'd ever felt before.

"Shhh," he whispered into my hair, and I realized then that I'd been making soft, strained noises. "Be a good girl and watch the show."

CHAPTER 31
SHAWN
FRIDAY MORNING

Verra Convention Center

"He was inside me all night," Lilly whisper-yelled to Mia as I walked into the kitchen.

I paused, leaning against the doorframe as Mia whispered back, "Okay, what the actual hell? How did you two go from hating each other to boning?"

Lilly sat with her elbows planted on the tabletop, chin resting on her palms, eyes hooded and hair lazily wound into a topknot. "We talked and... I don't really know. But it was the best sex of my life."

"Which time?" Mia asked wryly, staring down at her from across the table, arms folded.

She let out a breathy sigh. "All of them. I'm so sore. I might've reached my limit."

Mia looked her up and down, then said, "Normally

I'd tell you the limit doesn't exist, but it's like you're drunk on sex."

"And lack of sleep," I added, walking into the room.

Mia and Lilly both yelped.

"You asshole," Mia muttered.

Lilly looked up at me dreamily, and I couldn't resist. Mia scoffed as I bent to kiss her.

"I can't believe you two. Look at you. What happened to wanting professionalism at all times, *Mister Jackson?*"

I shrugged and walked straight to the coffee pot, pouring both Lilly and me a cup each. After last night, we both needed a few shots of caffeine. She sighed happily as I handed her the warm mug, bending to kiss her hair.

"As cute as this is," Mia said, "we still have a problem. Trevor the dickbag, remember?"

I put my mug to my mouth and said, "I'll handle it. I'll call the department and tell them I made a mistake. Once I know Lilly's in the clear, then I'll deal with Trevor."

Lilly shut her eyes and shook her head. "I can't let you do that. We should just talk to Trevor. Maybe if we let him know that we know, he'll admit it and apologize."

I grinned into my mug. She was as trusting as ever. Always willing to do the thoughtful thing, even if a shithead like Trevor didn't deserve it.

God, I loved her.

"That's a nice idea," I started. "But if Trevor owns up to tampering with emails and orders, he'll lose his job. He's not going to admit to anything."

Mia folded her arms. "There's got to be some way to prove that bastard messed with Lilly's computer."

"Maybe there is," I agreed. "But right now, I need to deal with the extra takeout cups before they become a problem."

Lilly lifted her chin, worrying her bottom lip with her teeth. She was gorgeous. I never stood a chance. "Without taking the blame, right?"

"I'll take care of it," I told her, and I would. I just needed to finish this coffee first.

Mia was smug. "Look at you, saving the day. Only took you five bloody years to get here."

Just then, as Lilly leaned on me, I could hear footsteps just outside the doorway. I wanted to keep her there, but Mia had a point before.

Technically, I was their boss, and the teachers here expected me to act professionally. My reputation could take a hit with the department, but if anyone saw me like this with Lilly, it wouldn't be good for her. Not while her job was still on the line.

I didn't want anyone twisting this thing between us into something that could hurt her.

I steadied Lilly, then stepped away, telling her, "I'll call the department now. I'll see you in my office in... twenty minutes?"

She nodded as I turned away.

Stacey was in the hallway. Her eyelids were at half-mast, and her pace was slow. If I was lucky, she might've been tired enough to let me slip by.

Later, I planned to ask about all the things she'd done to Lilly. All the shit I'd only just found out about. But this wasn't the right time for that.

First, I had to deal with the damage Trevor caused.

"Morning, Stace," I greeted her and kept walking, but she gave me an odd look and stopped short, right in front of me.

"You look happy. And tired." She glanced down at her notebook before I could answer. "You've got a call with the department heads in ten minutes, by the way. Something about budget overspend?"

Shit.

My hand flexed around my mug.

How did they find out about that?

I looked back at Stacey, but she was already heading toward the kitchen.

"Stacey, wait. What overspend?"

She shrugged and looked over her shoulder. "Don't know." She waved her hand. "But if you want me to look into it, you'll have to wait until I finish my coffee."

I made it to my office, shut the door, and loaded the computer. Scrubbing my hands down my face, I slapped myself a few times.

Whatever this was, I had to handle it before it made things worse for Lilly.

~

Shawn

"I don't understand." I squinted at Pedro, the Head of Finance.

My screen was divided into four squares, and each showed a beige or gray office behind a middle-aged, balding man. And they were all angry.

"Then I'll repeat myself," Pedro drawled. "Your volunteer, Miss Lilly Fares, wrote an email to the department last night. She admitted to forging an order."

I shook my head, trying to loosen the static there. This couldn't be happening.

"Could you read the email to me? Or forward it?"

Pedro let a breath shoot through his nostrils. "I'll forward it, but you can read the email in your own time. Right now, your job is to fire Lilly Fares."

The thought of that felt like a punch to the gut.

"Fire her?"

They must've heard something in my voice, because Tony, the head directly below Pedro, tilted his chin. "Yes, of course. After what she did, why wouldn't we fire her?"

"What happened wasn't her fault."

"Well, whose fault was it, then?" Pedro snapped.

I didn't like his tone.

"Look, I can't just fire her. We don't know the whole

story. And she couldn't have sent that email–she wasn't at her computer last night. She was–" with me.

I gritted my teeth. There had to be a way out of this that didn't make Lilly look bad, and telling the heads of the Education Board that she spent last night with my cock inside her wasn't it.

Pedro's eyes narrowed. "She didn't have to physically be in the office to send the order. She explained how she did it in the email."

"You'll feel better about firing her once you read it," Tony added.

Shit.

I had to do something–say something–here.

But I couldn't understand how this was happening.

First, the merchandise order was doubled, and we'd traced it back to an email that had an invoice attached to it that I didn't sign off on. We wound up with more coffee cups than we needed, all of them now sitting in Tristan's storage room.

Lilly said she never sent that email, and I believed her.

Then Mia saw Trevor sitting at Lilly's computer, logged into her profile. Which meant that if Lilly didn't do it, then maybe Trevor did.

But that explanation was a long shot, almost impossible to prove.

And now there was a second email? One from Lilly admitting to the forgery and overspend?

She didn't touch her inbox yesterday.

If Trevor was doing this, then he was doing it well.

He'd even beaten me to taking the blame.

A confession that pinned it all on Lilly meant there wasn't anything I could do to fix this for her. Because I didn't have any fucking proof that she didn't do any of it in the first place.

What could I do here? How could I fix–

Pedro cleared his throat. "We also need to talk about the money. Since your employees were forging orders under your nose, we've had to make some changes."

My insides twisted. There was a pause. Then Pedro spoke.

"The overspend will be taken from your percentage, whatever the amount turns out to be."

I nodded slowly.

Thirty percent of the fundraiser's proceeds—about three hundred thousand dollars—would go to my project. That amount would be enough to launch my Maslow initiative across schools in lower Manhattan.

Fifteen thousand wasn't that hard a hit.

I wasn't worried about that. I was worried about Lilly.

"And we've revised your share of the proceeds. Your project will receive five percent."

I jerked back, surprised. "Five percent? You can't be serious, Pedro."

He frowned. "Five percent is still fifty thousand."

"Not when you take away fifteen of it," I told him.

"What am I supposed to do with thirty-five thousand dollars? It isn't enough. This is a state-wide project. You've seen the numbers. You know what I need."

"And we were willing to give it to you, but you didn't tell anyone about yesterday's delivery. We should've known about it the minute it happened. This fundraiser isn't just about your initiative. We have other projects to focus on, and we can't afford to waste time worrying about your team. Honestly, you're lucky we're not firing you."

"Pedro," I warned, standing from my seat and looming over the monitor. "You don't mean that."

"Yes. I do." His voice had just enough threat in it to match mine. "If the fundraiser wasn't due to go ahead so soon, we would've replaced you with someone else. Be glad that this is all you have to deal with."

They hung up. My screen went blank. And I fucking *roared*. Angry, deep, and loud.

Teachers turned to watch me through the glass, their eyes wide, hands flying to mouths as I punched the concrete wall closest to me.

When the door opened and shut, I looked up to find Lilly staring at me, worried. She looked at my hand, came close, and gently touched my knuckles.

"Are you okay?" she asked quietly.

I shook my head. "No. None of this is okay."

I opened my inbox and found the forwarded email Pedro sent. Lilly stood at my shoulder, reading, her fingers squeezing the top of my chair.

"What is this?" she breathed.

The email read:

Dear Education Department,

My name is Lilly Fares. I teach at South Bronx Classical, and I've volunteered most of my summer break to work at the New York Educational Arts Fundraiser under Shawn Jackson.

However, due to a misunderstanding between Mister Jackson and myself, I thought one of our merchandising projects was under-ordered. I fixed the issue by adding more cups, and signed off on the order myself using Mister Jackson's signature.

I was trying to save time, but it turns out I'd gotten it wrong, and the order came to $30,000USD instead of $15,000USD.

Because of my mistake, the budget has gone over what was planned.

I've been completing my work for the fundraiser both in the office and out, and so, when I forged the order, I did it from my school faculty computer. You can find the logs attached.

I apologize, and I hope we can find a way to move past it.

. . .

REGARDS,

Lilly Fares
South Bronx Classical

I WAS SHOCKED. And so angry I couldn't fucking think.

And now... I had to fire her?

Once Lilly failed here, Trevor would use what happened as an excuse to let her go. An investigation would open, and she'd lose more than just her job at South Bronx. She'd lose her teaching license.

Her career was over.

"This... this can't be real. But–" Lilly cut herself off, bursting into a sob and sinking to the ground. I dropped beside her and pulled her to me.

"Why did I think I could do this?" she cried into my chest. "I'm such an idiot."

Fucking Trevor. I was going to kill him.

CHAPTER 32
LILLY
FRIDAY MORNING

Verra Convention Center

SHAWN GOT up from the ground and pulled his office door open so hard that the hinges screeched.

Through it, he yelled, "Stacey, get in here now!" and it gave me an idea of what we looked like to the teachers peering into the room.

They saw me on the floor, red-faced and crying. They also saw a side of Shawn they'd never seen before. He was furious, loud, and demanding.

What they couldn't see was the heaviness in my chest. Or the stunning certainty that I never really stood a chance. My career ended the minute I stepped into that staffroom to meet with Trevor.

And it was devastating.

I'd felt panicked before. I'd had anxious spirals that led me to believe my world was crumbling down around me. But I'd always come out knowing that everything would be okay.

This time, it wouldn't be. My anxiety finally won a battle. And it felt like I'd lost the war.

I wiped my cheeks with my sleeve, took a breath, and stood. Breaking down wasn't going to help. I'd done enough of that over the last five weeks anyway.

Stacey walked in with her arms folded, annoyed with the way Shawn shouted at her from across the office, and Mia followed, as excited as I'd ever seen her.

The door shut, and Mia let loose. "What'd she do? Was it bad?"

Stacey's neck snapped in Mia's direction, then back at Shawn.

He was an intimidating guy to begin with, at over six feet tall with broad shoulders. But with his face lined in a scowl, his hands flexing into fists, and his unblinking stare, Angry-Shawn was... pretty scary. I tried to remember the last time I'd seen him this mad, and couldn't.

Stacey gave him a look, then defensively asked, "What's going on?"

"Your fucking cousin," Shawn ground out before stopping to take a breath. He let it out slowly, then, a little more calmly, said, "He's been using Lilly's computer at South Bronx to send emails."

All three of us watched Stacey's face then, looking for something. For some kind of recognition. But eventually, all she did was ask, "What?"

"Your cousin is trying to get Lilly fired."

She scoffed. "Shawn, that's crazy."

"No," he said, and I could tell he was trying not to yell again. "It isn't. Mia saw him sitting at her desk."

Her blue eyes narrowed. "So?"

"So?" Mia erupted. "So? He's been fucking with Lilly's email and her orders. He's trying to get her kicked off the fundraiser."

"And it worked." Shawn's tone flattened out. Maybe watching Mia explode was sobering for him. "He sent an email from her computer last night to the department heads." He ran a hand through his hair, then down his face. "He pinned the merchandise issue we found out about yesterday on Lilly, and now they want me to fire her."

Stacey shot me a glance, like she just realized I was standing there.

"But... what makes you think it wasn't Lilly who sent those emails?"

I felt a spark in my chest, but it went away as quickly as it came. This was the version of Stacey I'd expected since we started working here. Of course she'd believe the worst about me instead of Trevor. Given my track record with the fundraiser, I almost couldn't blame her for asking that question in the first place.

Besides, Shawn was offended enough for both of us. It was in his tone as he told her, "Lilly couldn't have done any of it."

"Why not?" She cocked her head, pushing.

"She wasn't in the office or at her school."

"Do you know where she was?"

"Oh, you evil bitch," Mia snapped, stepping close to Stacey, forcing her back. "You're trying to protect your dickbag cousin, aren't you? Well, you can't. Because Lilly wasn't here or at the school. She was with Shawn."

"Mia," I warned gently, lacing my arms around her shoulders and dragging her back.

But Stacey wasn't intimidated. Instead, she looked exasperated. She raised a brow as she turned to take in Shawn's pinched and... guilty face?

"Was she?" she asked, almost resigned.

Shawn didn't say anything. The muscle on his jaw jumped as he nodded.

She laughed then, but it didn't have any humor to it.

"Really?" she asked. "You just couldn't resist, could you?"

"Stacey," he snapped, warning her, but she went on as if he hadn't.

"Remember how she made you feel? Remember what you told me?"

"Stacey, that's enough. This isn't about Lilly and me, it's about your cousin," Shawn said, but she only scoffed, then rolled her eyes at me.

"He avoided you for five years, Lilly. Are you really okay with that?"

My voice sounded surer than I thought it would as I answered, "We talked about it, and I forgave him."

Her smirk was an open-mouthed thing that made Mia tense in my arms. "Oh, that's great, isn't it? Well, I guess you're going to have to forgive him again, aren't you? Since he has to fire you now."

"Stacey," Shawn warned.

She turned on her heel, whipping around to face him. "Fire her. This is your job, Shawn. They told you she put the fundraiser at risk. Doesn't that mean she deserves this?"

Shawn's chest rose, his jaw clenched, and his eyes narrowed. He looked as if he wanted to breathe fire at her. Instead, he took her by the shoulder and turned her away, as if she needed to be close to hurt me.

"Listen," he told her. "She doesn't deserve to be fired. Your cousin is trying to ruin her career. He did this."

She let out a frustrated sigh. "Even if that were true, what does that have to do with me? Why am I here?"

Shawn opened his mouth to answer, but I beat him to it, asking, "Do you know why Trevor's doing this?"

I was numb. Yes, my pulse was thundering and my palms were sweaty, but I couldn't actually feel anything just then. Even my anxiety couldn't reach me. If there was a chance that I could fix this, I had to take it. It was possible that Stacey knew something that could help.

But based on the look she gave me, helping me was the last thing on her mind. "You think my cousin would do something to screw up a fundraiser I've been working on with Shawn for over a year, and tell me about it? Really?"

I'd forgotten I was still holding Mia back. She stiffened and said, "Maybe you're in on this together, then. Maybe you felt bad for Trevor when Lilly dumped him, and you promised you'd help him fuck her over."

Stacey rolled her eyes and threw out her hands. "And why would I do that?"

Mia opened her mouth, probably ready to list all the reasons why we couldn't trust Stacey, and why it made sense that she helped her cousin pull this off.

But I cut in and said, "You're right. You'd get nothing out of the fundraiser going over budget."

This fundraiser wasn't just the peak of Shawn's career; it was Stacey's too. If anything went wrong, it would reflect badly on her as well. It didn't make sense that she would jeopardize her career just to help her cousin with this.

That was if Trevor was the one who did this in the first place.

Something almost like sympathy flashed over Stacey's features as she said, "Exactly."

Then she folded her arms and turned back to Shawn, her voice almost gentle. "I know this isn't easy for you, but the department heads told you to fire her. There's no point in dragging this out. You don't have a choice, Shawn."

He looked at me, cursed, and said, "I can't."

Stacey let out a noise of frustration. "But everything

we planned for is on the line here. You can't let anything get in the way–this is too important. Think of all those kids going without a decent breakfast, or the kids who show up to school in ripped uniforms. We can fix that, but you have to do what they want first. Otherwise, they'll shut us down before we can get anything off the ground. We're so close, Shawn."

He shook his head. "We'll find another way. I'm not letting her go."

Hearing him say that made me feel sick. I didn't want him to choose me, not like this.

We believed he would walk away from this untouched. That the great Shawn Jackson would be able to take a hit like this.

But Stacey was right.

His initiative was on the line. He needed this fundraiser to go well. He'd already told me that more than once. And even if I wasn't the one who sent those emails, if I stayed, I would be the reason his plans went up in smoke.

I was ruining this for him. And I couldn't do that.

Letting go of Mia, I put a hand on my stomach and quietly told them, "I'll go."

Mia whirled around and threw her hands on my shoulders, then glared at Stacey like this was all her fault.

"I knew you were still a bitch," she spat.

Frustrated, Stacey ground out, "Yes, I'm a bitch. Now, will you get her out of here?" as Shawn closed the distance between us and quietly begged, "Wait, Lilly, don't go. We can still fix this."

But it wasn't up to him to fix this. And if I stayed, I'd only cause more damage.

I'd already lost what mattered most to me. I couldn't let Shawn lose, too.

I shook my head, and that was all Mia needed.

As Shawn yelled after us, she led me out of the room, angrily muttering, "I'm going to need something stronger than boozy bingo to deal with this."

~

Friday Afternoon
Lilly's Apartment
Lilly

TECHNICALLY, Shawn didn't fire me. He didn't have to.

Mia made sure I got home, and wasted no time coaxing me back into my pajamas before she left. She was a great friend. She didn't deserve to be dragged into... whatever this disaster was.

Now, I was lying in the same bed I was in only a handful of hours ago, hugging my pillow tight. The smell of Shawn's woodsy-coffee musk was still there, and it made my eyes water.

I wanted him to forget about me and focus on the fundraiser. That was the important thing here.

Not me and my... God, what was this? What was actually happening?

How was it that I went from teaching fulltime at the school of my dreams, to getting fired from a fundraiser my boss set me up to fail at?

All in a few weeks, too.

Okay, I had to stop before I spiraled. An attack would get me nowhere.

Taking a deep breath–in and out, in and out–I told myself that I was still young. No matter what my anxiety made me think, my life wasn't actually over. I could pick up and start something new. Maybe even go somewhere new.

But the thought of letting down my mom–that's what made this so hard. I'd already lost so much.

I lost my father to another family, my mom to cancer, and... but I had Uncle Henry. Without him, I'd never have started working at the coffee shop with Tristan, Nikki, and Shawn. And without them, I probably wouldn't have made it through school in the first place.

Wiping my tears on my arm, I let go of the pillow and picked up the notebook I left by my bedside.

Shawn was still at the fundraiser, probably working through all the new issues this morning left him with. The twinge in my chest spread to a full ache as I remembered the way he stood there in his office and refused to fire me.

But, for once, Stacey and I agreed on something.

The fundraiser had to come first. Too many students depended on the money he'd raise for their schools.

I'd figure out a way to come back from this. I just... needed a minute to think all this through.

I flipped my book open and started writing. Trevor was trying to ruin my career. Why?

1. Years ago, my grades were slipping, and Stacey asked me to date her cousin. If I did, I could keep my spot in Kappa Delta.

2. Trevor and I broke up after we started working at South Bronx, and he's hated me ever since.

3. The moment Trevor had a position of power over me; he threatened my job, and forced me to work over the summer break to earn my spot back at South Bronx.

I tapped my pencil against the paper, thinking.

Would Trevor really go to all this trouble just to get me fired?

If that was the case, then the entire past six weeks of my life started to look different... and now those calls from Trevor made sense.

He was disappointed when I told him I'd caught up on my tasks. He thought I'd fail on my own, but when that didn't happen, he created the coffee-cup problem. And that was definitely enough to get the job done.

Still thinking, I rubbed my chest, distracted, as if that could ease some of the pressure in there, when my phone rang, surprising me.

I picked it up, thinking maybe it was Shawn or Mia. Maybe even Nikki.

What I didn't expect was for Trevor's name to flash across my screen.

"You-you asshole," I sputtered, feeling hot and prickly all at once.

"Woah, easy there," he replied, not bothered at all by the way I'd answered his call. "What's going on? How are things at the fundraiser?"

"You know exactly how they are," I tried to snap as I stood from my bed and wandered around the cramped room.

He pretended to be confused. "I don't know what you're talking about. Did something happen?"

"As if you don't know I've been fired."

I could hear him breathing. I could hear the smile in his voice as he asked, "You've been fired? Why? What happened?"

"You know what happened," I yelled, wiping away the mucus that dribbled from my nostril.

I suddenly felt unhinged. Like I could climb through the phone and rip his arms from his shoulders.

"I don't." He could barely cover the joy in his tone. "I was calling to talk to you about Mrs Hernandez. I know you gave her your phone number. But I, oh, look at this. I just got an email from the Department of Education, and it looks like you're under investigation."

He made a happy hmph sound and said, "Mrs Hernandez was one thing, but I don't think your career can survive this."

I sank onto the bed. Tears pricked the corners of my

eyes. "Why are you doing this to me, Trevor? What'd I do to make you want to get rid of me this badly?"

"Lilly, Lilly, Lilly," he scolded, gently. "We might not get along sometimes, but I've always been supportive."

"That's such a lie."

He tsked at me, then, as if to prove his point, said, "What about the module I signed you up for? And the fundraiser? I was trying to help you."

Wiping at my wet cheeks, I scoffed. "That wasn't to help me. You messed with my computer while I was away from school."

"Why would you think I had anything to do with your computer problems?" he drawled. "It's not like I blocked your access to the server, or uninstalled your email remotely. I didn't have anything to do with sending that invoice to the merchandiser. And I wasn't the one who sent an email to the Education Board last night. Why would I do any of that to you? What you're accusing me of makes no sense."

Right then and there, everything paused, and I held my breath.

Investigation reports were confidential. Even head teachers didn't have the right to know the details behind them.

He was rubbing everything he did in my face without admitting it outright, and I still couldn't do anything to prove it.

"Ah, Lilly, I just don't understand why you decided to do this." His tone shifted. "And poor Shawn, having to clean up the mess you made. I hope his initiative works out. I mean, how bad would you feel if you ended up damaging your career, and his?" He sighed. "It's a shame you blew it; it really is."

My throat felt scratched raw, but I managed to choke out a soft, "You're horrible," which earned me nothing.

Not an inch of guilt was in Trevor's voice as he purred, "I wish I could help you, Lillybug. But it is what it is."

My stomach turned at hearing his old pet name for me.

"Your mom would be so disappointed if she knew about this. But, oh well. Maybe your old coffee shop boss will hire you back."

He hung up and I threw my phone on the ground, watching it bounce along the carpet. Then I put my head in my hands and dug my elbows into my knees. My chest, throat, and eyes burned with tears, until I couldn't hold them back anymore.

I cried then. Deep, long sobs that shook my shoulders.

Because there wasn't anything else left for me to do.

FOUR YEARS AGO

CHAPTER 33
LILLY
TUESDAY MORNING

South Bronx Classical

"HE TRIED TO KISS ME." I grimaced. "In the library."

Mia let out a noise of disgust. "In front of the students?"

With a slight nod, I answered, "Like a dog marking his territory."

Mia's lips twisted. "When are you going to dump him? This has already gone on too long."

I lifted a shoulder, then took another sip from the warm teacup in my hand. Mia and I were sitting in our staffroom. The students were gone for the day, and we were settled at our desks, ready to mark our latest round of assessments.

"I just don't want to upset him. He said he loves me." I couldn't repeat those words with a straight face. My nose wrinkled on its own. "And you know how he gets when he's upset."

"I know. His temper tantrums are exhausting. But I think it's worse to keep him on the hook like you're doing now. You should just end it and let him deal with it. Sooner is better than later."

I shook my head. "It isn't that simple. I can't just break up with him. We work together."

Mia shifted in her seat and started shuffling papers.

"Lilly, listen to yourself. It's been a whole year since we graduated. You're teaching at your dream school, and we get to work together. Stacey can't hurt you now. Why are you still forcing yourself to be with someone you don't want?"

I squeezed my lips into a flat line. It might've been over a year since then, but Stacey's threat still popped up whenever Trevor locked his arms around me. At first, I was just resigned to dating him. I thought I might, maybe, develop feelings for him. Eventually.

After all, forced proximity and fake dating were two of my favorite romance novel tropes, and they had to be rooted in something real. Right?

And Trevor was nice to me. Most of the time. Every now and then, something cruel slipped out of him. But before I could process it, he was apologizing, explaining, and moving us on like nothing had happened.

I couldn't ignore that something was missing, even if I didn't know what that something was. He just wasn't... the one for me.

Slowly, whether I wanted it to or not, my resignation turned into an almost ever-present nausea, and it was like Trevor could sense it.

He upped the ante, trying to kiss me at work. And now my stomach dropped every time I spotted him in the hallway.

What would he do next? Pull me into a classroom? Would a student catch us? And what would happen then?

It wasn't just that I felt uncomfortable with his... enthusiasm, it was also that I wasn't okay with him touching me.

Ugh, why did I put myself in this situation to begin with?

If I could've just taken an exam without feeling anxious... but Mia was right.

This wasn't fair for either of us.

I had to end this, and sooner rather than later. I just... wasn't totally convinced that Trevor would let me.

~

Lilly

"Mmm." The way Trevor moaned made my skin crawl. "God, I love your lips, Lillybug. I could kiss you for hours."

His hands slid around my waist, and he pulled me

closer. The urge to run as far as I could was strong, and I felt myself turning rigid as he nuzzled into my neck.

"Trevor—"

"Mmm?"

Another kiss, sloppy and wet, left a trail of saliva on my shoulder. I bit my lip, fighting the wave of nausea it brought up.

"You have to stop touching me. We're going to get in trouble."

He met my stare with a smirk. "That's half the fun, isn't it?"

He pushed me against the concrete wall and ground into me. I couldn't help it. My hands worked on their own as I shoved him.

"Stop it," I hissed.

As I looked around the still-empty cafeteria, he held up his hands and came closer, slow and cautious, like I was acting hysterical and had no right to feel uncomfortable.

"Okay, okay, I'm sorry. I didn't know you were so freaked out over getting caught."

I shot him a glance that said, *you would've known if you'd just listened to me.*

"You know what this job means to me, Trevor. If a student catches us, it could mean instant dismissal," I whispered.

He put his hand on my arm, and I shrugged away from him.

"Lillybug, come on. Nothing like that is going to happen. I just wanted to kiss you. It's not like I was going to fuck you against the wall."

"Trevor," I huffed. I really was going to be sick. And not just because of my anxiety.

He eyed me with a pout. "What's wrong?"

The words bubbled out of me before I could stop them. "I can't do this anymore."

His face went slack, fingers paused mid-air, as he asked, "Do what?"

I waved a hand back and forth between us.

"This. I can't. I know Stacey set us up because of the sorority, but she can't force me to be with you anymore. And I tried. I really, really tried. But I just don't feel anything."

His reaction was instant.

Trevor's spine snapped straight. He ran his hands through his blonde hair, and stepped back, giving me space.

His voice was low as he said, "But, I love you. Doesn't... doesn't that mean anything?"

My heart sank. "I'm sorry. It does mean something, just not... that. To me."

I wasn't doing this right. I was fumbling my way through this, and he was going to be hurt no matter how it went.

Seconds passed. We just stared at each other. He looked hopeless, and I felt like such an asshole.

Then his eyes narrowed, his tone hard as he

said, "I should've figured it out. You didn't want to meet my parents; you didn't want to move in together. You've been pretending this whole fucking time."

My stomach clenched, working into knots. He was hurt and angry, and he should've been. If I'd been honest about how I felt from the beginning, his feelings for me could've just been a blip from college. Easily forgotten, easy to move on from.

I would've gotten kicked out of my sorority, but maybe I deserved to be.

"I wasn't pretending. I was trying," I reasoned. "But I've given it more than a year, and it wouldn't be fair to you if I just... kept going."

He screwed up his face, then asked, "What now?"

Weakly, I lifted a shoulder. He was so mad at me that I didn't know what to say.

But he must've taken something from my silence, because he said, "I'm not leaving this school," as if I'd somehow implied it.

"I didn't think you would. I was hoping that maybe we could be... friends?"

I winced at the hope in my voice, because honestly, at this point, my insides felt like lead. I knew what he wanted, and it wasn't friendship.

He scoffed. "Friends?"

I nodded and stretched out my hand. He drifted out of reach. Then, without a word, he shook his head and left the cafeteria.

~

A Week Later
South Bronx Classical
Lilly

TREVOR CALLED IN SICK, and for four days straight, Mia and I worked his classes.

And I had to admit, it felt good.

No more looking around corners, hurrying from room to room, trying to avoid my 'boyfriend' while I pretended everything was okay.

Mia was right. This was what I needed.

It was a Tuesday when he finally came in, bleary-eyed and smelling like he hadn't showered in a few days.

And honestly? Guilt hit me hard.

Our breakup was a relief for me. But for Trevor, it didn't look like relief at all.

Mia squeezed my hand before heading out of the staffroom to teach her first class of the day, leaving Trevor and me alone.

And I wasn't sure what I was thinking, except that maybe I owed it to him to try and make this easier?

Maybe it was the people-pleaser in me, but I couldn't help it. I hated knowing that I'd made him this upset.

I went to his desk and tapped his shoulder. He looked up, tired and sad, and I swallowed before asking,

"Did you know pizza is the most photographed food on social media?"

I smiled weakly at him, and he rolled his eyes, scoffing.

"Just leave me alone, Lilly."

Well. At least he wasn't calling me Lillybug anymore.

"Trevor," I started gently, "do you think we could figure this out?"

Hope flared in his eyes, and my mouth dropped open, hands waving in front of me like a lunatic.

"I mean, could we figure out a way to work together?"

He slumped forward for a second, then stood, towering over me. The same old nausea made me stand back and stare up at him, but instead of reaching for me, he just nodded.

"Yeah. We'll figure... something out."

A year later, Principal Rutton started looking for a new Head Teacher.

NOW

CHAPTER 34
SHAWN
FRIDAY AFTERNOON

Verra Convention Center

"I can't fire Stacey," I yelled after Mia as she stomped back to her desk. At this point, I didn't give a shit about what the other teachers thought.

She whirled around and yelled back, "She probably helped Trevor fuck with Lilly's career. I'd say that's more than a good enough reason to fire her."

"I had nothing to do with–"

"SHUT UP, STACEY," Mia roared as she heaped her things into her bag and swung it over her shoulder. "I quit. Find someone else to manage the entertainment."

"Mia, you can't just leave–"

"Watch me." She stepped through the elevator doors before they closed, and I stood there surrounded by a group of shocked teachers.

I let out a breath and felt like complete shit as I raised my voice. "Everyone, be in the meeting room in fifteen minutes."

As I turned my back on them, whispers hissed behind me, and I felt every hour of lost sleep in that moment.

~

Shawn

As a boy growing up in Brooklyn, I was an only child living in a cramped two-bedroom apartment. My ceiling had mold, half of our appliances didn't work, and the hot water shut off after a half hour.

My family wasn't well off. Not by a long shot. But my parents, who both worked full-time, did everything they could. Sending me to our local private school was one of the best things they did for me.

I became one of those kids who thrived in the class-room. I was popular and smart. My teachers gave me praise and helped me mature. I loved every minute of it.

But I didn't know I'd become a teacher until I bumped into this kid at a downtown basketball court. Tryouts were in less than a week, and I needed the practice.

This kid, Jacob, wasn't there for that, though. He was there to throw rocks at people. And there I was, seventeen years old, standing in front of a kid who was about to hit me with one.

"What are you doing?" I asked him.

His arm was bent back, ready to throw. But he paused and said, "None of your business."

I drifted closer, watching him take a step back, the rock still in his hand.

I didn't think anyone had tried to stop him. Every time he threw a rock, people scattered. I could picture them now, muttering under their breath, their hands and faces buried in their coats as they walked away, maybe wondering if they should call the cops on this kid before he hurt someone.

I turned slowly and started dribbling. I could feel his squint on me, but the rock stayed in his hand.

The next time I looked at him, his anger was replaced with confusion. I gestured to the ball, then to the hoop, before throwing it in. It sank into the net, then hit the ground, bouncing and rolling on the court.

He took the hint, dropped the rock, and jogged over.

We played for a while, starting out with easy conversation that turned serious in a couple of hours.

He told me about his family and about the problem with his grades. If he couldn't raise them, his parents would send him to live with his aunt. When I asked him why he didn't want to go, the things he told me about his uncle made me sick.

I didn't know what else to do except offer to tutor him after school at the local library. All he really needed was to see the work from a different perspective, and it helped.

When his parents congratulated him on his latest test scores, he cried into a textbook I'd given him, telling me I'd changed his life. Not sure of what to say, I wound up just handing him a tissue.

We kept in contact. Jacob got married, had a few kids, and now he ran his own accounting firm.

There were so many times when I'd wondered what would've happened if I just walked down the street. If I saw the angry, dangerous kid, and left. What would've happened to him?

What would've happened to me?

Jacob thought I changed his life, but it went both ways. He changed mine too.

He gave me that feeling. The kind I still felt when a student's face lit up.

They got it. It clicked. And it changed the way they saw things.

Some people find their calling years after they leave school. Some switch, some have their careers forced on them, some swear they always knew who they were meant to be, and some people have a moment, like I did.

Sitting there with Jacob, I knew. I was going to become the kind of teacher who made a difference. Not for me—I wanted to do it for kids like him.

Maslow's Hierarchy taught me that for a student to thrive, their basic needs had to be met. Kids needed regular food, clean water, and a roof over their heads. They needed rest, and to feel safe.

More than that, kids needed to feel valued.

Once they had those things, they could reach their full potential.

It was a shock to learn about the number of kids who didn't get anything close to three meals a day. And about the students who came to school in the same clothes for a week straight. I'd seen kids beaten and bruised, showing up to school just so they could put their head on a desk, to have that minute of peace.

This job broke my heart so many times. But I couldn't stop doing it.

I had to do more. I had to do better.

So, after I... ended things with Lilly, I threw myself into my work and created an initiative based on student well-being.

Funding was approved, and every student would finally get the support they needed.

And then Trevor fucked everything up.

❧

Shawn

THE TEACHERS I'd been working with for the past five weeks looked up at me from the meeting room table, and I had to force every bit of frustration down as I met their eyes.

"Miss Fares and Miss Walker won't be working with us on the fundraiser anymore," I announced.

One sentence, and the room broke into a low hum. A few moments later, someone asked why.

Stacey came to stand next to me and cleared her throat. "Why Miss Fares and Miss Walker decided to leave our event doesn't matter. All that matters is how we handle the slack they've left behind."

I started issuing orders. Without much pushback, Stacey and I rearranged the rest of the tasks, giving them to teachers we trusted.

Once the meeting was done, I caught Stacey's attention and mouthed, "Stay."

The look she gave me was grim, but she hung around after everyone left.

Arms folded, she leaned against the table and sighed. "What is it now, Shawn?"

With no one else but Stacey around, I could finally scrub my hands over my face.

I was tired. Last night with Lilly was the best thing that ever happened to me, but I wasn't ready for today. I felt like I hadn't slept in days.

"I've decided something. And I don't think you'll like it."

She frowned, but waited.

"Stacey, we know Trevor did this. And I believe you when you say you didn't help him do it. Even though what you did to Lilly years ago was pretty shitty."

She let out a sharp breath. "For god's sake, how

many times do I have to go over this? I didn't force her into anything. All I did was set her and Trevor up on a date."

"Okay, but why?"

Stacey held up her hand, shifting on her feet like she was about to leave. She didn't want to talk about this anymore. I kept going anyway.

"I know you were going to kick her out of the sorority. I know she felt like she had to date Trevor–"

"That was on her," she snapped. "If she kept up with her grades in the first place, there wouldn't have been a problem. But that had nothing to do with my cousin."

"Then why set them up?"

Stacey shrugged. "He just wouldn't stop bugging me."

I gave her a look, and she threw her hands up. "That's really it. It wasn't some big conspiracy where I forced her into dating him. He asked me to introduce them, and I did. When they kept dating, I honestly thought she wanted to be with him."

I sighed and folded my arms. "Lilly probably thought staying with him would make you happy."

"Well... maybe," she agreed slowly. "But what happened between them wasn't my fault, and neither is this."

"I get that. But you do see how fucked up this is, right? The whole time, she was too scared to leave Trevor, and you knew how I felt about her."

Stacey's jaw clenched, and a line formed between her brows. "You and Mia think I bullied her."

I nodded.

Hesitating, she admitted, "Okay, fine, maybe... maybe I bullied her. But you know I wouldn't do something like that now. And I wouldn't risk the initiative. It's important to me too."

She was uneasy now, shoulders stiff as she fidgeted with her fingers.

Eventually, she said, "But Trevor's my cousin. Do you really think he'd do something like that knowing it'd hurt us too?"

"I don't know. But it's the only way this makes sense." I shoved my hands into my pockets and shook my head. "And I can't let Lilly take the blame for this."

"Then... what are you going to do?" she asked.

"I'm going to tell the department that it was my mistake. That I signed off on the invoice, and that Lilly was trying to keep me from losing the initiative."

"But," Stacey argued. "If you do that, you'll lose your job."

I shrugged. "I'd rather lose that than lose Lilly again."

The initiative meant a lot to me. But Lilly meant everything.

I turned to leave as Stacey said, "Shawn, that's crazy. You can't do something like that—you have to think this through."

I made it to the hallway before I turned back to her.

"You can take over the initiative. I know it'll be safe with you."

But her cousin wasn't safe from me.

If I was going to lose everything I'd worked for, I'd make sure I took Trevor down with me.

CHAPTER 35
LILLY
MONDAY AFTERNOON

Lilly's Apartment

OVER THE WEEKEND, Shawn sent me a single text.

S: *I'm going to fix this.*

I replied, asking, **L**: *What does that mean?*

But I got no response.

So I tried calling him a couple of times. All my calls went to voicemail, and I'd heard nothing from him since.

Which bothered me.

Where was he?

The knock on my door felt like it came at just the right time, pulling me out of my head before I could get too deep.

"Lilly, would you hurry up?" Mia yelled through the wood.

I shuffled to the door, letting her in.

"You haven't been answering your phone," she said as she pushed past me.

Just looking at her, I could tell I didn't have enough energy for whatever she was so excited about.

"Sorry. I was in the shower, and it wiped me out. But I was going to call you back."

I didn't have to explain anything. Mia knew this pattern. She knew how hard it was for me to get out of bed on days like this.

She looked at me with sympathy just as my stomach growled, right on cue. Then she pulled a box of donuts from her oversized tote bag and slapped them on my kitchen counter.

I moaned. "Mia, you're amazing."

"Eat while I talk."

I grabbed the box and took it with me to my sofa.

With a mouthful of original glazed, I asked, "What happened?"

Mia stood in front of me, looking around my cluttered apartment as she spoke.

"Shawn quit the fundraiser, and he's on his way to our school, right now, to talk to Principal Rutton."

"What? Why?" I gasped, and a bite of donut clogged my windpipe.

I coughed and sputtered as Mia smacked me between my shoulder blades.

"You okay there, love?"

No. I wasn't okay.

I left the fundraiser so Shawn could follow through

with his plans. If things had to fall apart, then they should've only fallen apart for me.

Oh god. I had to fix this.

As soon as I was done choking.

I made a rumbly, throat-clearing noise and asked, "He quit? What does that mean?"

"It means that he told the board that the merchandise issue was his fault. He's trying to get you your job back."

I snapped upright, opening my mouth to tell her that was the last thing I wanted, but Mia shook her head, cutting me off.

"No, no. I'm not here to sit and chat over tea and donuts with you. You need to swallow that down—wait, don't choke on it, Lilly! It's not Shawn's bloody penis, is it? Stop shoving it down your throat."

As I swallowed my last bite, Mia pulled me up and pushed me to the bedroom.

"Go get dressed. We have to leave. Now."

CHAPTER 36
LILLY
MONDAY AFTERNOON

South Bronx Classical

I WALKED into my school wearing a pair of jeans and a tank top. The summer heat was intense, and I dug my sweaty fingers into my belt loops, hauling the fabric higher over my ass as I waddled after Mia.

"Come on," she urged me on, half a step in front of me.

Mia led me down the narrow, quiet hallway, and I tried not to think about the fact that this could be the last time I'd ever see this place.

This school was more than just my job.

This was my reason for getting up in the morning.

And I couldn't believe Trevor did what he did just to take that away from me.

Mia was furious over it. I knew she wanted to do very violent things to Trevor, and I couldn't blame her.

But we were here for different reasons. Mia was here to support Shawn, and I was here to stop him.

I wanted my job back, but not at the expense of Shawn losing his.

It didn't make any sense to me anyway. That he could disappear for three days, then suddenly show up like this.

Did he really think he could walk in and solve my problems for me? Just like that? Without talking to me about it first?

No. That was *not* happening.

But my stomach was in knots. I didn't actually know what I was going to do. All I wanted was to forget that all this happened, and to yell at Shawn for leaving things the way he did.

I still didn't know what to think.

Was this all in my head? Did I have a right to be upset that Shawn didn't send me more than a single text?

It almost felt like being rejected by him all over again.

As we reached the next doorway just outside of Principal Rutton's office, Mia threw her arm across my chest and stopped me in place.

She pressed her finger to her lips, silently asking me to stay quiet. She looked like she was afraid of getting caught. It didn't take long to understand why.

"... ruined everything Shawn and I have been working on, Trevor."

Stacey. Her voice was mean and low, but it was definitely her.

"It's not my fault he decided to take the blame for Lilly. That's on Shawn, not me."

Trevor.

Mia turned to me with wide eyes, giving me a look that said, *holy shit*, and I knew I was giving her the same expression. She flapped her hands before reaching for her phone.

"But if you didn't forge that invoice in the first place, none of this would've happened."

"I had to. Nothing else worked."

We pulled our phones out and cringed at each other.

Trevor and Stacey weren't close enough to record. We could barely hear them as it was.

Were we too late?

"You should've just left Lilly alone and found another job somewhere else."

"No. She lied to me, Stacey. She deserves this."

Stacey made a noise of frustration. "I don't care if you think she deserves this. Do you know what your stupid plan cost us? We were raising money to help kids, Trevor. *Kids*. Don't you care about them?"

He scoffed. "Why the fuck would I care?"

Next to me, Mia made a face, disgusted.

"Well, what about me? Don't you care about me? This is my career."

Trevor sighed heavily. "Look, I'll help you with the initiative after this is done. This has to work."

"But what if it doesn't? What if Rutton gives Lilly her job back and Shawn loses his?"

"Then I'll just have to keep fucking with her test scores until she gets fired."

Mia and I swapped a wide-mouthed stare, and in an instant, my body flushed white-hot from head to toe.

I almost screamed.

That *bastard*.

He's been messing with my class test scores all this time?

My fists were so tight, my nails bit into my palms. I'd never wanted to hurt anyone like this before.

Stacey tsked, and I bit my lip hard enough to taste blood, forcing myself not to storm in there. But it wasn't easy. Holding myself back like this left me stiff and shaky, like it was burning energy I didn't have.

"Wasn't what you did with the invoice enough?" she asked.

"I don't know. It should've been, but if Shawn's meeting with Rutton works out, and she gets her job back, I might have to think of something else."

"Hey." Shawn. He sounded rough and threatening, like he was putting voice to everything I felt. "What the fuck are you doing here?"

Mia and I swapped another loaded glance as Shawn's heavy footsteps thudded down the hallway.

"I still work here. Where else would I be?" Trevor

snapped, and I could picture the scowl on his face as he spoke.

Mia grabbed my arm, and we stepped out. Stacey looked at us with surprise, but Trevor and Shawn didn't seem to notice.

"I'm going to break every one of your bones, you piece of shit," Shawn growled as he closed in, hands curling into fists.

Trevor stood there, looking as if he didn't believe Shawn would actually hit him.

"Mister Jackson," Principal Rutton called out, stepping from her office.

I could easily make out the shock on her round face. Shawn hesitated, stopping suddenly, his feet rooted to the ground. Rutton's eyes landed on Mia and me, as everyone else swung around.

There was a moment where we all just stared at each other.

An anxious, angry thud pounded in my head as Shawn looked at me and frowned.

"Why are you two here?" Rutton asked Mia and me, confused. "Miss Walker, this has nothing to do with you. And you don't teach here anymore, Miss Fares."

Mia folded her arms. "Hang on, things have changed, haven't they? Shawn's the one under investigation now, not Lilly."

Rutton shook her head. "Nothing's changed. She didn't make it to the end of the fundraiser."

"Are you–" Mia started, but I put my hand on her arm, cutting her off.

"Shawn," I snapped, still so mad that I couldn't hold it in anymore. "What are you doing?"

"Obviously, he's trying to make you happy. Because that always ends well," Stacey muttered, frustrated.

Shawn gave me a crooked smile and shrugged, and it was so at odds with the tension in the room that the way he looked at me hit me hard.

I read so much in his face. *I miss you. I love you. I'm doing this for you.*

But maybe I was seeing what I wanted to see. It wasn't as if Shawn had the most reliable track record.

He cut me out of his life for five years, told me he loved me, then didn't call me after everything that happened at the fundraiser.

That didn't feel like love to me. And him rushing in like this didn't feel like love either. If anything, it put me on edge.

"I came to talk to your principal," he said, ignoring Stacey, his eyes still on me. "I wanted her to know it wasn't your fault. I was about to ask her to give you your job back."

Trevor scoffed. "There's no way that's happening. This isn't just about the fundraiser; it's about her test scores."

Shawn took a threatening step toward Trevor, and I shot a hand out in front of his chest, holding him back.

"He isn't worth it. None of this is," I told him.

"What you're doing could help so many kids, and my career isn't worth ruining that. I'll be okay. I'll find something else."

His jaw clenched tight as he searched my face. "I'm not letting you give up your mom's school because this–" He pointed at Trevor "–asshole thinks he can get away with fucking everything up for us."

Rutton made a horrified noise. "Mister Jackson, what's going on? Are you two... seeing each other? Is that why you've decided to take the blame?" She looked to her left, to Trevor. "And what does Mister Atkins have to do with any of this?"

"Everything," Shawn growled. "He's the reason–"

Shawn cut himself off and listened to the tinny noise coming from Stacey.

"It's not my fault he decided to take the blame for Lilly. That's on Shawn, not me."

Every head snapped toward her.

"But if you didn't forge that invoice in the first place, none of this would've happened."

She held her phone up, scowling as she played her recording.

"I had to. Nothing else worked."

Trevor was shocked. His mouth dropped open, his brows furrowed, but then he gritted his teeth and lunged at his cousin.

"You should've just left Lilly alone and found another job somewhere else."

Shawn grabbed Trevor's shoulder, forced his weight

down on him, and as Trevor's knees buckled, Shawn wrapped an arm around his neck.

"No. She lied to me, Stacey. She deserves this."

Mia stepped forward.

"I don't care if you think she deserves this. Do you know what your stupid plan cost us? We were raising money to help kids, Trevor. Kids. Don't you care about them?"

Cocking her arm back–

"Why the fuck would I care?"

–Mia slammed her fist into Trevor's face.

"Well, what about me? Don't you care about me? This is my career."

As Trevor's legs crumpled underneath him, his grunt of pain echoed in the hallway.

"Look, I'll help you with the initiative after this is done. This has to work."

Shawn let him drop to the ground.

"What if it doesn't? What if Rutton gives Lilly her job back and Shawn loses his?"

Mia shook out her fist.

"Then I'll just have to keep fucking with her test scores until she gets fired."

Principal Rutton gaped at Stacey's phone, almost like she couldn't believe what she'd just heard, let alone what she'd just seen Mia do to Trevor.

"Wasn't what you did with the invoice enough?"

"I don't know. It should've been, but if Shawn's meeting with Rutton works out, and she gets her job back, I might have to think of something else."

Stacey paused the recording, lowered her phone, locked eyes with the principal, and said, "Trevor's been trying to get Lilly fired for months. Shawn doesn't deserve the blame for any of this, and neither does she."

"Stacey, you fucking bitch," Trevor yelled. "You said you wouldn't say anything."

Shawn looked like he was ready to murder him, and Mia stepped back like she was about to kick him right there on the ground.

But it was my turn.

After everything he put me through, I was ready to make him regret it.

But when I opened my mouth to speak, tears pricked my eyes, and my voice shook. "I can't believe you've been trying to get me fired for the past year."

Holding his nose, Trevor glared at me and shouted, "You can't believe it? Lilly, you made me think you loved me for eighteen fucking months."

At that, my chest fell—but no.

I wasn't supposed to feel bad now. Not now. Not after everything he did. I wasn't supposed to want to fix this feeling for him. I wasn't supposed to feel the urge to apologize to Trevor of all people.

No. Anxiety or no anxiety, I was done trying to please people like him.

"So you did all this just because I didn't want to be with you anymore? You can't treat people like this, Trevor. You can't... fuck with people's lives."

"I'll fuck with you as much as I want."

I couldn't believe it. He didn't regret what he did at all. He didn't care that what he did hurt not only me, but Shawn, and his own cousin. It shocked me that he could—that anyone could—be so selfish.

Principal Rutton raised her voice, and all of us turned to look at her as she called out, "That's enough. I want all of you in my office. Now."

CHAPTER 37
SHAWN
MONDAY EVENING

Lilly's Apartment

AFTER WE LOCKED Trevor in the principal's office, the department heads were called, and Trevor had a decision to make.

He could deny everything and force Stacey to play the recording again, or he could come clean.

He chose to come clean.

Principal Rutton was shocked. And the apologies Lilly received were music to my fucking ears.

The satisfaction I felt was almost savage.

Stacey was oddly quiet. She kept staring at her cousin like she was trying to figure him out, but couldn't.

And Mia? Trevor glared at her as she shimmied and sang 'bye-bye Treviboy' right there in Rutton's office.

She was obnoxious and chaotic, thrilled that Lilly could get her life back on track.

I guess I could understand why Lilly loved her so much. She was loyal down to her bones. And I had to respect her for that punch she landed on Trevor's nose, even if it did make me pretty damn jealous.

Trevor never apologized, and I never got to kick his teeth in like I wanted, but Lilly's job was safe.

That's what mattered.

Back in her apartment, the half-empty box of donuts caught my attention as Lilly turned to face me. She was tired, but based on the way she put her hands on her hips, I could tell she wasn't happy.

Actually, she'd been upset for hours. I thought she'd be relieved that she got her job back, but I knew her well enough to know something else was going on.

Her voice was quiet, but sharp, as she told me, "You shouldn't have quit, Shawn. I never wanted you to do that."

I watched her for a second, caught off-guard by what she said. Was she upset... with me?

"I know, but–"

"Where were you?" she interrupted, moving behind the kitchen counter, putting it between us.

"At the center. Talking to the department heads."

She pinned me with a look that could peel paint. "For the entire weekend?"

"Yes. I was trying to fix it."

"By taking the blame?" she shot back quickly, like she was ready for it. "I didn't ask you to do that. Why didn't you just call me?"

"I couldn't."

She wasn't impressed with my answer.

"You couldn't call me? Or visit me? Not even to check on me after I'd just been fired?"

I felt like an idiot for not seeing it sooner.

As I walked around the counter, her eyes flicked up to mine.

"I'm sorry. I should've called. I wanted to see you, but I knew that if you found out, you'd try to stop me."

She gave me a look that told me she wasn't convinced. "Really?"

"Yes. I was trying to help."

She chewed her lip, fidgeted with her fingers. I let out a breath, annoyed with myself. I should've seen this coming. After what I did to her years ago, it made sense that she'd worry I'd do it again.

"Lilly, listen. I'm not going anywhere. Not this time. Not until you tell me to leave."

I put my hand over hers. When she didn't pull away, I counted it as a win. Gently, I pulled her into me, letting her head rest on my chest.

"But you can tell me to leave if that's what you want."

She wound her fingers in my shirt, just like she used to, and shook her head. "No. I want you to stay."

Relief made me hold her tighter. "Then I'll make it up to you."

She let out a breath, frustrated.

"I hate that this was my fault," she said, her voice clearer than before.

"Lilly, nothing about what he did was your fault."

"But he wouldn't have done all those things if I ended it when I knew I didn't want to be with him. I should've done it before graduation. I just... I didn't know if I needed to give it more time, or if some of the things I didn't like about him were just in my head."

She pulled away and sighed. "I should've been honest with him. I should've accepted that I'd be kicked out of the sorority."

"You felt like you didn't have a choice."

"But that doesn't make it okay. Look, I'm not trying to make excuses for him. I know what he did was bad. But what I did hurt him, and I hate that I understand why he did it."

She wrapped her arms around her middle, hugging herself as she quietly said, "But I'm not doing that again. I won't let people take advantage of me anymore."

I gave her a look then, because that wasn't exactly easy to believe, and asked, "You won't?"

"I won't," she said firmly. "I swear."

I folded my arms and raised a brow at her. "So no more giving your number to parents like Mrs Hernandez?"

She groaned, and it made me laugh. "I need to change my number, don't I?"

I came to stand behind her and took her by the waist, dragging her back into me.

"I'm glad you're done people-pleasing. You should put yourself first. Your mom would've wanted you to."

I'd been thinking about it all weekend—why South Bronx meant so much to Lilly, how deeply losing her mom had impacted her.

Trevor could never have done what he did if she hadn't been so desperate to protect what her mom left behind.

She turned in my arms, looking up at me with a small line between her brows, just visible under her bangs. "My mom? You think she'd tell me to be selfish?"

"It's not selfish to take care of yourself," I told her, brushing her hair from her eyes.

Her brows knit together like she was going to argue with me. "But my mom told me—"

"Lilly," I interrupted, warning her. "If you think your mom wanted you to work yourself into the ground just to teach at the same school she once taught at, you're wrong. Your mom would never have wanted any of this for you. She would've wanted you to be happy."

She worried her bottom lip between her teeth, making me want to lick that sweet little pout.

But then, in a voice steadier than before, she said, "But I am happy. I love it at South Bronx. It's... home for me."

A small blush crept across her cheeks, like she was embarrassed to admit it. She had nothing to be embarrassed about, though. I loved how much she cared about the kids she taught, about the people she worked with.

I ran my thumb over her cheekbone, so fucking elated that I could touch her like this. That I didn't have to hold back anymore.

"But you're right," she said, that little line between her brows back in place. "Mom didn't want me to struggle the way I did. And she would've hated what happened with Trevor. That's why I have to–"

"–change your number?" I cut in, and she playfully nipped at my finger with a laugh.

"And if you're lucky, maybe I'll give it to you." Then, her smile fell just a little. "As long as you stick around."

She had to be kidding. She couldn't really believe I'd actually let her go a second time.

"Lilly, come on. You know I want you."

She made a noise of disbelief, and tried to shrug out of my arms, but I held her tighter. She needed to hear this.

"No, hang on. I'm serious. You're it for me."

She paused, looking up at me with worry.

"I know it took me a long time to get here, but I'm *here*," I told her. "And I'm staying."

She hesitated, then said, "You say that now, but–"

"No. There is no 'but'," I interrupted. "You're the only one I want, and you always will be. I love you."

I tilted a finger under her chin and kissed her then, taking it slow, enjoying the way she melted into me.

It'd take time for her to trust that this was real. But I could be patient.

I'd waited this long. And she was worth it.

CHAPTER 38
LILLY
FRIDAY MORNING

Verra Convention Center

THE CENTER WAS full of color, light, and sound. The smell of fried dough and roasted garlic drifted from one end to the other, blending into something that made my stomach growl.

"This is amazing," I yelled over the music. Shawn squeezed my hand and winked down at me. He was suited up, and so was I.

After everything that happened, the department decided to let us work the fundraiser. I took my duties back from the teachers who'd been covering for me and oversaw the delivery of all the merchandise I'd arranged.

And honestly? It felt good to be back. It felt good to finish this.

Even better? Shawn had his thirty percent back, and I figured out what to do with those extra coffee cups.

Tristan waved at us from his stall, where a small crowd of women stared and pointed at him, not even trying to hide it. But I wasn't sure I could blame them. With his salt-and-pepper stubble and hair, he was pushing forty, and was still a thirst-trap.

It wasn't until he curled an arm around Nikki that the ladies started to mutter at each other, disappointed. Tristan didn't notice. He never did. Years later, it was still our longest-running inside joke.

"This was a great idea," Nikki shouted, as she pulled me in for a hug. "Have you seen all these people? They'll be at our shop ordering refills before the week is over."

Once we knew my job was safe, I remembered an old idea and called Tristan.

Back in college, whenever I made a set of merchandise for a Kappa Delta fundraiser, Tristan would keep some of the stock to help me raise awareness. But the most effective campaign was a run of coffee cups I designed for one of the charities.

We kept them at his shop, and he sold them with the offer of discounted refills for the rest of the month.

I put the offer out everywhere we stocked our merchandise, and the boom of customers was more than we could keep up with.

Once people had Tristan's smooth coffee roast and a taste of his homemade pastries, regulars tripled and our hours extended.

Now, we were doing it again.

Tristan agreed to host a stall, and I got to work writing to the Board.

The initial approved thirty thousand cups were here, being sold. But the rest were at *Tristy's*, where my old boss would sell them with the same offer over the next eight weeks.

The profit from the sales would go directly to the fundraiser, but Tristan would keep the customers.

Simple, mutually beneficial, and it left the door open for future donations. Once the contract was signed, the relief left me drained.

I'd been running on adrenaline for weeks, and I could finally accept that everything was going to be okay.

And now, today was the day. Nothing could ruin this.

Shawn stood with Tristan behind their makeshift counter, talking, while Nikki kept the line moving. As soon as the band kicked in, Mia appeared at my side to grab a round of coffee for them.

"Bloody divas," she muttered, picking up a takeout tray. "How'd I let you talk me into doing this again?"

I fluttered my lashes at her. "Because you love me?"

She rolled her eyes. "You're lucky I do. That frontman's a real asshole."

Lifting onto my toes, I checked out the stage, spotting the tattooed, well-muscled guitarist she hated most. With that ripped shirt and spiked hair, he looked like he'd been pulled straight out of the nineties.

And it was a good look for him.

I waggled my brows at Mia. "Would you say he's a fit asshole?"

She scowled. "He might be nice to look at, but he's no Shawn. He's just an ass."

I sniffed the air, then teased her with, "I smell an enemies-to-lovers story coming."

She gave me a horrified look, picked up her loaded tray, and hissed, "You have to stop reading those horny novels. I'm not going to fall for that bloody guitarist."

She stomped back to the stage as I giggled, watching her.

I'd noticed the way she blushed whenever he was around. She'd probably never admit it, but this guy had gotten under her skin.

I gave Nikki and Tristan a quick goodbye, and Shawn followed as I made my rounds to the other merch stalls. Stacey caught up with us, bouncing on her toes and smiling like she couldn't hold it in.

It was déjà vu. I hadn't seen her like this in years.

"Can you believe how well this is going?" she asked, her eyes flicking between Shawn and me. "At this rate, we're going to beat our target."

Shawn grinned, and before I could feel a twinge of anything, he squeezed my hand again. "You did a great job managing this, Stace. It really came together."

"It did, didn't it?" She looked around the center,

hugging her notebook. But then her eyes dropped back to me, and her smile slipped. "Lilly, could we talk for a second?"

I worried my bottom lip. We hadn't talked since Principal Rutton's office, and after the way she'd defended me and Shawn, putting words together around her wasn't easy.

But Shawn nudged his chin at Stacey, giving me a look that meant, *Talk to her*, and then he was gone, making his way through the crowd.

"Lilly, I just want to tell you that I'm sorry. About back when we were at school." Her voice was firm, but kind, like she knew she owed me this, and wasn't embarrassed to say it. "I might not have forced you to date Trevor, but I made you take on work you didn't have time for, and–" she shrugged "–honestly, Shawn told me it was a pretty shitty thing for me to do, and he was right."

She shook her head. "I get why you and Mia acted the way you did when you first got here. If someone treated me the way I treated you, and I had to work with them? I'd probably shove them into a stack of chairs too. But then there was my cousin. And god, what the hell was that? Right?"

I squinted at her, not sure of what to say as she gave me a good-natured, probably polite, laugh. Then the question burst out before I could blink.

"Shawn's making you apologize, isn't he?"

She hesitated, then said, "He can't make me do anything. But... he did ask me to."

Okay, I had to admit, I wanted to laugh then. But instead, we started talking over each other:

"Stacey, you don't have to—"

"No, but I should—"

"It's okay, *I* should've—"

We stopped, laughing awkwardly at ourselves.

Finally, I said, "Look, Stacey, it was years ago. And you helped me get my job back." I held up two fingers, thinking about that day she arranged a tutor for Jessica. "Twice. I think we can call it even."

Staying mad at Stacey wouldn't get me anywhere. I was okay now. Better than okay. My job was mine again, Shawn and I were happy, and Trevor was finally out of my life.

The least I could do was forgive her.

"So, we're good then?" she asked, not sure it was safe to believe me.

I nodded, surprised to see the relief on her face.

"Great. Thanks, Lilly. This is my last project with Shawn, and I wanted to start the school year with a clean slate. I'm glad we could work it out."

And that was how I left things with Stacey.

The fundraiser was a success, the Education Board's faith in Shawn was stronger than ever, and my career was safe.

There was only one thing left to deal with. My class exam scores.

CHAPTER 39
SHAWN
MONDAY MORNING

South Bronx Classical

I WAS GOING to jump out of my skin. This was going to be so fucking fun.

"Are you ready?" Principal Rutton asked as she opened her office doors.

I nodded, following her as she led the way through South Bronx Classical.

"I was surprised to hear from you, Mister Jackson."

She turned another corner, and I slowed down to stay in step with her.

"You were offered a position with us years ago, am I right?"

I cleared my throat to buy a second or two. I was only half-listening to the principal. My mind was on Lilly.

I couldn't wait to see the look on her face.

"I was, but I went with Brooklyn. It was hard to pass on the offer they gave me."

I tried not to regret turning down that offer from South. Yes, it kept me from Lilly, but it also gave me the start I needed.

But things were different now. Lilly and I were making up for lost time. And this was another way I could make it up to her.

We turned another corner, then stopped in front of a narrow doorway. Down the hall, students laughed, passing phones around, but they weren't loud enough to cover the voices floating out of the staffroom.

"I can't believe they found another teacher so bloody quickly," Mia grumbled. "I hope he isn't another dickbag."

"Mia," Lilly hushed her. "The students might hear you."

At the sound of her voice, a familiar heat crept down my spine.

"Oh relax, they've heard worse."

"But what if it's a woman?" Lilly asked. "You don't know that we're getting a guy."

"Actually, I do," Mia said, exasperated. "I overheard the math teachers. They're excited about having another sausage join their party."

Lilly's laugh—bright, bubbly, and warm—drifted into the hallway as Principal Rutton looked over her shoulder at me. Judging by the way she raised her brows, she wasn't finding this as funny as I was.

I had to bite the inside of my cheek to stop myself from laughing.

"I'm sorry, Mister Jackson," the principal said, voice low. "Miss Walker can be... a bit to handle, sometimes. But she's an excellent teacher."

I nodded and gave her a small smile.

Then Principal Rutton rolled her shoulders back and walked in. I didn't follow her this time. Instead, I stood out of sight just behind the doorframe.

"Ladies, how are we today?"

"Good, and you?" Lilly answered.

"My scoliosis is acting up," Mia told her, probably palming her back and twisting her neck like I'd seen her do before.

"That's... too bad," Principal Rutton said, a little thrown.

But then she cleared her throat and went on with, "I wanted to wish you both a good start to the school year. I hope this one will be... better than the last. Our last head teacher definitely caused some issues, but they're nothing we can't recover from."

An understatement, if I'd ever heard one.

"I have a couple of announcements this morning. First, we have a new teacher joining us."

She waved a hand behind her, surprised to find no one there. She did a double take, then watched as I walked into the room.

Judging by the gasp in the right corner, Mia was surprised. But Lilly was all I could see.

Her face went from mild expectation, to wide-eyed disbelief, to open-mouthed shock. Then she squealed, jumped from her desk, and crashed into me, wrapping her arms around my neck as I stumbled back, laughing.

"So you two already know each other," the principal joked. She knew what she was getting into when she hired me.

"What's he doing here?" Mia asked, standing as Lilly nuzzled her cheek into my chest.

"Babe," I warned her, shooting a look at the principal.

My girlfriend flushed as she realized what she'd done in front of her boss, but to her credit, Principal Rutton waved it away.

"As long as the students don't see it, I don't mind."

Mia crossed her arms and complained, "Are you kidding? You hired him to be our new head teacher? He's going to lord this over us for years."

Lilly gave Mia a look, practically begging her to be okay with this, but Mia just gave her a smile and winked. She wasn't really mad that I was here. She was just acting up for the fun of it.

"He'll be a great head teacher," Lilly said, letting go of me. "I bet you've already planned our entire year."

Principal Rutton cleared her throat again as I shook my head.

"I don't have any plans," I told her. "And I'm not your head teacher."

"Oh." Lilly frowned, confused, turning back to look

at Mia, probably thinking she'd see the same expression on her best friend's face.

Because if I wasn't head teacher, who was?

But Mia wasn't confused at all. With her hands behind her back, she smiled wickedly at Lilly, looking like the satisfied troublemaker she was.

Principal Rutton was the one who spoke next.

"Mia and I had a chat over the holidays, and we talked about who the next head teacher should be. I thought Mister Jackson would be the best choice, but he can't give this department the attention it needs."

"With my initiative rolling out across lower Manhattan," I added, "I don't have time to lead a faculty."

"So, that left the two of you." Rutton shared a look with Mia, let out a surprising laugh, then turned back to Lilly. "As much as I respect Miss Walker, we both agreed you'd be a better choice."

Lilly's mouth dropped open. Her hand floated to her stomach. She started to look panicked. On instinct, I took her hand and made her look at me.

"Hey, this is a good thing," I said, trying to reassure her. "You're going to be great at this."

But it didn't seem to help. She stuttered, "But I can't–I'm not–I mean, I was almost fired–"

"We all know what happened," Mia said softly, interrupting her. "No one blames you for it."

There was a pained look on Lilly's face as she turned to Principal Rutton.

"But you and Trevor agreed. You weren't happy with me. This was supposed to be my second chance, right? I can't just get promoted. It doesn't make sense."

The principal cleared her throat for the third time.

"We all know the exam procedure in our school isn't perfect, but the fact that your test scores were tampered with only made your situation worse."

She did this thing where she sucked on her teeth, making a sound that made me wince.

I glanced at Lilly. She was on edge. She held her breath, and her shoulders were up by her ears. It made me want to unwrap her and smooth out all her tension.

"But, after we looked into it," the principal went on, "we found that your students showed, if anything, better critical-thinking scores than others. Which was actually quite impressive." She sighed then, as if it was work to have to share this news with Lilly. "So, whatever your method is, Miss Fares, it works. This department will probably improve because of it."

That was what Lilly needed to hear. She relaxed then, looking lighter, like she'd thrown off a weight.

The principal toyed with her teeth again, then said, "I've already sent letters to our parents apologizing for the system 'issue' that gave their children the wrong grades, and the students involved have been moved to their correct classes. I've informed them that you'll be working as Head Teacher from this term onwards."

The principal held out her hand. Lilly took it.

As they shook, Lilly asked, "So, I'm... a good teacher?"

Rutton let out an amused huff. "Yes, Miss Fares, you are. I'm sure you'll make the school proud."

"Too right she bloody will," Mia shouted, tackling Lilly and almost knocking the principal over in the process.

"I have to go. I've a meeting in five minutes." Rutton turned to me. "You'll be all right from here?"

"I'll be fine."

"Uh," Lilly piped up once Mia let her go. "Thank you, Principal Rutton, for the opportunity. I'll do my best."

She waved away Lilly's gratitude. "After what you've been through, it was the least I could do."

Biting back a smile, Lilly and I shared a look as Principal Rutton nodded her goodbyes and left.

Then Lilly surprised me. Once Rutton turned the corner, she bit her lip, walked her fingers along my shirt, grabbed my tie, and pulled on it, bringing me down to her.

As she kissed me, her lips soft and teasing, Mia playfully grumbled, "All right, all right. I'll go. All you had to do was say you wanted some privacy. Guess I'll have to start knocking before I walk into my own staffroom."

The door shut softly behind her, and now that we were alone, I wasn't sure that this was the smartest choice.

Working with Lilly again.

Knowing what she did to me, was this smart?

I pushed her onto the closest desk, already knowing my answer. But right now, I didn't care about being smart.

Her legs opened around me, and her dress rode up. Running my hands up her thighs, I nipped her lip, and kissed her again.

She tightened her legs around me, breathing out, "This is going to be the best semester of my life."

"Because you're Head Teacher?"

"Because you're finally here."

I reached the seam of her underwear, and she tilted her hips just a little as I ran my fingertip along it.

"We still have to be careful," I told her.

She looked up at me through her lashes. "Why?"

"Well..." My eyes drifted to the shut door. "We can't let anyone see us if we–"

"Mister Jackson," Lilly warned, her voice teasing, but stern. "There won't be anything to let anyone see."

She pushed my chest and I stepped back, confused, but loving the sound of her laugh.

Then, she switched into professional mode, telling me, "Touching and kissing isn't appropriate while on school grounds. Is that understood?"

Without waiting for an answer, she slid off the desk and put her hands on her hips, repeating something I'd said to her weeks ago: "We're here for work, Mister Jackson."

I folded my arms, eyeing her, not sure if she was just teasing me. "So, you mean–"

"I mean," she interrupted, clearly enjoying herself. "If you want to get busy with your head teacher–" she poked my chest "–then you'll just have to see me after class."

She winked then, and I laughed, jerked her close, and kissed her.

When she pulled back, she was genuinely serious this time. "But I can't screw this up, okay? No sex at work."

I almost laughed again, but the look on her face made me hesitate.

I shrugged, trying to lighten the mood again. "I guess I can keep my hands to myself if I have to. You're the boss, *Miss Fares*."

She looked so relieved then, that I couldn't resist. I put my mouth to her ear and whispered, "But when I get you home, I'm in control."

She gasped as I ran my teeth over her earlobe. I couldn't get enough of the sounds she made. I took her hands and pinned them behind her.

"And I'm going to tie these wrists to the headboard, and lick your pretty little pussy 'til you scream."

Her eyes glazed over, but she managed to look annoyed with me. "That's not fair. You can't just come in here and do that."

"Do what?" I asked, letting her go.

The blush on her cheeks was my favorite thing to

watch, but I also liked the way she put her hands on her hips and huffed, "You can't turn me on before I have to teach."

She turned to pick up her folder, complaining, "Now I have to go to the bathroom and fix my underwear."

I laughed as she whirled around and rushed out the door.

Satisfied, I put my hands back in my pockets, grazing my still-hard cock.

Yep. This was going to be so much fucking fun.

Want more spicy, slow burn, enemies to lovers goodness?

Scan the QR Code HERE to Start Reading *Apparently, I'm Trouble*.

Mia and Theo's story is just beginning...

~

APPARENTLY, I'M TROUBLE
Inside Book 3

MIA
8 WEEKS LATER
Wrinkled Pages
Saturday

"No, I didn't hook up with that asshole guitarist. Why would I?"

"Because you're randy and he was cute," Lilly drawled.

I scoffed into my phone. I didn't care how cute he was—an asshole was an asshole.

"I shouldn't have taught you that word."

"What? Randy?"

"No one says it anymore."

"Stop trying to distract me. I love Shawn, but that guitarist was one of the greatest things to come out of that fundraiser, and you know it."

I rolled my eyes but gave in. "He *was* a bit ridiculous, wasn't he?"

My best friend's laugh was a shot of serotonin straight to my brain. I was smiling at strangers on the sizzling sidewalk, and they were staring back at me like I'd lost my mind. I held my phone tight against my ear and kept walking.

"He was. Forget about the band, we could've met our goal if we charged admission just to see him. Women were drooling. Those eyes and that hair? Are you kidding me? It's not right for a man to look that good."

"Especially one that's as big a grump as him. Nice to look at, awful to talk to."

Lilly sighed, and it sounded almost wistful. "Maybe you *should've* hooked up with him. Enemies-to-lovers is my favorite trope."

I huffed out a laugh and said, "Excuse me, have you been reading your horny novels again?"

"Mia, they're not horny novels."

I turned a corner and dodged another surge of sweaty New Yorkers. The summer break might've been over, but this bloody heatwave wasn't.

"If an author forces two complete strangers into having sex, it's a horny novel."

I could picture her rolling her eyes now.

"Other things happen. It isn't just sex from page one."

I let out a laugh, and the person across from me gave me a look of disgust. I understood. No one should be laughing with beads of sweat rolling down their back. Most people were covered in suffocating business wear, which was just *wild* for a Saturday. Meanwhile, there I was in one of my usual breezy boho dresses and sandals, swishing along the sidewalk like a British hippie from the seventies. I definitely couldn't relate to these poor sods in suits.

"Knowing you, you're only reading them because they make your panties tight."

I walked by a store, and as their sliding doors opened, a gust of cool air hit my neck. I almost groaned. Why did the bookstore have to be so far from the subway?

"Cowboy romances are your favorite, right?" I teased. "Do we need to put Shawn on a horse?"

Lilly grumbled, "Shawn doesn't need a horse, and I'm not reading them for the sex. There's more to them than that."

I scoffed. "If there was more to them, they'd be part of the syllabus."

"But there *is*. Romance is about change. And healing. We could teach a whole unit on transformation through positive relationships."

"They get their fill of that with Shakespeare, and we give them too much of him as it is."

She blew a breath through her nose, and my phone made that awful staticky noise in my ear.

"That's a fair point."

I could practically hear the gears turning in that people-pleaser brain of hers. After that meeting with Rutton yesterday, she was on edge. I had to talk her down, or she'd shackle herself to her laptop, and then I wouldn't see her until the semester started.

"I know Rutton messed with your head, but you're

thinking too hard about this. Our classes are set for the rest of the semester. Just enjoy it."

She scoffed. "Oh, like you're enjoying it? What're you doing right now?"

"It's one bloody book, Lilly. It's not like I'm donating a library."

But expectations *were* pretty high.

It wasn't lost on me that, though she could've handled it better, Rutton was right. The A.P.P. was the most prestigious program we offered at our private school, and after what happened last semester, our reputation couldn't afford to take another hit.

But my mind was on Lilly.

For the sake of her career, she needed this class to go well. She was counting on me.

And I was going to teach the shit out of this program.

Every year, a select group of private schools competed for advanced placement into Ivy League universities, and this time, the theme was *Breakouts: Texts That Shatter the Cultural Glass Ceiling*. My class was going to study a literary fiction piece titled *Misplaced*–a story about a teen going through loss.

I had a new student joining us on Monday and didn't have a single copy I could loan her, which was why I was on my way to the closest bookstore I could find. My students wouldn't show up to my class with blank faces. Not even the girl I hadn't met yet. Too much was riding on this.

"It would've been fine if she didn't have it for a day," Lilly reasoned. "She probably needs time to settle in."

Not on my watch.

Lilly's argument was a moot point anyway, because there it was—the bookstore sign. I'd never been happier to see the words *Wrinkled Pages* in my life. I turned the corner into the sliding glass doors, desperate to get out of the heat, and smacked straight into someone.

Immediately, my stomach dropped, and so did my tote bag. But I couldn't look for it until I'd dislodged myself from this bulky blue wall of a person. He smelled of musky soap and felt firmer than anyone had a right to be.

The bulky wall grunted, took half a step back, and gripped my elbows. As I looked up, the surprise of seeing Theo's face made me forget about my tote. I didn't even notice that something had rolled out of it.

Still holding my arms, Theo led me away from the entrance as Lilly asked, "Mia? You okay?"

"I'll call you back," I answered, jamming my thumb on the end-call button.

As he let me go, I watched, stunned, while he bent to pick up my things.

Well. What were the odds?

I'd *just* been talking about him with Lilly. The last time I'd seen him was onstage during the fundraiser. He was a tattooed, broody nightmare. When it ended, I thought I'd never have to see him again.

And really, what was the point of living in a city as big as this if I was just going to run into him anyway?

His broad shoulders were tense as he handed me my bag, his blue eyes refusing to meet mine as he said, "Is this yours?"

Sitting in the palm of his hand was my purple bullet vibrator. Of course it slipped out and rolled across the floor–because why wouldn't it?

I snatched it from him and refused to feel embarrassed. A woman does what she needs when she needs to. No one was going to sexually shame me, especially not some asshole guitarist in an expensive blue polo shirt.

"What're you doing in a bookstore?" I asked. "I thought you could only read sheet music."

His brows lifted, and for a second, I almost thought he was fighting a smile, which would've been a better look for him than his usual scowl.

With his stubbled jawline and tousled honey-brown hair, he reminded me of a midwestern cowboy who had just moved to the big city to 'figure life out'. I could picture him in flannel and denim, which wasn't a stretch considering he already had an actual honest-to-god *tan*, which seemed like something a man got out in a field while wrangling cattle. He would've fit perfectly in one of Lilly's horny novels.

Someone just had to get rid of the business-casual polo shirt and dark slacks he was wearing.

I sucked in my bottom lip, thinking about panties

tightening, as he stared down at me and said, "I just picked up a book for my daughter."

I eyed the brown-paper-wrapped book in his fist. "Well, that makes more sense."

He gave me the kind of nod that would've looked better if he had a wide-brimmed hat on his head, and *oh my god,* what was I doing thinking a thought like that? Lilly and her damn horny novels were getting to me.

"It's nice to see you again, Mia."

I scoffed. "No, it isn't. I know you and the band hated me as much as I hated all of you."

His lip twitched again, still fighting that smile, but he managed to control it as he said, "I don't remember saying that."

"You didn't have to."

"I missed rehearsals because I was busy."

"Busy doing what?"

"Working."

"On *what?*"

"My job, which is what I should be doing now."

I gestured behind me and moved aside. "Well, if it's so important, don't let me get in your way."

Something that almost resembled a smirk crossed his features before he went back to his default setting of unbearably broody.

This man *towered* over me. Not that that was saying much. Most people did. But his body almost leaned toward mine, like he was a breath away from caging me against the stack of books at my back. A shiver pulsed low in my stomach, and I pushed the thought away as Theo passed by without another word.

I watched him through the glass doors, and finally let out a breath. I didn't realize I'd been holding it in.

There, I told myself, *He's gone, and I'm fine. No damage done.*

Now, if the next semester could hold that sort of luck for me, I might have a fighting chance at getting those spots.

"Okay, let's focus here," I muttered to myself. "I just need that book."

*

Scan the QR code HERE to read the entire book now!

DEAR READER

Thank you so much for spending time with Lilly and Shawn. I hope they made you laugh, swoon, and maybe even tugged a little at your heart.

If their journey left you smiling (or shouting at the pages), I'd love it if you shared your thoughts in a quick review on GoodReads or Amazon.

Reviews are how books like mine find new readers, and yours would mean the world to me.

And if you'd like to keep the bookish fun going, I'd be thrilled to welcome you into my **Book Club**. Each month, we read, chat, and celebrate the kind of stories that make us feel something special.

You can join us here: https://www.demiblaize.com/newsletter/

Thank you again for being part of this adventure with me. I can't wait to share more stories with you soon.

With love and gratitude,
Demi xx

ALSO BY DEMI BLAIZE

Apparently, We're The Problem

Apparently, I'm A Bitch

Apparently, I'm Torture

Apparently, I'm Trouble

READ THE WHOLE SERIES BY SCANNING THE BELOW

QR CODE

Author's Note

To the incredible members of the Scribblers Guild: **David Leys** and **Cheryl Thomas** - thank you for your time, encouragement, and thoughtful feedback. Your insights made this book stronger in every way.

A special thank you to **Sarah Maree Boyd** (also known as my favorite co-conspirator) for your unwavering support, patience, and sharp editorial eye.

And to **Kirsten Oakley (KJ West Writes)** — you went above and beyond, reading the entire book and offering feedback at every stage. Your dedication, honesty, and friendship mean the world to me.

It takes a village to write a book, but it takes a handful of extraordinary hearts to make it shine.

Thank you for being mine.

About the Author

Romance author Demi Blaize doesn't like the anxious hold love has on her... so she writes the feeling into smart, ambitious heroines and cinnamon-roll men. She lives in Australia, avoiding any and all social interactions in favor of Netflix and Chilling with her hubby once her two adorable kids have gone to bed.

Not afraid to get into all things spicy, Demi writes with angst, swoon and humor. Picking up one of her books **guarantees** a good time.

Check her out on Instagram and TikTok, and don't forget to subscribe to her newsletter for a complete list of books and her bookclub picks.

Connect with Demi online!

instagram.com/demiblaizebooks

tiktok.com/@demiblaizeofficial

www.ingramcontent.com/pod-product-compliance
Lightning Source LLC
Chambersburg PA
CBHW050114120726
47904CB00004B/1340